C000060718

In
Ice

DAVE SIVERS

Copyright © Dave Sivers, 2022

Cover design by Jessica Bell

Published by Dave Sivers

The right of Dave Sivers to be identified as author of this work has been asserted.

All rights reserved. No part of this publication may be reproduced, stored, or transmitted in any form, or by any means electronic, mechanical or photocopying, recording or otherwise, without the prior permission of the copyright owner.

In Ink is a work of fiction. Names, characters, places and incidents are the product of the author's imagination or are used fictitiously. Any resemblance to actual events, locales or persons, living or dead, is purely coincidental.

ISBN: 978-1-9997397-4-4

DAVE SIVERS

Dave Sivers grew up in West London and has been writing all his life. His books include the popular crime series featuring the Aylesbury Vale detectives, DI Lizzie Archer and DS Dan Baines.

The Scars Beneath the Soul and *Dead in Deep Water* were both top three bestsellers in the Amazon Kindle Serial Killers chart. *In Ice* is the second in the DI Nathan Quarrel series.

His other works include the Lowmar Dashiel crime fantasy novels.

Dave also writes plays and other material for the amateur stage and is a founder of the annual BeaconLit festival of books and writing. He lives in Buckinghamshire with his wife, Chris.

To keep up with Dave's news and upcoming releases, subscribe to his newsletter at www.davesivers.co.uk.

Also by Dave Sivers

Archer and Baines
The Scars Beneath the Soul
Dead in Deep Water
Evil Unseen
The Blood That Binds
Too Long Gone
Die in the Dark

DI Nathan Quarrel
In Ink

The Lowmar Dashiel Mysteries
A Sorcerer Slain
Inquisitor Royal

Short Stories
Dark and Deep: Ten Coffee Break Crime Stories

For

Fred Sivers (1921-2021)
and
Maurice Kennard (1931-2021)

1

She tests the restraints again, but finds nothing but resistance. Attempts to cry out behind the gag, knowing it is futile. It's all she can do, and she knows it's hopeless, and might incur punishment.

What form that might take, she doesn't even want to think about. And, of course, the more she tries not to think about it, the more her imagination dwells on it. All that has happened to her so far could be a picnic, compared to the possibilities she has glimpsed.

She's already losing track of time in this dimly lit place, wherever and whatever it is. She's pretty sure it was only last night that a day she hadn't thought could get any worse had abruptly descended into the stuff of her darkest nightmares. She'd regained consciousness to find herself here, gagged and secured to this bed, with no idea how long she'd been out. Soon after, she'd heard the door handle turn and the pain and horror had started.

Afterwards, that leather tool roll, with its ominous dark stains, had been opened and shown to her whilst, in matter-of-fact tones, she'd been told she was now property, to be disposed of in any way considered fit. That she was operating on a reward and punishment system.

The punishment for disobedience or defiance lay in that roll of tools.

The reward for absolute compliance was that she might not get the punishment.

And she wonders if there's anything she won't do to reap that reward.

The worst of it is, no matter how ridiculous the notion may be, no matter that sole responsibility for her predicament lies with the person – or maybe people – doing this to her, she feels it is somehow her fault, some karma she has called down upon herself.

She wonders if she has been missed yet. If anyone is looking for her. If there is any hope at all that they might find her.

Footsteps on the stairs, halting outside the door. The sound of the handle turning. Cold sweat bathing her as her stomach knots with terror.

He is coming.

2

Four days earlier.

Even on a day off, neither Nathan Quarrel nor his partner, Laura Shaw, were quite able to break the early rising habit. He was a Detective Inspector with Hertfordshire Constabulary, often working unsociable hours, while she did shifts as a crew leader at Hertfordshire Fire and Rescue. On the rare days they had together, they liked to be up and doing things.

After some wet weather during the week, today's forecast promised dry with sunny intervals. A long walk was planned and so, breakfast done and dishes stowed in the dishwasher, they sat in the hall of their three-storey house in the hamlet of Dudswell, pulling on boots. Nate was looking forward to getting out in the fresh air with the woman he loved and stretching his long legs. Laura had already promised they could make a stop for coffee and a sweet treat.

They stepped out of the house and he turned to lock the door behind him. The Grand Union Canal ran beside the house, and weak shafts of sunlight glinted on the water. A few ducks were dabbling. The forecast said it should be mild for late October. It was going to be a good day.

As he shoved his key into a pocket, his mobile trilled. He pulled it out, read the screen display, and sighed.

"The station," he said through gritted teeth.

She looked half-irritated, half-amused. "Why am I not surprised?"

"I ought to take it."

"Of course you did." She rolled her eyes. "So get on with it."

He answered the call and listened. Checked some details.

"Okay," he said, resigned. "I'm on my way."

He ended the call and stuffed the phone back in his pocket with a hint of savagery.

"You're not going to believe it," he said. "I have to go to Wigginton."

Laura barked a laugh. "How long have I had you? I knew it was too good to be true."

"I'm really sorry." And he was. "We never get a break, do we?"

She shrugged. "Why are you still here?"

*

Less than a quarter of an hour later, Nate was wincing at the scraping noises made by vegetation against the sides of his Volvo estate. It wasn't as if the old girl was in pristine condition, and a fair few battle scars had accumulated over the years, but he still hated inflicting fresh indignity upon her.

In his door mirror, he could see the young uniformed officer who'd waved him through after checking his ID. He was grinning and seemed to find this amusing.

The driveway inclined upwards and bent around to the right before Hall House was really visible. It was a good size, detached and very secluded. You certainly couldn't see it from the road.

He pulled up behind a patrol car and applied the handbrake. A second uniformed officer in a yellow hi-vis jacket was talking to Detective Sergeant Katie Gray and Trainee Detective Constable Isabel 'Izzy' Cole. The latter lived in Tring, closest to the scene, and had evidently beaten both of them to it. She was already in crime scene overalls and Katie was pulling her own on.

"Whoever owns this place isn't exactly a keen gardener, are they?" Katie observed as he got out.

"Even so," said Izzy, "surely you'd hack it back from the driveway entrance, at least enough so it doesn't scratch your car."

"Maybe they don't have a car," Katie suggested.

"In Wiggo?" Izzy lifted an eyebrow. "The back of beyond?"

"Hardly that," said Katie. "It can't be more than two miles from where you live!"

The fact was, Wigginton was a fair-sized village, mentioned in the Domesday Book, and with evidence suggesting a settlement here as far back as the Iron Age. Nate doubted the inhabitants would appreciate Izzy's description.

"Do you remember Harry, sir?" Izzy said, as Nate opened the tailgate to retrieve his own overalls. "PC Chris Harrison?"

Nate, good with faces, recognised him. Harrison, an erstwhile colleague of Izzy's before Nate had plucked her from the Tring unit to supplement a murder investigation team. She'd done well, and he'd kept her on at Hemel Hempstead under a trainee detective scheme.

Nate nodded an acknowledgement. "I gather you managed to get into the house?"

"Yes, sir, round the back. There was a key in the French door on the inside and it looks like someone broke the glass to get at it. They evidently found the cellar and, like our anonymous caller said, there are three chest freezers down there. One's been opened – the padlock forced – and there are two bodies inside. Women. Naked. Hard to put an age on them when they're, you know, frozen."

"So you looked inside?"

He tensed. "I needed to check." He faltered, a little defensive. "We, that is, I thought we should check, sir." He frowned. "Have I messed up?"

"No, you did right." The young man visibly relaxed. "Did you need to open it, or was it already shut?"

"Shut, sir."

"Good. The pathologist's going to have a hard enough job, without decomposition setting in. And it can be rapid, with a frozen body, I know that much. You didn't open the other two?"

Harrison shook his head. "Both still padlocked shut. We thought we should leave that to the CSIs."

"Good." He finished zipping up his overalls and looked the young man up and down. "I don't suppose you suited up before you went inside?"

"No, sir," Harrison mumbled, looking slightly sheepish. "For all we knew, it was a wild goose chase. We did put gloves and booties on."

"Well, that's something." It was more than some might do. "Tell the crime scene manager when she arrives, though. She'll need to eliminate you."

He stepped back and looked around him. The front garden had run wild. He found himself wondering how that fitted in with the grim discovery inside. How long had those bodies been there? And who and where was the owner?

The anonymous 999 call that had blown Nate's quiet, domestic Saturday out of the window had been made by a young woman, and traced to a call box in the centre of Aylesbury – some nine miles away, over the Buckinghamshire border. She'd described this house and its rough location, said there were bodies, then hung up quickly, perhaps wrongly believing the police needed a little time to trace a call. In fact, that hadn't been the case for decades.

"So," Katie stepped over to join him, while Izzy continued to converse with Harrison. "Shall we wait for CSI, or go in?"

He smiled, guessing that waiting was her strong preference.

"Go in," he said. The corners of her mouth duly drooped. "I want to see what we're dealing with without getting in Debbie's way."

Once Debbie Brown, the crime scene manager, got here, this place would be hers. Her team would be busying themselves, doing what they did extremely well. Debbie would engage with the detectives, but they would not be her focus.

Harrison led them through an open gate, into a rear garden as neglected as the one at the front – if anything, more so, as not only had the weeds taken a death grip on the beds, on the knee-high lawn, and even some of the cracks between paving slabs, but what was actually *meant* to be growing here had also run riot. The roses, in dire need of a prune, somehow made Nate think of some ensorcelled fairy-tale castle.

The Georgian style patio doors were also open: paint was peeling in places on timber that was also past its best. Nate observed the smashed glass that the PC had mentioned.

"The gate and this door," Izzy said. "Were they open when you got here?"

"Yep," Harrison confirmed. "And there's rainwater on the floor inside the door. It hasn't rained since yesterday morning, so I'm reckoning the door has stood open for at least the best part of twenty-four hours."

"And the call only came this morning?" Katie pursed her lips. "So what do we think? A burglar breaks in and stumbles across something that scares them? And they get an attack of conscience and eventually decide to tip us off?"

"Something like that," Nate agreed. "I can't see a scenario where our caller is directly connected to the bodies, but the girl must have been involved in the break-in – or known someone who was. We need to find her, and anyone else who was in on it." He turned to Harrison. "Where's this cellar?"

"Come with me."

"No, just tell us where to go. Best you wait here for CSI."

Inside the house, Nate noted that the kitchen was of good quality. A layer of dust indicated that it hadn't been cleaned lately, but the dust on the work surfaces had been disturbed in places. The burglars, the residents, or someone else?

Moments later, he stood at the top of the stairs leading down into the cellar and glanced at his two colleagues. Katie Gray, a first-rate homicide detective, and one who admitted to being a former Goth, looked characteristically squeamish about what awaited them. Izzy Cole, young and fiercely ambitious, had no such qualms.

"Well?" Izzy asked. "Are we going down?"

He smiled, amused by the contrast. "I guess so," he replied, "we won't find out much standing around up here."

The cellar doorway was less than standard size, and he had to stoop to get his lanky frame through without striking his head. The stairs creaked under his feet as he led the way down. Izzy was close on his heels, Katie bringing up the rear two or three steps behind, in no hurry to view the horrors that awaited them.

The three chest freezers stood in the middle of the floor in a neat row. All three were closed, two of them padlocked shut.

The lock was missing from the one to the left. Nate's gaze scanned the floor, spotting the lock lying nearby, its shank twisted out of shape.

He looked at Izzy. "First impressions?"

His voice echoed dully in the space.

She paused for a moment, gathering her thoughts. He liked that she didn't rush to give an opinion. "Well," she said finally, "so far no surprises. We knew what to expect, and we at least know what's in the freezer with the busted lock. We're surmising that the other two are the same. But something seems off."

"Go on."

"What's bothering me is, why padlock them at all? Who's being kept out, and why?"

"A cleaning lady?" Katie suggested. "A family member who's got no idea what's been going on?"

"Maybe. Except you're going to be curious enough about why anyone would have so many big freezers in the first place, aren't you? If it was me, I'd just keep the cellar door locked and make up some reason why."

She cast her eyes over the freezers again.

"Unless…" Her expression changed as she reached the same conclusion Nate already had. She moved closer to the unlocked freezer. Laid a gloved hand on the handle.

"May I?"

He shrugged. "One of us should."

She lifted the lid then. Nate moved closer, then Katie followed suit. He stole a glance at her, hoping fainting wasn't on the agenda today.

One woman lay on top of the other. Both were dark haired and lay in rough estimations of foetal positions, their skin as pale as alabaster. They were naked, the layer of frost on their hair somehow making their condition all the more pitiful.

"Oh, sweet Jesus," whispered Izzy.

Her finger traced the network of scratches on the inside of the lid. The red smears vivid against the white background. She pointed to the more visible hand of the topmost body. The broken and bloody nails.

8

Nate was conscious of Katie stepping back, her hand moving to her mouth.

"You okay?" His tone sounded harsher than he intended. He made himself soften it. "Only, if you feel sick..."

He felt pretty sick himself. He knew that was mostly down to the inside of the lid, red on white: a pattern that still had the power to unsettle him after all these years.

He felt sad, too. And angry.

"No." Katie's voice was hoarse as she shook her head. "No, I'm fine. But, Christ. Those poor women."

"It's pretty obvious now what the padlocks were about, isn't it?" he said.

It was Izzy Cole who answered him. "Yes, sir. They weren't to keep people out. They were to keep the victims in."

3

While Nate waited for Debbie Brown and her CSIs, Katie and Izzy had been dispatched to speak to neighbours. The nearest property to the murder house was the larger of a pair of semis. Sharon Carlton had been having a lie in, and answered the door in a towelling robe. They showed her their warrant cards and said they had some questions about Hall House and its occupants.

"Is it just you?" Katie asked.

The woman shook her head. "Normally, there'd be my husband, Mike – but he's away on business. He's an IT consultant." She looked up and down the road. "You'd best come in. I could make coffee?"

The fact that the women in the freezer were naked suggested a sexual motive, and sexual predators and violence against women were particular hates of Katie's. So the grim discovery next door had left her angry. And chilled to the marrow. She would have happily killed for the coffee and warmth Sharon offered, but Nate had suggested that he would come and find them when he was done at the house. So they talked on the doorstep.

"There was just the one woman living there," Sharon said. "Lynne. Lynne Redding. All a bit sad, really. According to the people we bought this place from, it's the house she grew up in. Like a lot of grown-up kids these days, neither she nor her brother had got round to moving out. One weekend, Lynne's parents and her brother were on their way to Watford, I think, and had a bad crash with a lorry. All three killed."

"When was this?" Katie asked.

"Must be ten years ago. Maybe more. Lynne was left with everything – the house and a tidy sum, or so our predecessors said. But she herself became a bit of a recluse." Her expression clouded. "Actually, make that a *lot* of a recluse. We moved here about four years ago. She never went out, as far as we knew. I don't even think she had a car. She did take a couple of parcels in for us though. If she hadn't, it's entirely possible we wouldn't have ever met her at all. As it was, we only passed the time of day. She wasn't exactly Mrs Chatty."

"But..." Izzy frowned. "Food, clothes. Medicines..."

"Ocado delivered every week," said Sharon, "and there were couriers."

"What about visitors?" Katie wondered.

"Not as such, I don't think. She had a cleaning lady, Eve Banks. I vaguely know her. A garden guy came maybe once a month."

"Not recently though?" But the state of the garden was answer enough.

Sharon smiled. "You've been there? What do you think?"

"I notice you keep talking about her in the past tense," Izzy said.

Sharon shrugged. "Yeah. She went away. Got to be maybe eighteen months ago." She shook her head. "It was most odd, actually."

"In what way odd?"

"Look," she said, "like I said, we didn't really know her at all. Then, one morning, we found a note on the mat from her. Must have dropped it in really early, because I'm not exactly a late riser – apart from weekends." She glanced down at her dressing gown.

"The note?" Katie prompted.

"Yeah, sorry. It was typewritten, I remember that. Said she'd had to go abroad for a while. She didn't know how long she'd be away, but she thought she should let us know, as her nearest neighbours. I reckon she dropped it in so early to minimise the chance of seeing anyone. Most likely she left the house more or less straight away after that. Taxi, I'm guessing."

"I don't suppose you've still got that note?"

Sharon shrugged. "I very much doubt it. It will have been long since recycled."

"You're sure?"

"I suppose I can look, although I'm not sure where. We'd have no reason to hang onto it."

"And the gardener?" Izzy interjected. "The cleaner? They didn't come any more?"

"Nope. She must have contacted them too. Told them she didn't need them." She frowned. "Oh, but there's this one guy who does turn up now and again. She told us about him. In the note. She was having bits and pieces of jobs done while she was away."

"Did you ever see him?"

"Yeah. One of the first times he was there, Mike wandered up to say hello. He's pretty nosy, is my hubby, to be honest. Fancies himself as a DIY legend." She chuckled. "Wanted to know what she was having done. Guy's called Steve. Seems okay. Most of what he was going to do was inside. A bit of decorating, some shelves. He said he was fitting it in with other jobs, so he'd be coming and going."

"So did your husband take a look at the work?"

"Well, no. I think he would have liked to, but the guy didn't invite him in. Can't really blame him. Maybe he'd feel awkward inviting people into someone else's home. Anyhow, he said Lynne had told him he could sleep there if it worked for him, so not to be surprised if his van was there overnight. It meant he could make an early start or work late. Not that you could see the van from the road," Sharon added. "Especially since the gardener stopped coming."

"And gardening wasn't part of Steve's job?" Katie asked.

"Well, if it was, he's not been doing it." Sharon shrugged again. "Not that it's any of our business."

"Did anyone else ever visit Lynne before she went away?"

"We saw the odd car turning in or coming out, I think. Not often. Guys in suits. Mike was taken with a Jag and a Merc."

"That's very specific," Izzy said.

"I suppose because it was so rare. And nice cars, too."

"Could you describe them?"

"Not really. Oh, one of them might have had a bit of beard."

"What about this Steve?"

12

"Oh, yeah. Bushy grey hair and beard. Scruffy. Glasses. Always had a Watford cap on. The football club? And he had some sort of West Country accent." She raised an eyebrow. "Are you sure you can't tell me what this is all about?"

"Sorry, not for the moment," Katie said. "And it would be really helpful if we could trust you to keep this chat to yourself for now."

Sharon nodded. "No problem." But there was a glint in her eye that made Katie wonder.

"I don't suppose Steve gave you a business card or anything?" Izzy suggested.

"Not to my knowledge. I can't see Mike asking, and why would he offer?"

"Did any of the other neighbours know Lynne had gone away?"

"If they did, they haven't mentioned it. But then, neither have I. I didn't think it was wise to broadcast it around that the house was standing empty." But she didn't meet their gaze, and Katie found herself wondering again if she was as discreet as she made out.

"One last question," Katie said. "Did Lynne do anything for a living? Or was she just living off her inheritance, do you know?"

"I think she said she was some sort of freelance editor," said Sharon. "Editing what, I'm not sure. The people we bought the house from told us." She looked uncertain, then grinned. "Don't tell me she'd been running something dodgy there all these years?"

"You've been helpful." Katie handed over her card. "Will you ring us if you think of anything else?"

Back in the street, they paused. "Is it just me?" Izzy asked.

Katie shook her head. "This whole thing feels off to me. Someone who never sets foot outside the door suddenly ups and goes abroad for over a year? And then we find bodies, frozen in the cellar?"

"And this Steve," Izzy said. "Is he blissfully unaware of the bodies? Or has he seized the opportunity of having the house to himself to take women there and kill them?"

"And what about Lynne?" said Katie. "What if she didn't leave at all?" She shivered briefly, and it had nothing to do with the chill of an autumn morning.

"That's what I'm wondering," Izzy agreed. "Maybe Lynne Redding went nowhere. Maybe she's right there in the house, in one of those freezers."

4

Debbie Brown and her CSI team had arrived and had got down to business. Not too far behind them had been Dr Jordan Stoddart, the ridiculously youthful-looking pathologist. Meanwhile, more uniforms had arrived to help secure the scene. Normally, the owners' consent would have been obtained before the police and their colleagues had moved in in numbers like this, setting up lamps, carrying out searches, taking photographs, dusting for fingerprints and subjecting the property to other forensic indignities. But nothing about this situation was even remotely normal.

Under Debbie Brown's direction, the other two padlock shanks had been cut through and the icy coffins opened. The older one in the middle contained two more bodies. The one on the right, only one. The lids were closed now, to preserve the remains.

"Three freezers, five bodies," Debbie said. "So many questions."

"A lot of work for you here, Doc," Nate suggested to Jordan Stoddart. "I'm especially interested in whether they were all frozen at around the same time, or over a longer period?"

"You're thinking, if they were all killed together, it might be less likely there'll be more?" The harsh lighting glinted on a nose ring that always seemed at odds with a serious scientist.

"Something like that," Nate agreed, knowing it would guarantee no such thing.

"I fear I might not be able to help much with that, Inspector," Stoddart said. "Freezing makes time of death incredibly difficult to pin down. I'll do my very best, of course, but these poor women could have been dead for anything from days to years."

"*Years?*" Nate thrust his fingers through his untameable mass of grey hair. The thought that women might have been systematically killed and their remains stored like this over such a long period made him feel they'd been failed in some way. And that he was a part of that failure.

"One thing we do know," said Debbie. She pointed to the middle freezer. "This one looks much older than the other two, and three of them are a hell of a lot of freezer space, unless you're some sort of survivalist nutcase. So I'm thinking the two newer ones at least were bought specifically to store bodies. My guess is we'll find the killings took place over time and the newer freezers were bought in advance."

"Okay." He attempted to gather his thoughts. "The most pressing thing, I suppose, is who they were. Surely someone has missed them. Did any of them live here, in this house? Were they visitors? Or were they brought here by force?"

"You're thinking the owners of this place must be responsible?" suggested Debbie.

"I just don't know. This place bears all the hallmarks of having been unoccupied for quite some time. So where are the owners now?"

"What I *can* tell you for sure," Stoddart said, "is this isn't going to be a quick process. For starters, each body will have to be defrosted before I undertake a formal post mortem. Even before that, I would put every body through CT scanning before defrosting, making a permanent visual image record before anything destructive is done."

"How will you get them to the mortuary?" Debbie asked. "I assume you won't attempt anything here?"

"Good God, no!" He puffed out his cheeks. "I've got my work cut out as it is. We'll have to transport the freezers with the bodies in. Once we get them to the mortuary, we'll need a plan for removing them from the freezers and processing them."

"A *plan*?" Nate didn't like the sound of this. "How long are we looking at?"

"Well, it takes about a day for a body to thaw. Not helped by how cold the mortuary is, by the way. We might anticipate doing two post mortems a day but, since we have an odd number of bodies to deal with, I'm inclined to start with the freezer with the single occupant."

"Why's that?"

"The double occupants are going to be frozen together, remember. Think of a packet of frozen sausages."

Nate's stomach roiled. "I'd rather not."

"Yes, well. The point is, we need to do our best to identify these women and also to detail any injuries. I'm guessing, to be honest, they'd have suffocated."

"Not frozen to death?"

Stoddart shook his head. "They'd have run out of air first. It's probably a mercy, if you can call it that. Anyhow," he continued, "doing that one on the first day will give me an idea as to how long it might take. If we mess up, at least it's just the one."

This was a man whose trade was death and the dissection of human remains. Yet he looked as horrified as Katie and Izzy had been, and Nate felt.

"We may never know exactly what they went through before they died," he continued, "but we can at least do our best to record what we find. I'm afraid it could be a very lengthy process. I'm thinking I should start on Monday. Depending on how that goes, we might be able to do the next two in a day. There again, we might have to take those two out to defrost and, once they're properly separated, pop one back in a mortuary freezer for later. Worst case, we might have to restrict it to one post mortem a day. If we have to work through the weekend, I'd be prepared to do that."

"The whole week?" Nate felt impatience gnawing at him. "And you wouldn't start today?"

"We're not going to be twiddling our thumbs," the pathologist said with no sign of rancour. "Before we even get going, that first body has to defrost, which, as I said, will take about a day. But the bodies will need to be imaged inside the freezer and then imaged again on removal."

"My guys will want to photograph each freezer after the body or bodies have been removed, too," Debbie added.

"And each body will need to be photographed in detail – both whilst still frozen and again after defrosting," said

Stoddart. "So I'm afraid we really are talking Monday to do the first post mortem."

Nate could see the scale of the task, even if he didn't like what he was hearing.

"Can we at least get fingerprints?"

"Best done when they're defrosted," said Debbie. "The ice crystals that form on the skin can disrupt the pattern otherwise."

Although he wasn't a swearing man by nature, this was one of those rare occasions when Nate felt like it.

He sighed heavily. "Fair enough. You two know your jobs. It's not as if we're looking at a critical first twenty-four hours."

5

The board in the major incident room at Hemel Hempstead's Combe Street police station had acquired the nickname 'Wall of Death' somewhere in the murky past, and it had stuck. At present, it was pretty barren. A couple of exterior photographs of the murder house; some early images of the victims lying in their icy tombs; a few notes. A photo album had been found, and a snap of Lynne Redding had been extracted, her likeness confirmed by the neighbour, Sharon Carlton.

It was early afternoon. Nate's boss, Detective Chief Inspector Rachel Sharp, stood alongside him at the front of the room, waiting for the team to settle. Nate would lead on the case, but Rachel liked to kick off major investigations personally. She'd interface with the Divisional Commander, Superintendent Ian Taylor, and other more senior staff. She'd also try to manage the message going out to the media, although Taylor always fancied himself in front of the cameras and liked a press conference. This was going to be big once the word got out, and the Super wasn't above a bit of unhelpful ad-libbing.

"Right," Rachel said, "let's make a start." She was slim and immaculate as ever in a grey trouser suit, her blonde hair short but stylish. "This is a shocking case in the heart of a small, quiet village. DI Quarrel will fill you in on the details, and I know a number of you have got down to work already."

DCI Sharp ceded the floor to him and he briefly outlined the scene they'd found earlier this morning. Katie provided a roundup of what had been gleaned from Lynne's neighbours – which wasn't much. The Carltons next door seem to be the only ones who'd had any contact with her.

"Half the neighbours claimed never to have even seen Lynne, nor to know anything about her. More than one of them had imagined the house to be empty for much longer than it had, simply because they'd never seen any signs of life there."

"And we don't know anything about this Steve character, or Lynne's other regular visitors?"

"Hardly anything," Katie said. "But there's a regular postie who would have interacted with her from time to time. Name of Pete."

"Postman Pete?" Ricky James guffawed. The self-appointed joker in the team, he evidently imagined he was cooler than he really was. Last year, he'd been channelling some 70s cop show, all leather jackets, jeans and tee shirts. Recently, he'd taken to suits, and even ties, although he insisted on wearing the latter at half-mast with his top shirt button undone. "Don't tell me he's got a black and white cat?"

Nate gave him a hard stare. "Very good, Ricky. As a reward, you can track him down. I want him interviewed today." He turned back to Katie. "Anything else?"

"Well, we know Lynne Redding's parents and her brother are dead, but she must have a next of kin of some kind. Should we be notifying them?"

He'd thought about this. "Not until we have a better idea what we're dealing with, but let's try and identify them in the meantime. Aliya, can you work with Libby on that?"

"On it, guv," DC Aliya Nazir said. Steady and dependable, she seemed especially cheerful these days. Nate kept meaning to ask Katie if she knew why.

PC Libby Statham was nodding. A trained Family Liaison Officer, it would be her role to support families of local victims, but Nate also liked having her and her insights on the team for major investigations.

He turned to Izzy Cole.

"Izzy, did you arrange for that police artist to work with the Carltons on a likeness of Steve?"

"Yes, sir. I've put him in contact and he knows it's urgent."

"Good, thanks."

"There's one thing, though, sir," she said. "It strikes me that all that hair and beard, the glasses, the cap... I mean, you won't see much of his actual face, will you? Which is convenient, don't you think?"

"You're thinking it's a disguise?" He'd half-wondered the same himself.

"I'm thinking, if this guy's the killer, and he's known to Lynne – and knows that relationship will come out if his crimes ever come to light – then if he *is* spotted coming and going, a completely different appearance would be convenient."

"It wouldn't be the first time someone changed their appearance to throw us off track," Katie added. "And a West Country accent? You only have to listen to *The Archers*, don't you?"

"Good points," Nate agreed. "Still, I want that likeness, and I want to be ready to issue it when we start going public."

Next up was Debbie Brown.

"We're still processing the scene," she said. "So far, there are a few things of note. The first is that we've found several sets of fingerprints, as you might expect. We're going to see if there are matches for any of them on the national database. We've got to assume that Lynne Redding's are amongst them, wherever she is now. But obviously it's the others that really interest us. Is our killer amongst them? Is this so-called handyman? And are he and the killer one and the same?"

"The woman who called it in must have been in there," Nate observed. "Finding her, and anyone else who broke in, is key, even though I doubt they had anything to do with the murders. They might have information they don't realise is important. I know Ricky and Aliya have been checking out CCTV, but let's finish with Debbie first."

Debbie paused while notes were scribbled.

"Secondly, there's evidence of a fair bit of cleaning going on there. Use of cleaning products to an extent you'd normally describe as anything from excessive to obsessive. Fortunately for us, blood is one of the hardest substances to clean. It has a way of bonding to anything it comes into contact with and, just because the traces might not be visible after cleaning, that doesn't mean they've been eliminated. Maybe our killer didn't know that."

"So you found blood?" said Nate. "Where, and how much?"

Debbie nodded. "Mainly in one of the bedrooms upstairs. Although nothing suggestive of the sort of quantities that makes me think anyone was killed up there. I think every victim met her end inside a freezer."

"I don't get it," said Aliya. "Why even bother cleaning up when there are five bodies in freezers?"

DC Ricky James grinned. "Bit of a giveaway, right?"

"Let's not get too hung up on that," Nate said. "It's a question we might have to catch our killer and ask. But can you tell us a bit more about the blood, Debbie?"

"I'd say the bed linen had been washed, but the stains were revealed under ultraviolet lighting. And there's another thing. The bed frame is an old fashioned style with a metal headboard and foot rail." She held up a couple of photographs. "I'll add these to the Wall, but you can probably make out the vertical bars, and the rails. There are abrasions that must have been made by something rubbing on those rails."

She paused again.

"You're thinking restraints," said Rachel Sharp. It wasn't a question.

"We're thinking restraints," Debbie agreed. "It's possible each of the victims was secured to that bed and put through Christ knows what before the killer decided it was time to lock them in a freezer."

Nate had been around cops long enough to know it took a lot to really shock them. It didn't mean they were immune to the things they saw; the evil people are capable of doing to each other. Sure, there was a degree of desensitisation, he supposed, and sometimes black humour offered a much needed release valve. But he knew he wasn't the only one who sometimes couldn't sleep, or had dark dreams when he did.

Last year, when a serial killer had been active locally, some local cops might have imagined that was a once in a blue moon case. Now it seemed possible that another serial killer had been at work amongst them even before that, undetected. Either luring women to that house or kidnapping them, and then putting them through hell before their ordeal ended in a dreadful death.

He didn't have to turn around to know that the sick feeling in his own gut would be reflected in most of the faces in the room.

Debbie finished her report.

"Aliya, Ricky," Nate said, "how are you getting on with the cameras and stuff?"

"Thames Valley CSI have been processing that public phone," Aliya said. Aylesbury lay over the border in Buckinghamshire, so the phone used for the anonymous call was in a different jurisdiction. "I've been warned that the problem might be too many sets of fingerprints."

"That doesn't matter," Debbie piped up. "If we think she was one of the intruders, then there's a chance we'll find a print or two at the murder scene that matches something on the phone."

"There's more, though," Aliya said. "There's a CCTV camera covering the square where the phone is. The DC I spoke to over there – Natalie Chen – is getting hold of the footage from around the time the call was made."

Ricky raised a finger. "I'm still waiting on footage from cameras around Wigginton for the last week or so. If we get really lucky, maybe we'll recognise the girl who used that phone."

"I don't want to dampen enthusiasm," said Rachel Sharp. "I know that break-in led to the tip off, but it's probably the least of our worries in terms of identifying our killer. Or our victims, come to that."

"Very likely," Debbie said. "But we can't be absolutely certain none of the intruders is actually involved in the murders, can we? And, even if they're not, then at least if we can eliminate them; then any other prints or DNA at the scene might help us narrow down the field."

"Fair point," Rachel acknowledged.

"And we recovered a computer and tablet from the house for analysis, so they might also yield something useful."

"You've handed them over to the techies?" Nate checked.

"Of course."

"Okay." Nate had resumed his place at the front. "This is obviously one where it could take us some time to identify all the victims," he said. "It's just possible they were in some way known to Lynne Redding, the owner of the house, and that some third party will know them all. But we can't take that for granted. We don't even know at the moment whether Ms Redding–" he tapped her photograph on the Wall "–was involved in the murders or is one of the victims."

"The post mortems should help with identification, sir," Izzy suggested.

"I hope so, although it's possible they won't leave us any the wiser for some victims. We should eventually get fingerprints, but whether all or any of them will be on the database, we'll have to wait and see. We'll also look for matches on the National Crime Agency's missing persons database, as well as circulating details to local forces. Someone must be missing these women. We just don't know for how long."

"What *is* obvious," Rachel said, "is that Hall House is unlikely to be the start of our killer's career. Even if he hasn't killed before, he'll have some sort of crimes of violence or sexual offences under his belt. Either he got away with them, or he's somewhere in police files. I know we're already checking out known sexual offenders in the area, but while we're talking to the NCA, let's see if they can find anything that chimes with what we've got here."

"Meanwhile," Nate said, "we need to find the person who made that anonymous call, have a chat with the local postie, and try and track down Steve the handyman."

"What about that note, purportedly from Lynne, to the neighbours?" said Rachel. "Do we think it's genuine?"

"It doesn't sound as if we're going to get a look at it, but that's always possible. If it *is* genuine, I reckon there are two possibilities. Either Lynne's involved in the murders and some, or probably all, of the women were already dead when she went away. Maybe she got scared she was about to get found out, or maybe she had a partner and they both decided to move on for some reason."

"If that's the case, maybe Steve is the real deal, and maybe he'll be turning up for work on Monday."

He smiled. "Wouldn't that be nice? But it seems strange, to say the least, to give a handyman the run of the house, knowing there are bodies in the cellar."

"You said there were two possibilities?" Rachel said.

"Or maybe the note's still genuine," he suggested, "but then Steve, whoever he is, starts killing women and storing their bodies in her absence."

"Far more likely the note is fake," Katie said. "Lynne is a victim herself, and it was Steve who typed and delivered it, explaining away both Lynne's absence and his own comings and goings."

"You may well be right. But I don't want to close down any avenues of inquiry for the moment. As far as Steve is concerned, let's just hope he's left fingerprints and DNA at the scene."

He scanned the faces in front of him one more time. "Anything else, anyone?"

"We're still checking out paperwork found in the house," piped up PC Sophie Monahan. Like Libby Statham, a mainstay of the uniformed contingent in major investigations. "But it's starting to tell an interesting tale. For starters, her passport was still in the house. It's long since expired, and doesn't look officially cancelled. So unless she went abroad under an assumed name, possibly with fake documentation, I'm thinking she must still be in the UK, even if she isn't in one of the freezers."

"Can you check with the passport office and make sure it hasn't been renewed?"

"On it, guv. The other thing that's interesting is that all the documentation relating to stuff like Council Tax and utilities bills was organised on the coffee table in the lounge. Not much else in the way of post, apart from a small pile on the front doormat. Although, if she's that reclusive, she might not *get* anything else."

"Or someone's been handling the official stuff," Izzy suggested. "Making it look like it's business as usual at Hall House."

"Something else for you to follow up on, Sophie," Nate said. She nodded and scribbled a note.

"What about media?" Rachel said. "I suspect Superintendent Taylor will be chomping at the bit to issue a statement."

"We need to hold off on that for as long as we can," Nate objected. "As far as we know, our killer has been pretty much coming and going as they pleased, maybe for at least eighteen months. For all we know, he could be planning on going back there at any moment. We don't want to tip him off that his lair has been compromised if we can help it."

"I get where you're coming from," Rachel said. "But the neighbours won't have missed the police activity. They'll tell their family and friends, even if they don't tell the press. And these burglars, or crackheads, or whoever broke in…"

"They're not going to be broadcasting their criminal exploits, are they?"

"A tip off to some rag in exchange for a nice little finder's fee and a promise of anonymity? Who knows? But in any case, I'll be very surprised if the Super isn't determined to at least make some vague statement today about an unspecified number of bodies being discovered at an unspecified location in Hertfordshire."

Nate thought even something as brief and unspecific as that was likely to have headlines writing themselves. If he was the killer, he'd err on the side of caution and assume that the police were all over his killing ground. He would stay well away for now.

Meanwhile, Wigginton had no idea what was about to hit it. A full-scale media circus, with everything but the big top, was going to descend on them. Parish Councillors, the Vicar of St Bartholomew's, and other community leaders, would all be asked for sound bites. There would be vox pops with 'ordinary people', short on information but long on opinions. It would be the main topic of conversation at The Greyhound pub, in the community-run shop and café, even in the swanky Champneys health spa up the road.

And coppers going about their duty would have to endure the bellowed question from across the road. The microphones and cameras shoved in their faces.

He returned to his office, replaying the briefing in his mind. One house, five dead women. There could be any number of scenarios behind those bald facts but, if he was a gambling man, his money would be on them being killed over a period, by someone driven to kill and kill again. If he was right, that urge wouldn't disappear. Sooner or later it would become overwhelming. The itch would be scratched somehow.

And Nate had no idea when or where.

6

By day, the centre of Watford is busy and bustling. Whether it's the Atria shopping centre, with dozens of stores under one roof, or the other shops, or the banks, cafés, restaurants, betting shops and other amenities scattered around the town centre, there is plenty to attract people.

They all go about their business, getting on with their busy lives. Most of them don't notice Courtney. She doesn't know it, but the town was ranked thirty-sixth highest for homelessness in a recent survey, with well over six hundred people in temporary accommodation and more, like herself, sleeping rough.

Few of those who give her a glance make eye contact and, for those who do, it is nearly always fleeting. A brief look and look away.

They have no idea how easy it is to become just like her. How those busy, bustling lives they are leading hang by a thread that can snap in an instant. Once you start falling, it can seem impossible to stop until you hit rock bottom.

She too had a life once.

Since she found herself here, friendless and penniless, she's had the odd night's respite in shelters, but she's yet to find a permanent room where she feels safe and comfortable.

So here she is, another long night on the street ahead of her.

The town centre is never quiet but, as the sun goes down and shadows lengthen, it seems to her to take on a more threatening character. Who knows what that darkened doorway may conceal, or whose footsteps are passing by? For a woman alone, it can be terrifying.

Only a couple of weeks ago, when she was so new to all this, she'd been approached by two men passing by. Two men with beer breath, cheesy grins and a certain look in their eye, setting her alarm bells ringing immediately, and no one else around.

They were trying to get her to drink from a hip flask, and growing more belligerent, when a tall figure with birds-nest hair had surged out of a nearby shop doorway. One moment, Courtney didn't know she was even there. The next, she was standing beside her, drawn up to her full height, chin jutting aggressively.

"She said no," she said evenly. "Why aren't you taking no for an answer?"

Hip Flask Man stared at her. "What business is it of yours?"

"I'm making it my business. So why don't you piss off? Get back to your wives, your wanking, or whatever it is you do with your scrawny little pricks."

It wasn't exactly diplomacy, oil on troubled water. For a moment Courtney's heart had been in her mouth, convinced this was going to end badly. Then the other man had barked a laugh.

"Sorry, Butch," he said. "This one never said she was spoken for. We'll leave you dykes to your muff munching, or whatever you do with your big, wet—"

Rosie slapped him hard across the face. "Mind your manners around ladies. If there's one thing I hate, it's bad fucking language."

The man had laughed again, rubbing his cheek with his palm. "Sorry again, Your Majesty." He turned to his mate. "Time we were going anyway. See what you get for being friendly."

Only when the men were far enough away had the woman focused on Courtney. "You need to be on the front foot if you're gonna survive on the streets, hun. You need to toughen up, or you won't last five minutes."

From that moment, Rosie had taken her under her wing. She isn't around so much during the day, and Courtney never likes to ask where she goes with that big wheelie shopping bag of hers. After dark, though, she's never far away, and it makes Courtney feel that bit safer.

But this is Saturday afternoon, Rosie is off somewhere, and Courtney is sitting on a low wall, trying not to draw too much attention to herself. She isn't actually begging, but she's found there are some decent people around who might slip her a few coins, maybe a sandwich or a coffee.

The outreach workers do their best too, but the one shelter they've enticed her into scared her too much to stick around. The sound of loud arguments, what sounded like fist fights at 2am, waking up to someone in her room, trying to steal what little stuff she has. Rosie says it can be like that, and that she feels safer on the streets.

At the same time, she needs some way of getting back on her feet. As things stand, she can't go back, and she can't move forwards.

"You look like you could do with one of these." A male voice breaks into her thoughts, and she looks up to see a guy holding two takeaway coffees.

She's not seen him before, and her suspicions are immediately aroused. But he must see that in her eyes, because he says, "I got an Americano and a latte. If you like, you can choose which you want, and I'll drink the other one, so you can see there's nothing funny about them. I know you can't be too careful."

He's scruffy, with a shaggy beard and longish hair straggling out from under a battered baseball cap. A parka that's seen better days, open to reveal a baggy, rust coloured jumper. There's something reassuring about his slightly shabby appearance and his open smile. Nothing like the vulpine look of a predator.

Still, "You drink the Americano," she says.

He takes a few sips, and then offers her the latte again. This time she takes it, thanking him.

There's something of the old-fashioned gentleman about him, and his eyes seem kind. He asks her how long she's been on the streets, and how she came here. And, to her surprise, she finds herself telling him.

The domestic abuse. Fleeing to her parents, only for them to appoint themselves as mediators and invite him down with a view to brokering a reconciliation. By then, her partner had manipulated her out of her job and cleaned out the joint bank account he'd insisted they have. Her parents had been mortified, their apologies grovelling, but the damage had been done. With little cash in her purse, and bank cards that didn't work any more, she'd walked out anyway, first sofa surfing with friends, but increasingly scared by him turning up on their doorsteps looking for her.

She'd run again and somehow fetched up here. Sometimes she wanted nothing more than to phone her parents, forgive them, and try to rewind, but she'd fallen so far, she could see no way back.

"You do know there are shelters and things?" he says gently. "It's not safe out here, especially at night."

So she tells him of her distrust of those places.

"I know what you mean," he says, "but maybe you were unlucky. Look, I work for a small charity that works with homeless people and with the local outreach teams. I could keep an ear to the ground for something that'd suit you if you like. Not all places are that bad, and there are some good schemes coming through. What do you think?"

She's far from convinced, but at least he seems to be talking about her as a person with her own individual needs. She likes that. She thinks she might like *him*.

"Okay," she says. "Might be worth a try."

He smiles. "Good. Just leave it with me. I'm Paul, by the way."

He holds out a hand, and she shakes it.

"Courtney," she says.

7

Ricky James's efforts to get hold of Wigginton's regular postie had proved a bit fiddly, but he'd eventually found an out of hours contact at Royal Mail and been assured that one Pete Savage would be contacted and asked to call Ricky urgently. He was pleasantly surprised when the call came through less than half an hour later.

"No, no," Savage had said when Ricky had offered to visit his home, "I'll come to you, rather than give the neighbourhood gossip factory any ammo."

"We're detectives," Ricky assured him, "and we'd be in an unmarked car. No one will know we're police."

"Round here? You'd be surprised."

So Ricky had Pete Savage in one of the nicer interview rooms, such as it was. The guv had asked Izzy Cole to sit in. Ricky knew that shadowing 'proper' detectives was a major part of her training and she seemed to crop up everywhere.

He supposed some might resent a protégé of the boss, especially a young woman, getting involved in so much of the interesting work. But Ricky wasn't complaining, especially when he was the one being shadowed. At least it presumably meant the boss thought of him as someone Izzy could learn from.

He still thought she was hot, even if she'd made it pretty clear she didn't do workplace relationships. Sometimes wondered if he might stand a chance if he or she transferred out of West Herts Division.

Probably not, he decided.

Pete Savage was about five-nine and slim, with short dark hair and a cheerful smile. He was also no fool. As soon as Wigginton was mentioned, he nodded.

"I thought so. This is about those murders in the news, right?"

"Suspicious deaths," Ricky amended. The M word hadn't yet been used in any public statements."

"Whatever," Savage said. "So whose house is it? I know them all. You can learn a lot about people as a postie. There's one guy in who gets all these packages in those big grey plastic mailing bags. You've seen 'em?"

Ricky wasn't sure he had, but he nodded to save time.

"Well, it turns out he's some sort of tribunal judge and those packages are all the papers for his hearings – bundles, he calls them. Then another woman—"

"Good to know," Ricky cut him short, but not rudely. "You'll have some really good insights then." A bit of ego-stroking never went amiss. "So your round is from when to when?"

"Well, my shift is 7am to about half two. I'm usually doing Wiggo around lunchtime."

Ricky gave him Lynne Redding's address. "What can you tell us about her?"

He looked shocked. "Ms Redding? Really? I'd never have put her down as someone to get herself murdered – or a murderer, come to that." Even as he spoke, there was a subtle change in his demeanour. "What exactly happened?"

It was rich that this guy had labelled his neighbours as gossips, when it was already clear that he loved a spot of tittle-tattle himself. He was almost drooling, his ears practically flapping.

"We can't discuss the details," Izzy cut in. "But I'm sure you understand that?" She flashed her killer smile at him. It seemed Ricky wasn't the only one who knew how to stroke an ego.

"Oh, sure." He reached for nonchalant. Ricky didn't think he cut it. He nodded sagely. "You'll be holding back information only the killer would know."

"We really can't comment," Izzy said.

"Course you can't." He actually winked. "I watch the crime shows. Wow," he added, "this is cool."

There was no disguising her distaste. *"Really?"*

Postman Pete at least had the grace to look mortified. "Sorry. Christ, I can't believe I said that. Not cool for the people who died, obviously."

"But you've seen Ms Redding?" Izzy persisted. "You've met her?"

"Yeah, course. Only when I had to knock the door like, with something too big for the letter box or needing a signature. Or something for next door. But I haven't seen her for..." He frowned. "It must be well over a year, and there hasn't been anything to knock about for at least as long. Not so much post for her these days, either, now I think of it. Bits of junk mail. You can't stop that, can you? Well, you can a bit, but—"

"What were your impressions of her?"

"Nice. A bit quiet." He looked thoughtful. "Shy, maybe. Always seemed to be home – I never had to leave a card that I recall."

"Did she ever have visitors when you called there?"

He frowned. "There was sometimes a van – a gardener, there was a sign on the side. Oh, and one of those little Fiat toasters was there about once a week. I saw that at other places too, though. A lady. Does cleaning gigs all over the village. I guess she did Ms Redding's place. They're not really visitors though, are they? And the Carltons next door reckoned she was some sort of hermit. A recluse?"

"The Carltons talked to you about her?" Ricky interjected.

"Well, yeah. We always have a chat. Mostly her. I'm sure she mentioned it about Miss Redding when I had a parcel for her. I thought it was pretty sad. As I say, she was really nice."

He leaned forward. "Actually, when I say no visitors, that's not quite right. I remember seeing an Audi parked there a couple of times and, I suppose after the past year. Look, can you at least tell me if she's okay?"

"What about a handyman, name of Steve?" Ricky suggested. "Have you ever seen him? Talked to him, maybe?"

"Don't think so. When would this have been?"

"Since about May last year?" The date of her farewell note to the Carltons.

"Don't think so," he said again. "What's he look like?"

Ricky weighed giving the description. A likeness of Handyman Steve would be released soon, so it wasn't going to be under wraps for much longer.

"Bit of a scruffy individual, by all accounts. Grey hair all over the place, straggly beard, shabby clothes. Watford baseball cap."

"Watford?"

"The football team?"

"I wouldn't know. I don't follow football at all. Delivering letters is my sport," he added with a chuckle. "But no. Never seen him."

"Okay," Ricky said. "Coming back to Ms Redding... you must have had conversations with her."

"Not really. As I say, she seemed nice, but it wasn't like we put the world to rights. The odd bit of small talk. The weather mostly, I think. 'How are you?' 'Fine, thanks, and you?' That sort of thing."

Ricky suppressed a sigh. "Maybe you can you think back to when you last saw her? It might have been nearer to eighteen months ago?"

"Blimey, that's a long old time. I'm not sure *when* I last saw her, to be honest. But why?"

"We wondered if you remembered anything different about her?"

"It's clear you've got good memory," Izzy flattered.

He looked pleased. "Yeah, well. But no. No, I can't recall any difference."

"Did she seem on edge, for example?"

He puffed out his cheeks. "Not that I remember now, but it was a long time ago." He looked suddenly earnest. "Look, I love my job. Out in the fresh air, seeing people, getting exercise... it suits me, you know? But one day's much like any other. All I can say is there was nothing stuck in my mind." He paused. "Thing is, she *always* seemed a bit on edge, like she couldn't wait to shut the door."

"So what do you think about him?" Ricky asked Izzy after Savage had departed.

She shrugged. "Bit of a dick. But he's not a serious suspect, surely?"

"Seems that way, but…" He made a rocking motion with his hand. "He could easily have been the last person to see Lynne alive. And, if we really think the killer based his whole agenda on having that house to himself, then Pete the Postie definitely had plenty of opportunities to see that potential."

"I guess, whoever the killer is, they're not going to have MURDERER stencilled on their forehead," she conceded.

"Great idea, though." He grinned. "Make our job a lot easier."

8

Katie and Libby had spoken to Lynne Redding's cleaner. Eve Banks had worked at Hall House around six years and thought Lynne had seen more of her than anyone else. Most likely, she'd been the only visitor who had the run of the house. She'd gone in the cellar twice a year, just to deal with dust and cobwebs, and saw it as mostly a dumping ground, with just one chest freezer down there.

"We'd got into a bit of a routine," Eve told them. "Lynne would make tea as soon as I arrived, and we'd sit together and drink it. Lynne told me she knew people must think she was odd, but she suffered with agoraphobia. Counselling hadn't helped, and having so little interaction with other people served to make her nervous about seeing anybody. Taking me on must have been a big step for her."

Eve had come to see her as a friend, so she'd been gutted by the way she'd been let go. That short, sharp email had felt like a sacking, and also made her feel like a fool.

"After all that stuff about not being able to go out at all, she was going abroad. As if she'd been lying to me and laughing behind my back from the very beginning."

She admitted her husband had gone "absolutely Tonto" about it, and one's spouse being dismissed from a couple of hours' a week cleaning might be a cause for annoyance, even anger, if it was handled badly. But a motive for murder, let alone five murders? Still, it was as well to keep an open mind. Could he have killed Lynne in a fury over his wife's sacking and then found he liked it? Or had the knowledge that the house had been standing empty been the incentive to act out a sick fantasy?

Eve had been able to provide a name and contact number for the gardener, Brian Small, and mentioned an accountant "or some such", who occasionally dropped in. Adam somebody. Handyman Steve she'd neither seen nor heard of.

It was getting on for 7pm. Laura answered Nate's call just as he feared it would go to voicemail.

"Hello, you," she said.

"Hi. Look, sorry about today. I can't say much about the case right now, but it's pretty horrible and there's been tons to do."

"That's what I get for falling for a murder detective, I suppose." He heard the smile in her voice. "Don't worry, I've been fine. I did the walk anyway."

"To Aldbury?" A ten-mile round trip from home.

"Yep. It's been a bit of a grey day, but it was good to get out."

"I suppose you stopped off at the Musette?" The farm-based café was big on its authentic Vietnamese street food, but Nate's sweet tooth drew him unerringly to the magnificent range of cakes on offer. Laura maintained that several of them amounted to a coronary on a plate, but Nate insisted that the five-mile hike home was more than enough to counterbalance the calories. Certainly, he never seemed to gain an ounce.

"Well," she said, "someone had to do it. I had the healthiest looking cake on the menu, which isn't saying much. A little something for you seems to have found its way into my backpack too."

He smiled. "Have I told you I love you?"

"Might have mentioned it."

"Anyhow, I just rang to say I shouldn't be here much longer."

"Calling it a day?"

"Yeah. It's tempting to keep everyone here, chipping away at the case, but it's that bit more difficult getting hold of people on a Saturday night. I might just drop by the mortuary before I head home though."

Dr Stoddart was planning on removing the single body from its freezer to thaw, and he wanted to be there.

"So you'll be how long?"

"Should be home before eight."

"Good. I made that stew earlier, so it'll just need heating up."

After they hung up, he checked his email one last time before standing up, intending to pack everyone off home. He was halfway to his office doorway when Katie appeared, accompanied by Ricky and Aliya.

"News?" he demanded.

"It's suddenly coming thick and fast," Katie said. "I'm not sure where to begin."

"Well, come in," he said, finding their enthusiasm infectious. A thought occurred to him. "Is Izzy about?"

"Yes, good thought," Katie said. "Useful for her to sit in."

"I'll find her," Ricky said.

A few minutes later, the five of them were squeezed around Nate's small meeting table.

"As I said," Katie told him, "a lot has happened in the last half hour."

Nate opened his notebook, pen poised.

"First of all," she said, "CSI are still checking any fingerprints they find at the scene against to the national database. And they found a match – one Owen Simmonds. Seventeen years old, from Aylesbury."

"Aylesbury again?" It couldn't be a coincidence. "Why are his prints on the database?"

"Minor drug offences about a year ago. But there's more on him. Ricky, you tell it."

"Guv, we've got some interesting stuff from the local cameras," Ricky said. "Thursday night, on the A41, a mile or so from Wiggo, a Vauxhall Corsa was caught by a mobile speed trap. Just before 10.30pm, doing ninety-one miles per hour. Registered to the same Owen Simmonds. And that's not all. We've identified a CCTV camera just down the road from the murder house, and we've picked the same car up on that one."

"We need to get him in," Nate said.

"Yeah, but it gets even better, guv."

Ricky had brought a slim folder in with him. Now he opened it and placed a photograph in front of Nate. "Not long before Owen boy's car gets caught on camera, we see this lot running from the direction of our crime scene. Three males and two females by the look of them. You can view the footage for yourself, guv, but they look to me like they're in a panic."

Five grainy figures. All in hoodies, three of them with hoods up.

"Not great pictures," Nate commented.

"Sure, but…" Ricky laid out two more images. One was a driving licence. "This is Owen Simmonds."

The thin-faced youth, staring sullenly at the camera, looked younger than his seventeen years.

"And this is one of the figures from that group, blown up," Ricky continued, tapping the second image. "Okay, he's got his hood up, but I reckon you can see enough of the face. As you say, guv, it's not the best of pics, but I reckon it could easily be him."

"I'm pretty sure it *is* him," Katie added.

Izzy was squinting at the blurry image. "I see what you mean. I wouldn't like to swear on it though."

"We're still working our way through the cameras," said Ricky, a slight defensiveness creeping into his voice. "I'm hoping we'll spot the car closer to the crime scene. But I haven't finished."

He pulled another sheet from his folder. "We blew up the other kids in the first picture. Take a look at this one…"

He produced another grainy, expanded photograph. A girl this time, her hood down, blonde hair in a ponytail, or maybe a plait. Even the poor quality of the image couldn't disguise how pretty she was. Or how scared she looked.

Aliya had brought her own folder, from which she produced a still, again from a CCTV camera. Same average quality, but good enough to clearly see the features of the girl in running attire, walking away from a public phone next to what looked like a lion statue in a town square. Nate and Izzy both studied the two images.

"There are earlier pictures of her using the phone at exactly the time our anonymous call was made," she said. "There's no doubt she's our caller. And I've no doubt she's the girl in Ricky's picture."

"Nor have I," Izzy said.

"I'm inclined to agree," admitted Nate. "Whether they'd convince a jury..."

"I know it's not perfect, Nate," Katie said, "but there's a narrative, I think. There's every chance we'll marry a print from the phone up with one from the house, pretty well putting this girl there on Thursday night."

"Yes," he said, "I agree. I think we're looking at these five kids breaking into the house. Hoping to steal something? A bit of vandalism? Let's park the motive. We're seeing them running away, probably scared by something they've seen – we can guess what that is, can't we? They pile into young Simmonds' car and he takes off, foot to the floor, hits the A41 and flies through that speed trap."

"We always doubted that the break-in was connected to the murders," Katie said. "And these kids..."

"...surely weren't involved," he agreed. "No, I think this is all about eliminating them from our inquiries. Except..."

Something was ticking at the back of his mind. But it was Izzy Cole who articulated it.

"Except they almost certainly *knew* that house was standing empty," she said. "I mean, come on. Kids from Aylesbury – well, at least two of them were from there, we reckon – busting into a house somewhere like Wigginton?"

"One of them had found out it was empty," Katie agreed. "The question is, who told them? And who else knew?"

"My money is on it stemming from Sharon Carlton," Izzy said. "I thought she had 'gossip' written all over her face, and the postie has confirmed it."

"Right," Nate said, "one step at a time. Great work, by the way, everyone. We need to bring this Owen Simmonds in and lean on him. Can you speak to your contact in Aylesbury, Aliya?"

"Sure," she said. "Do we want them to pick him up now?"

He was tempted to say yes, but he found himself hesitating. "It's the evening. He could be out with his mates, and then we'd have to find him." He made a decision. "You know what? Ask if they can do it early tomorrow. Nothing like dragging a suspect out of bed to put them on the back foot. I'd like you and Ricky to be there. Izzy, too."

"Do you want Simmonds brought here?" Aliya asked.

"Yes, I do. Stick him in a squad car, bleary eyed, and drive him twenty miles to Hemel. That'll put the wind up him. Oh, and make sure he knows he's entitled to an appropriate adult. One of his parents would be good. And find out who the duty solicitor's going to be, in case he wants them."

"I already checked the list for the weekend," said Katie. "It's Margaret Lunn."

Nate rolled his eyes. "Wonderful." Lunn was a woman of truly indeterminate age, with purple-streaked hair and a fondness for big spectacles. She eschewed the usual women lawyer's uniform of black suit and white blouse in favour of brightly coloured faux-fur coats in the winter and a range of dazzling diaphanous dresses all the year round.

If her look was somewhat unconventional, her style was one hundred per cent by the book. You didn't get an easy ride with Margaret Lunn. Which was fine by Nate. It could drive him mad, but he knew in his heart that she was good for justice.

"Okay," he said. "Let's get that arrest set up and then we'll interview him. Katie, would you be okay to lead on that? I might be around, but it depends on when the doc's starting his post mortem. Unless you want to cover for me there?"

He managed to keep his face straight, even when Katie shuddered.

"No," she said, "you're fine. You keep your rendezvous with the dead and I'll interview the living."

9

Being 'head hunted' from her uniformed role in a small town backwater to join the CID team as a trainee detective had been a dream come true for Izzy Cole. It was hard work, with study and exams, as well as hands on experience. But she relished it all. She'd passed her National Investigators Examination, completed her Investigator Training Course, and was now building a professional development portfolio that would provide evidence of her competencies as a detective.

She was also in regular contact with her Detective Tutor Constable at Hertfordshire Constabulary's Welwyn Garden City headquarters. And she was thoroughly enjoying learning from, and being mentored by, detectives she rated. Both DI Quarrel and Katie Gray seemed to take her development seriously, not just making sure she got to crime scenes and sat in on meetings and interviews, but actively seeking her opinions and ideas.

In a few weeks' time, Izzy hoped her work would be validated and she would be confirmed as a substantive Detective Constable. After that, she had her eye on the Senior Investigation Officer Training Programme, which would eventually qualify her to lead major investigations including murder, manslaughter, kidnapping and terrorism.

She was conscious that, around now, Dr Jordan Stoddart would be taking his first tentative steps towards finding out what those five unfortunate women had gone through at the house at Wigginton before finally relinquishing their hold on life. The scene there had sickened and appalled Izzy but, at the same time, she had to admit that working a case like this could do her career development no harm at all.

What was left of Saturday evening for her would involve a takeaway curry from the Tamarind in Tring High Street, some fairly mindless TV and an early night. With work so full-on, it was probably just as well that she had no social life to speak of.

The thought prompted her to check her phone. No texts, no WhatsApp messages, and no emails from friends and acquaintances. The only thing of note was that the battery was down to less than ten per cent of its power. Again. Even though she'd not exactly been hammering it today. She probably needed to make time to get a new phone before this one died altogether, she thought as she attached it to the charger.

That'll be a bit of an event for you, Iz, she thought sardonically.

Back when she'd first been seconded to DI Quarrel's team, she'd had a best friend she'd thought she could count on through thick and thin, and a boyfriend who probably wasn't going to last, but whom she'd still enjoyed being with. Fast forward a few weeks, and she'd dumped them both in a single moment of mortifying madness.

Now you're turning into one of those sad cows who lives only for your work.

"Piss off," she told the voice in her head, but it had spoken true.

More than once in recent months, she'd contemplated online dating. Everyone seemed to be doing it these days. Ricky seemed to get through dates like a pig in a pie factory, and she knew Aliya had met her latest squeeze that way. To her mind, she met enough bloody weirdos in a day's work, without actively going looking for them, but maybe that was being unfair to legions of people just as lonely as her.

Maybe she should talk to Ricky about how he broached the whole being a copper thing. No, not Ricky. He'd asked her out once, and she fancied she still occasionally caught him looking a little too fondly at her. Best not let him know she was looking for love.

Aliya, then. She'd resisted all her mum's schemes to set her up with a nice Moslem boy, only to find one anyway through a dating app. Izzy got the impression that was going well.

Aliya's mum was in Seventh Heaven. "He's only a dentist!" Aliya had told her. "I mean, not a doctor or a lawyer, but good enough for her. He ticks most of her boxes."

Indeed, if Mrs Nazir had anything to do with it, the wedding would already be arranged, but Aliya insisted she was just enjoying life and wanted to get to know Hamza properly, not scare him off by getting too heavy too soon. Fortunately, her dad got it and insisted she *"Leave the poor girl alone"*.

Still, Izzy was pleased for her. And, as she'd joked, "You never know when a friendly dentist might come in handy."

"Yeah," Aliya had agreed, "when he first complimented me on my smile, I half-wondered if he was being romantic or professional."

So maybe Izzy needed to ask her for a few pointers.

Meanwhile, she wasn't about to complain about being part of the Wigginton investigation. Shining on a case like this could do no harm to her prospects.

Maybe, a few years from now, it would be her calling the shots in major inquiries and answering to 'guv'.

For now, though, she had a more mundane task to address.

She reached for the takeaway menu.

*

As the day had wound down, Nate had found his feelings about the case conflicting. A lot of progress had been made in building up a picture of what might have happened in Hall House, and there was still a great deal of legwork to do. But he really hoped some concrete leads and viable suspects would emerge soon.

He'd been in this profession long enough to know how dangerous it could be to get too entrenched in any speculative theories, and that the killer could yet turn out to be some random individual who had not crossed their radar. But at this stage, his gut told him that the killer's name might have already been mentioned.

Postman Pete Savage, perhaps. The husband of Eve Banks, the cleaner…

Then there was the gardener, Brian Small and, apparently, an accountant and some sort of psychologist. And what about the flappy-tongued neighbours, the Carltons?

Who else was in Lynne's life?

The dream scenario was somebody making a slip of the tongue while being questioned. But he wasn't about to hold his breath.

Laura was watching a film on TV when Nate finally got home.

"It's crap," she said, "but there's only about twenty minutes left. Do you mind?"

"Course not. Tea?"

"Please. And there's plenty of stew, if you're hungry."

He nuked the stew in the microwave while making tea in the mugs. He took Laura's drink to her, ate the food when it was ready, then took his own mug in to join her. The credits were just rolling on her film, so she turned the set off and asked him how his day had been.

He yawned. "Frustrating. Sad. And you've got the whole weekend off and I can't be here. What will you do tomorrow?"

"Oh, I dunno. Maybe go for a walk up along the canal. Bake a cake. I might go over and see Mum and Dad. Catch up on bowls and dancing and their clubs, and get told all about people I've never met, as if I've known them all my life."

He laughed. "Parents, eh? Katie's always moaning about that. Not an issue for me, of course," he added, with rather less humour.

Nate's father was dead and he had been estranged from his mother for decades until April last year. That meeting had left him confused about his feelings, and about everything he'd thought he knew about her. But it certainly hadn't been what he'd call a reconciliation.

Since then, he'd made one brief, awkward call to her, making it clear that if they were to have any further contact it would be when he was ready.

By mutual consent, it wasn't a topic of conversation in their house, so they talked about other subjects. Laura enthused about the autumnal glory of the landscape on her walk, and told him she'd seen a deer in amongst some trees. He'd been planning to take his new camera with him, and wished he'd been with her to try it out.

Later on, he went upstairs to the top floor of their three-storey house and the room he used as his office. Thoughts of his mother were still buzzing at the back of his mind. The large cork board he had attached to the wall over his desk last year was covered up by an old sheet, which he now removed to reveal his own Wall of Death, festooned with printed off photographs, copied newspaper clippings, and notes relating to a case some forty years old.

Some of the material had been copied from the original case file, which he'd obtained under dubious pretences and copied for his own use before returning it. He would likely have some explaining to do if it became known that he'd done so. Quite likely it was a disciplinary offence.

And for what?

All those hours he'd spent poring over documents and photographs, trying to find something that might change the narrative of the case, had come to nothing. On the face of it, it was a simple, tragic case of domestic violence, its only singular feature being that this had involved a woman with a temper and a tendency to drink flying into a rage and stabbing her husband – the father of her son – to death in their Yorkshire home, on a winter's day with snow on the ground outside.

The trouble was, the woman was Nate's mother. The dead man his father. Apparently it had happened in front of the six-year-old Nathan, but he'd repressed the memory. The jury had not believed the self-defence plea, and Nate's mother had spent over twenty years in prison while he had been raised by his paternal grandparents, who hadn't believed it either.

After her release, she'd made repeated efforts to re-establish contact with him, but some wounds went too deep. He'd grown up without either of his parents, raised by people older than the parents of his peers. He'd had few friends, none of them close enough to be around any more, and trust, to put it mildly, had never been his strong suit.

In his efforts to be rid of her, he'd moved south, changed his name from Bowman to Quarrel, and hoped to drop off her radar. But she'd found him and, somehow, he'd agreed to take a look at her case, to what end he wasn't sure. There was nothing in the file, nor on the Internet for that matter, that contradicted the verdict.

He sighed. He should either condemn the contents of the board and all the paperwork in his desk drawer to a bonfire; or have the courage to do something with it. But what?

The ghost of an idea that had nagged at him for months slipped into his mind once more. Maybe it was time.

These days, the only person he trusted completely was Laura. It wasn't that he didn't invest any trust at all in others: his team were a case in point. But this was different. This wasn't just about professional confidence. It went way deeper than that. The case obsessed him, and he needed help, if he was ever to be free of it.

He went over to the window and looked out into the darkness. It was a clear night and the sky was full of stars. He could see them reflected on the surface of the canal. It somehow felt like a metaphor for pinpricks of light in his own darkness.

He took the copied case file from the drawer, located the report he was looking for, and re-copied the pages. Then he sat with them at his desk, took a heavy black marker pen from a mug containing miscellaneous writing implements. Paused. And began redacting the documents.

10

Izzy had slept like a baby until the alarm had woken her, and she felt fresh and sharp.

By contrast, she guessed that the duty solicitor wasn't a mornings person. Margaret Lunn stifled a yawn whilst Izzy set the recording equipment going and the detectives introduced themselves.

"So can we crack on?" Lunn prompted, once everyone said their names for the record. "The sooner we've gone through the motions, the sooner my client can go home and get on with his weekend."

Katie shrugged. "We'll decide whether Owen is going anywhere, Ms Lunn."

Owen Simmonds sat between Lunn and his father. Pale and thin faced, he wore his brown hair with a long fringe at the front. It flopped down over his eyes every time he moved his head and he kept sweeping it away with the back of his hand.

His expression spoke of something between insolence and apprehension. It had been pretty obvious during that early morning swoop, when his father had brought him downstairs, bleary-eyed and hastily dressed, that he'd known exactly what this was about. Simmonds Senior had ordered him to keep his trap shut until he'd spoken to a lawyer, and had accepted the offer of the duty solicitor "for now".

Katie looked at Owen. "Let's talk about Thursday night. What were your movements?"

The young man had been cautioned and arrested on suspicion of breaking and entering. If he was wise, he'd have confided about the events of Thursday night in the time he'd been allowed to consult with Lunn. Izzy wondered how his father would have reacted, especially as the young man had been in trouble before. She also wondered what Margaret Lunn would have advised him to say.

It didn't take long to find out.

"My client would like to save himself and the police a great deal of trouble by giving an honest account of the evening in question," Margaret Lunn said. "We hope he'll be given credit for that, and that what amounted to no more than youthful high jinks will be seen in that way."

"Let's not prejudge that," Katie said. "Will your client be naming the people who were with him?"

"It was just a laugh," Owen spoke for the first time since his arrest. "I was on my own."

"We know that's not true," said Izzy.

"This whole 'youthful high jinks' angle isn't going to work, Owen," said Katie. "Not if you lie to us the first time you open your mouth." She glanced at Izzy. "DC Cole?"

Izzy removed a sheaf of photographs, printed on A4 paper, from a folder and spread them in front of him. Pushed one towards him.

"Thursday night," she said. "This is your car being caught on a speed camera on the A41. The time stamp is 10.27pm. I'd imagine the summons is in the post." She pushed a second photograph his way. "This is the same image enlarged. Hard to make out faces, but it looks like five of you in the car." A third image. "Shortly before this, caught on CCTV, five people running from the direction of a house in Wigginton where your fingerprints were found. And this," she moved a fourth picture his way, "is that picture enlarged." She indicated one of the faces. "Not great, I know, but that's you, isn't it?"

He nodded. "Yeah."

"So we'll need the names of your companions."

He licked his lips. "No comment."

"Oh, dear," Katie said sadly. She eyeballed his lawyer. "Ms Lunn, haven't you told your client? Owen – can I call you Owen?"

He shrugged, staring at the photographs. "Whatever."

"Owen, this isn't how it works. Not if you want us to give you some credit for cooperating with us. We know you were in that house, and we know what you found in that cellar. We need to know exactly what happened, and exactly who else was there. Loyalty to your mates is admirable, but we don't have time to mess about." She stabbed the picture of the five running figures. "So who are the other four people in the picture?"

Margaret Lunn leaned across Owen's back and whispered to his father, who nodded.

The older man looked at Katie.

"He's not a bad lad, Sergeant," he said. "He's lost his way a bit since his mum died. We thought maybe, new school, new start..." He trailed off, then turned his gaze upon his son.

"Owen," he said, "you should tell them."

The teenager looked up then. Clutched at his head, his expression pained. Then looked at Katie. "Can you cancel my speeding ticket if I tell you?"

She burst out laughing. "Don't push it."

*

Hemel Hempstead Hospital, which housed the local mortuary, was just ten minutes' walk from the Combe Street police station. No matter how many times Nate went there, the chilliness of the place never failed to unsettle him. Drops in the temperature had disturbed him all his life. Snowfall was the worst. Laura longed to go to Iceland or Norway to see the Northern Lights, but she knew he wouldn't be going with her. They both knew how it could freak him out.

Even knowing *why* the cold had such an effect on him didn't help him to cope any better.

But there was no escaping the mortuary in his line of work. He might let Katie Gray off post mortem duty, even though it was something she was going to have to confront at some point in her career if she wanted to progress; but he couldn't let himself off. He owed it to the dead to listen first hand to what they had to tell him.

As always, the scrubs and personal protective equipment Jordan Stoddart wore somehow contrived to make him look even younger. Lab assistants were busying themselves in the background.

"I'm afraid we made a start without you, Inspector," Dr Stoddart said. "We've got as far as getting her out of the freezer – which, believe me, you didn't want to watch. Painstaking and not very pleasant. But you'll want to see her."

He led Nate over to the slab and removed the plastic sheet that covered the body. Rigid and in the same semi-foetal position as the other dead women Nate had seen.

"There are freezer burns," Stoddart said, "and some patterning caused by the position of the body, its contact with the inside of the freezer. We did our absolute best to get her out intact. She left a few bits of skin behind. Debbie's CSIs are coming to remove the actual freezer for processing. For us, it's a waiting game."

The sight of this young woman, in her early thirties, reddish-brown hair, evidently healthy before her last moments became a living nightmare – naked and somehow vulnerable even in death – caused a wave of sorrow to wash over Nate.

"I can't begin to imagine what her last moments must have been like," said Stoddart. "Panic, fighting in vain to get out. So cold. Air running out. I'd guess, in the end, she was in total despair, just doing her best to keep warm."

Nate thought he was right, and cold anger joined the sadness he was feeling. He tried to reach for a little dispassion as he studied the corpse.

There was something about the face. Was it familiar, or was that just wishful thinking? He studied the hands. Like the bodies in the first freezer he'd looked inside, fingernails were broken and bloody, but there was more here.

"Some fingers and thumbs are missing," he observed.

"Some toes, too," the pathologist indicated. "Pretty amateurishly done by the look of it. We'll know more when she's thawed, but I'm betting the wounds were sealed with something like superglue."

"As if his sole aim was to avoid making too much mess with the blood?" Nate speculated.

"I know from Debbie he's a clean freak. What it does say is, she was alive when those amputations happened."

Nate was looking at the right shoulder. "Is that a tattoo?"

"Looks like it." They both looked closely. "I think it's a humming bird."

Nate thought so too. Small, and good work. He knew a little about tattoos from a previous case.

"Cover her," he said. "She's suffered enough indignity. Not the face yet, though." He watched as Stoddart did as he was asked. "I wonder if the severed fingers are part of his MO, or whether they're part of a pattern of escalation."

"We'll have a better idea when we start getting the others out. But what are you thinking?"

"I'm thinking if he'd wanted to send them to family members or the police, with ransom demands, or just as a taunt, wouldn't he have done that with all of them? This has been going on for well over a year, we believe, and no one's reported any such thing. Or did he want souvenirs? Or is it all about plain, old-fashioned cruelty? Getting more creative? Maybe trying different things as he went along, to see what he liked best? If so, then it was important to do it while she was alive. No fun going back and doing it to the dead ones."

He felt a fresh wave of anger and sadness, along with one new thought. "We're already falling into the trap of calling the killer 'he', aren't we? But I'd bet quite a lot on the person responsible for this being a man."

"Or a couple?" suggested Stoddart. "Male and female?"

"Fair point." It happened. Brady and Hindley. The Wests. The 'Angel Face' killers, Kieran Bardsley and Edina 'Eddie' Maxwell. It never did to keep a closed mind. "If that's the case, maybe the house owner was the female half. Lynne Redding. I texted you that photo, but you said on the phone that so far you couldn't identify her in any of the freezers."

"That's true," Stoddart agreed, "but, as I also said, we won't get a proper look at the faces on the bottom where the killer's doubled up. And it seems logical to imagine that, if she's one of the victims, she would have been the first, so that's where we'd find her, and most likely in the older freezer. If all goes according to plan, we'll take those two out tomorrow."

Nate didn't respond to this. The pace was frustrating, but he trusted the pathologist to know what he was doing.

"I suppose, if the violence *was* escalating, that might give you another guide to the order of killing?"

"It might," Stoddart agreed.

Nate looked at the dead woman's face again. "I can't help thinking I recognise her."

"Funny you should say that," said the pathologist. "We think so too. I just can't put my finger on who it is she puts me in mind of."

"I'd like some photographs, if that's possible," said Nate. "The face and that tattoo. Chances are it's nothing. She might just look like someone on TV. But then again, maybe we can identify her sooner rather than later."

"We'll do that now," said Stoddart. He went and spoke to an assistant. Came back. "Yes, she'll take some pics and text them to your phone."

"Thank you." He hesitated. "Actually, can I have a private word?"

Jordan Stoddart looked surprised. "Yes, of course. In my office?"

"Perfect," said Nate.

11

Owen Simmonds having given up the names of his four companions, Aliya had contacted DC Natalie Chen at Aylesbury. By the time Nate returned to the station, all four had been rounded up and were being brought to Combe Street. The team was split and, by lunchtime, the entire cohort had been questioned.

The inconsistencies in their stories had been somehow reassuring. Five suspects singing from precisely the same hymn street would scream collusion. As it was, their stories might not have been a perfect match, but between them they supplied more than enough information for the events of Thursday night to be pieced together in a way that made some sort of sense.

Owen's friends were Thomas Green, Daniel Hardy, Olivia 'Liv' Fenwick and Jessica Cable, all of them sixteen going on seventeen. Nate's team had already guessed there had been a pact between the group not to report their sinister find. Thomas, Daniel and Jessica hadn't had a clue that someone had broken ranks, but Liv was clearly the girl on CCTV who'd made the anonymous call, and she certainly seemed the least shocked to find herself here.

Thomas Green was the nephew of Sharon Carlton, Lynne Redding's next door neighbour. It seemed his aunt's stated discretion about Lynne's apparent sudden departure abroad hadn't applied to her family at least, and an empty house, just standing there, secluded and virtually invisible from the road, had stuck in the imagination of a sixteen-year-old looking for the ideal place to do whatever he liked.

Reading between the lines, what Thomas liked was kicking back and smoking the odd joint. It was pretty evident too that what he *would* like to do was to get into Liv's knickers. Liv was sort of his girlfriend, but they hadn't gone much beyond the kissing stage so far.

His best mate, Daniel, had similar designs on Liv's bestie, Jessica, and the boys had hatched a plan to get into the house for what promised to be a bit of a harmless adventure. It wasn't entirely clear how the two boys, who'd never been in any trouble before, had talked themselves into actually implementing their pipe dream, nor what had persuaded the girls to go along with it. But Nate had seen before what a heady mix of peer pressure and teenage hormones could do.

On the face of it, Owen Simmonds was something of a fifth wheel. New to the school, he'd kind of latched onto Thomas and Daniel, and he might have been a gooseberry in the context of the plan, but an essential gooseberry. A few months older than the others, he'd taken and passed his driving test and had a car. Wheels were needed for the enterprise, so Owen was in.

In the event, the evening hadn't exactly gone smoothly. Daniel had boasted of lock-picking skills but, even if his piece of bent coat hanger wire might have actually worked, he was immediately stymied by a key in the lock on the inside, which resolutely refused to be pushed out. Perhaps as much out of embarrassment as bravado, he had put his elbow through one of the panes and slipped his hand through to turn the key.

Once inside, they'd set about exploring the house. They'd found the downstairs rooms pretty boring, but the cellar was suitably spooky, the three chest freezers intriguing. Jessica had speculated about a mountain of ice cream, while Daniel had joked about planning for the zombie apocalypse. Then Owen had pulled a huge large screwdriver out from inside his coat. He claimed to have thought it might come in handy. He used it to force the padlock, but it had been Jessica who had grasped the handle on the lid and lifted it.

And Jessica who had screamed, a scream so piercing, it had echoed off the walls as she stumbled away.

Liv was all for dialling 999 straight away, but Owen said he'd been in bother with the police before, so admitting to breaking and entering wouldn't do him a lot of good, and it wouldn't be good for the rest of them. In the end, they'd all promised not to tell, never to speak of it, not even between themselves. To pretend it never happened.

But Liv couldn't. Leaving the dead women there like that, knowing whoever had killed them could carry on, she was unable to sleep. So yesterday, she'd set off for her morning run and gone into town, where she knew there was a payphone.

Would any of the others have cracked in time? Nate wasn't sure.

"That's all for now, I think," he decided. He looked at Liv's mother. "We've taken her fingerprints and a DNA swab. You can take her home. People will be coming for the clothes she wore on Thursday night. You said they wouldn't have been washed yet?"

"I tend to do a load of washing on a Sunday." The woman looked almost as scared as her daughter. "What's going to happen?"

"We're going to have to report the break-in," he replied, "but we'll certainly say how helpful Olivia has been. I know how much courage it must have taken to go against your friends."

He doubted any of these five would get jail time for this offence, not even Owen Simmonds, with his minor previous drugs offence. Especially since the bodies would still be lying undiscovered if not for the break-in. If not for Liv's anonymous call.

Still, he was going to let her sweat a little bit longer. "But I can't promise anything."

12

The last of the kids had departed, every one of them pale-faced and scared-looking, with the exception of Owen Simmonds who, whatever he was feeling inside, still continued to affect a little bit of bravado. Katie reckoned it was nothing more than an act, and Nate trusted her instincts.

Nate had called a catch-up meeting. No one who'd sat in on this morning's interviews saw the teenagers as having anything to do with the bodies in the cellar, although there was a definite intention to speak to Sharon Carlton about how many other people she'd told about Lynne's departure. More to the point, how many people had she made aware that Lynne appeared to be a vulnerable woman living alone in a secluded house?

"I'm not sure how far she's ultimately going to take us, to be honest," he said. "Everyone she told has potentially mentioned it to who knows how many of their own acquaintances, who would have doubtless mentioned it to some of theirs. For all we know, there are people in Australia who know all about it."

"Do we think some random person knowing Lynne's situation is a serious candidate for the killer anyway?" asked Katie. "It seems to me that part of the attraction would be the cellar and the original chest freezer. Surely that points to someone who's been inside the house?"

"I agree that's most likely, always assuming Lynne herself is a victim and not a killer," Nate concurred. "But let's not rule it out. It's perfectly plausible that some random maniac found the set up at Hall House attractive enough, without that sort of in depth knowledge. He forces his way in somehow, does whatever he likes to Lynne, but also noses around the house. Finds the cellar and freezer and sees the potential for taking women, bringing them there, and repeating the process."

"It makes the Carltons rather weaker suspects, doesn't it?" said Rachel Sharp. "If you're using a house for those purposes, you're hardly going to draw attention to it by telling all and sundry that it's standing there empty and the owner has suddenly upped and left."

Nate thought she was probably right.

Izzy raised a finger. "The freezers seem to mean something to the killer, don't they? And I can see two possible reasons. It could just be convenience: instead of disposing of the bodies, with the risk that they'll be found – no matter how meticulous you've been about removing forensic traces, you can't be sure CSI won't pick up some miniscule clue that you missed. So just keep them frozen in the cellar, out of sight, and no nasty smells to upset the neighbours."

"Could be," he agreed. "You had a second possibility?"

"Yes, and it's a bit darker. The missing body parts – fingers and toes? Our killer wouldn't be the first serial killer to take that sort of trophy or souvenir."

"Yeah," said Ricky. "Chances are he's got those parts in a Tupperware box in his freezer at home, next to the fish fingers."

"Thanks for that image," said Katie with a visible shiver.

"My point is," Izzy pressed on, "most likely the killer likes to look at what he's kept from the victim, either to feed whatever sexual fantasy is associated with the killing, or as a reminder of how brilliant he is. And good to have a few fingers handy – no pun intended – at home."

"Sure," Nate said, "Ed Kemper and Jeffrey Dahmer did, and Ed Gein even made things like lamp shades and corsets out of human flesh. What's that got to do with the chest freezers?"

"So imagine having the whole body stored in a freezer, right where the victim died. You can look at them any time you wish, remembering exactly what their last minutes were like. Once he put them in alive, I wouldn't be surprised if he sat there, listening to them trying to get out, their cries getting weaker and fainter. If he got off on that, maybe he'd get something of that rush again just opening the lid and looking in on them."

"It doesn't mean he had to know about Lynne's basement, or her freezer, to start with," Aliya said. "Could be a bonus."

"Anything useful from the National Crime Agency yet?" Rachel Sharp asked. She was in what looked suspiciously like gardening togs. She'd opted not to come in for the day and get in the way, but had asked to be told when the briefings were, so she could keep up to date.

"Nothing concrete," Katie said, "but they suggest, once we know a bit more about our victims, we ask SCAS to put our cases on ViCLAS. It could just be that there are individuals on there who share some characteristics with our killer."

The Serious Crime Analysis Service had been created in the aftermath of the Yorkshire Ripper inquiry, and the Violent Crime Linkage Analysis System was a database of serious sexual offences committed in the UK. It captured specific details of both the offence and known or unknown offenders, and helped the service to compare cases and identify similarities.

"Let's make sure we do that," Nate agreed. "Now, let's move on. What else have we got? Have we unearthed anyone else who might have visited Lynne?"

"I'm still going through stuff recovered from the house," Sophie Monahan. "There's an address book. Not many names in it, which seems to sum Lynne up, but there's a Steve Redding in Milton Keynes. Must be some sort of relation, I'd imagine."

"Steve? As in the handyman?"

"It's a common enough name, guv."

"Sure, but we need to speak to him. If nothing else, he might be able to tell us more about Lynne. Katie, there's quite a few follow-ups to be done. I take it you've got notes?"

"I'll divvy the tasks up."

"Thanks. Now, there's one more thing." He picked up some sheets of paper from the table beside him, carried them over to the Wall, and attached a couple.

"The doc's got our single body out of the freezer to defrost, and we've got a picture of her face. Also this distinctive humming bird tattoo. So we can at least start trying to identify her. All the usual places. Missing persons databases to start with. We'll have more tomorrow, including fingerprints."

"Hang on, guv," said Libby Statham.

"Libby?"

She rose from her seat and walked up to the board, where she studied the dead woman's face. Then she looked at him.

"It looks like…" She frowned.

"I know," he said. "Dr Stoddart and I were trying to remember who she reminded us of."

"No," Libby said. "I know who it is. It's just…"

"Who do you think she looks like?"

"I think it's Donna Mason."

The name struck a chord, something just on the edge of Nate's memory.

"By God, she's right," said Ricky.

"I know the name," Nate said. "Remind me."

"She was all over the news a couple of months ago," Libby said. "She was from Cambridge, I think. On a hen weekend in Brighton, somehow got separated from her friends."

"Of course." Now he remembered. "They expected to find her back at their hotel, but she never showed up."

"It's dropped off the headlines," Ricky said, "but I guess they must be still looking for her. I don't think anyone was ever arrested, were they, Lib?"

"Not that I recall," she said. "I'd have to check. Wasn't there a guy they wanted to talk to?"

Nate could see Katie's thumbs flying across her phone's keyboard.

"Got it, guv," she said. "Hang about. Yeah, 11th of August she went missing. There's pictures here. Six of them, all wearing pink tee shirts printed with…" She squinted. "'Team Becca'. And they've all got tiaras, except, I'm guessing it's Becca, who's got one of those little bridal veil headband things."

Nate eyed the photograph on the Wall. "And we really think this is her?" Donna had disappeared some fifteen months after Lynne Redding had been supposed to have left the country.

Katie came and joined Nate by the Wall, holding the picture on her phone screen up next to the dead woman's image. A woman with reddish-brown hair and a carefree smile. "What do we think?"

In spite of the radically different circumstances in which the two photographs had been taken, the similarity was striking.

"I think you might be right," he admitted. "Is there anything about the tattoo?"

She scrolled. "Not that I can see. But you can imagine them maybe withholding something like that."

He could. "Can you get onto the Brighton police and see what they reckon?"

"Sure," Katie said. "I don't know who'll be there on a Sunday, mind you."

"Push if you have to. Or let me know and I will." He looked at the picture on her screen once more. "But both Cambridge and Brighton are a long way from Wigginton. Did she have connections around here, do we know?"

He was praying there was some motivation, some coherent agenda behind these killings, something they could focus on. An invisible thread they could start to follow that might just lead them to the individual responsible.

"I can find out," said Katie.

"Do that," he said. "And find out what else they're not releasing."

13

Members of the team were making calls, checking out every tentative and half baked thought in the hope that something might produce a giant stride for the investigation. Every step forward, however small, could be vitally important.

Katie had rustled up a DI Seagrove in Brighton who was working on the Donna Mason disappearance, and Izzy was sitting in with her on a video call to him. He was more than willing to drop everything if it was possible that Donna had turned up. Aliya and Libby had driven up to Milton Keynes to see Steve Redding, who it turned out was a cousin.

The interviews with Lynne's gardener, Brian Small, and another chat with Sharon and Mike Carlton were going to have to wait. Meanwhile, Nate was feeling uncharacteristically surplus to requirements.

It was late afternoon when PC Sophie Monahan knocked and entered Nate's office along with a willowy young woman, about Izzy's age.

"Sir, this is Shauna O'Connell," Sophie said. "You asked me to liaise with the tech experts who were working on Lynne Redding's computer?"

Nate looked at Shauna. Sleek black hair in a ponytail. Nate guessed her sharp suit hadn't come from one of the budget high street stores. They must be paying the techs more than he'd have imagined. She carried a bulging plastic folder.

"Good to meet you, Shauna." He stood up and offered his hand. She shoved the folder under her arm and shook it, smiling. "I haven't seen you around, have I?"

She laughed. "Probably not." There was a gentle lilt to her voice. Irish, he thought. "You know us nerds. They keep us in a cage and throw in the occasional Quorn sandwich and nettle smoothie."

"I can believe that," he said. "But don't tell me you've got something for us already?"

"I think we've got a few morsels, yes. Lynne wasn't the most imaginative when it came to passwords, and CSI found a notebook where she'd written half of them down. Kid's stuff, to be honest."

He gestured to his small meeting table. "So what have we got?"

They all sat down.

"I can't take all the credit," Shauna said. "I've been poking around in her online banking and a colleague of mine's going through her emails. But my colleague had to get away, so it's just me, I'm afraid. Anyway," she continued brightly, "finance first. I gather Lynne is supposed to have gone abroad about eighteen months ago, but there's been interesting activity – or lack of activity – on her accounts up until quite recently."

"Interesting in what way?"

"Well, she's got a current account, a savings account and a credit card. Thing is, the credit card hasn't been used for... well, about eighteen months, with two exceptions. There's a direct debit from her current account that pays off the whole balance, so nothing's been spent and nothing's been paid since around May last year."

"You're sure there's only the one card?"

"Pretty sure, unless she's got financial activity that isn't showing up on her computers. I know Sophie is going through her paper records, but most people who do online banking tend to do all their business online. So on the face of it, if she *is* living abroad, I'm not sure how she'd be financing herself."

"Drawing cash out of the bank? Debit card?"

"None of the above. Looking at her online banking, no cash has been withdrawn pretty well forever, and there are no card transactions either. I'd say, up until spring last year, everything was paid for either by card – mostly online – or direct debit, standing order or e-banking."

"And then it stops?"

"A bit more interesting than that, actually. There's a flurry of activity cancelling standing orders and so forth. Subscriptions, stuff like that. All that remains is the direct debits for council tax, utilities and the like. So the gas and electric, the water rates, landline, broadband and mobile phone, even the house insurance, have all gone on being paid."

"By the way, guv," Sophie said, "you'll recall that stack of opened post on the coffee table in the lounge was strictly stuff like bills. I reckon the rest has been chucked away, but the killer's monitoring the post in case anything needs action. Like reading a meter, for example. So nothing would happen, or *not* happen, to arouse suspicions or have anyone come snooping around."

He pondered. "So after those other regular payments are cancelled, nothing happens except the essential stuff, going out on direct debit?"

"Not quite," Shauna said. "There's a payment to an accountant. That's interesting, but I'll come to that. Also a couple of bespoke payments to the taxman. Most interesting of all, though, is the transfers from the savings account to the current account. Basically, the current account gets topped up so the direct debits are covered."

"So wherever she is, she *is* managing her finances?"

"*Someone* is. I've established that all that activity was conducted from Lynne's home computer in Wigginton."

"Really?" This wasn't making a lot of sense. "But why would she tell her neighbour she was going away, if she wasn't?"

"You got me there."

"So tell me more about this accountant."

She nodded. "So I cross-referenced the banking activity as best I could with the emails my colleague is looking at. Around the time the various direct debits were cancelled, she – or somebody – emailed what appear to be a cleaning lady – Eve Banks – and a gardener – Brian Small – dispensing with their services."

"We know about them You saw the actual emails?"

"Yup. No frills. They just said she wouldn't be needing them again, and thanks for their services. There's also an email exchange with said accountant, saying she was ceasing whatever work she did and could he wrap up her tax affairs as quickly as possible. His name's Adam Downes, by the way. So then she confirms she's signed and mailed her tax return back to him, which I'm guessing he sent on to the tax people. On the bank account, she pays him and then there are those tax payments."

"You said she was wrapping up her business?"

"Apparently, yeah. There's a round robin email to all clients saying basically sorry, but she's no longer offering her services. Jobs she had in progress, the manuscripts or what have you were returned to the clients and she – or someone – reimbursed any advance payments by bank transfer."

"And that's it?"

She looked pained. "I thought it was quite a lot, actually. Yes, that's *almost* it. All you need to do to disappear off the grid and no one be any the wiser. Everything needing human interaction terminated. Just the essentials, ticking over." She gave a small shrug. "I mean, you're the detective, but I can't see she went *anywhere*. She certainly didn't buy any train or plane tickets, or buy petrol, unless she paid cash."

"I don't think she even had a car."

"Well, I'd say either she wanted to become invisible, or someone else wanted her to."

"Back up, though," he said. "You said that was *almost* it, as if there was a 'but'. And didn't you say there actually *had* been a couple of credit card transactions?"

"Yeah, there were two uses of the credit card. One in February and one as recent as July. Both to an electrical goods company."

"I don't suppose we know what was purchased?" Although the back of his neck was already tingling. Because he had a good idea what the answer was.

She nodded. "As a matter of fact, we do. Again, we cross-referenced with emails around those times, and sure enough, there are the orders: two identical chest freezers."

"Almost unbelievable, isn't it?" Sophie said. "I'm thinking, once a freezer's got two bodies in it, and getting a bit crowded, they just coolly order another one."

Nate was thinking exactly the same.

He looked at Shauna. "Same company?"

"Yep. Details are in this folder, along with other relevant printouts."

"There's no way of knowing if her accounts were hacked?"

"Oh, there are ways. I don't believe that's the case here though. As I say, Lynne's rubbish at strong passwords. So someone else could have guessed them, or found her written list. Anyhow, we've printed off the emails I thought you'd be wanting. Exchanges with the accountant, Downes, and with the cleaning lady and the gardener. Those freezer orders. Oh, and some sort of psychologist, a Dr Ross."

"Didn't the cleaner say she'd had some counselling?" Sophie suggested.

"She did," Nate confirmed. "Likely this Ross is the guy."

Shauna handed him the folder. "They're all in there, along with the bank and card activity, such as it is. There's an electronic signature for Adam Downes, with phone numbers and an address in Maxted Road, and details of the freezer company, but you'll have to do some detecting for the others."

"I'll go through Lynne's address book again," Sophie said.

"Ah, there you go," Shauna said, "maybe you're halfway there already."

*

"It certainly looks like Donna," DI Seagrave said over Zoom as he squinted at the photographs Katie had texted to him. "And that tattoo… yes. We kept that out of the public domain to help us sift out some of the timewasting calls, but it looks just like Donna's, and in the right place too."

Izzy thought he was about fifty: grey hair, lines in his face, and just a hint of flab stretching his polo shirt. She knew he was at home, but he'd got one of those fake neutral backgrounds going on, so he could have been anywhere. From his expression, the news that his search for Donna Mason had ended badly might not be a surprise, but it still hurt.

"And you led the investigation when she disappeared, sir?" Katie checked. "What do you remember?"

"Pretty well everything. Donna was thirty-three and had been divorced for about a year," he continued. "It seems they both wanted kids, but it just wasn't happening. Donna was willing to adopt, but the husband – Grant – hadn't been interested in that, and she didn't fancy surrogacy. So then Grant started playing away, got his girlfriend pregnant and dumped Donna to live with his more fertile lover."

"The ex sounds a real prince."

"That's one word for him." He wasn't smiling. "Still, her family said she'd really found out who her friends were, and Becca and the others had kept her going. The 'Gang of Six', they called themselves. All of them were married with kids, apart from Becca, who was soon to tie the knot herself and, of course, Donna."

"So how did she feel about the hen weekend, after what she'd gone through?" Katie asked.

"Apparently she said she was looking forward to it, insisting it was exactly what she needed. You know, a nice time away with no hassle."

"And it was all going fine, up until her disappearance?"

"Sounds like it. They arrived at their hotel in time for dinner on the Friday night, had a few – maybe more than a few – drinks at the bar before bed. Spent Saturday 'doing' Brighton – you know, the Royal Pavilion, the pier, the i360, the aquarium... they walked along the beach, had a paddle in the sea..."

"You really have got a good memory," Izzy commented, wondering if she'd recall such details so effortlessly.

"Yes, well. Some cases are like that."

"And that day. Presumably you asked if they noticed anyone suspicious hanging around them? Maybe the same face popping up everywhere?"

"We did ask. The answer was no. Although I suspect observing their surroundings wouldn't have been high on their agenda."

"Can you talk us through what you know about the night of Donna's disappearance?" Katie asked. "The Saturday night? I mean, we've read the accounts online..."

"Of course. The plan for that night was a pub crawl, all mapped out, starting with a meal and ending up at a club. Maggie Mae's was their third stop on the crawl and, just as they were moving on, Donna popped into the loo. Somehow the others were almost at the next bar – the Tempest – before they realised Donna wasn't with them."

"How far is that?" Izzy asked.

"Less than half a mile. Maybe ten minutes' walk."

This was something that had puzzled Izzy when they'd first realised that one of the Wigginton bodies might be Donna's. "Ten minutes? And none of them missed their mate?"

She remembered when she and Bethany were as close as friends could be. How they'd always looked out for one another, right from their early connection at school, all they'd gone through together. Standing up to the bullies. Holding each other's hair as they puked into the toilet. Tears and tissues and sympathy over failed relationships. Good times too. Exam results, job offers. Bawling out Katie Perry songs in the car.

Bethany telling her Matt was a keeper and asking if she could have him if Izzy finished with him.

She pushed that last thought away. The thing was, even when they'd been out with a bigger group, she'd always kept an eye out for Bethany, and Bethany had for her.

Seagrave held up his hands. "I know. It sounds ridiculous, but I believed them. Maggie Mae's is popular, and they all said there was quite a hubbub in the bar – which sounds about right. And everyone we spoke to – not just the girls – said Donna was always a little softly spoken. Not surprisingly, the others were squiffy and chatty. They just didn't notice. I'd imagine they're still beating themselves up over that now."

"And when they *did* finally miss her?"

"The chief bridesmaid and chief organiser was Millie. She was about to call her when Donna beat her to it. She offered to go back and find her, but Donna insisted she'd find it with a little help from the map app on her phone, 'like a functioning adult'. And even though they all knew Donna was pants at finding her way anywhere, app or no app, they took the line of least resistance and agreed. Half an hour later, she still hadn't made it, and she wasn't answering her phone. She was never seen or heard from again."

"But you appealed to the public for sightings?"

"Oh, yeah. And several people came forward who remembered a tipsy woman in her thirties in a silly tee shirt and a sillier tiara, trudging the streets of Brighton, looking lost, waving her phone about and stopping people to ask for directions to the Tempest. The tiara turned up in a gutter, a couple of blocks away, but it was as if Donna had disappeared into thin air."

"CCTV footage?" Izzy asked.

"Yep, we picked her up a few times. Found a few people in frame we thought worth a chat, but nothing came of it. If she went off with someone, or was taken against her will, no one saw or reported anything. We had the ex in, too, just in case, but he had a cast iron alibi. She was just..." He shrugged. "... gone."

"We're getting an artist to work up an image of someone we're interested in," said Katie. "I'll get that to you as soon as we have it, but basically average height and build, shaggy hair and beard, maybe wearing a cap. Ring any bells?"

He didn't answer immediately. Izzy could almost imagine him thumbing through the contents of a mental filing cabinet.

"No," he said finally. "I mean, we've still got the footage so, when I have the picture I'll get someone to look, but no one like that cropped up, not as far as I can remember."

"We'll need someone to formally ID the body."

He nodded grimly. "I'll speak to the family. Not something I'm looking forward to. I always thought this day would come, and in their hearts they must have too. But there's always hope, right? Until there's no hope."

"I'm so sorry to be the bearer of bad news," Katie said.

"Yeah, well. It's the job, isn't it?"

"That doesn't make it any easier, does it?"

"No," he agreed, "it doesn't."

14

Steve Redding was probably late thirties, maybe early forties, with dark, well-cut hair. A little on the chubby side, what Aliya's parents might've described as 'prosperous looking'. On the face of it, nothing like the unkempt 'Handyman Steve' described by Lynne's neighbours. But she knew people could change their appearance. It wouldn't be the first time.

Aliya already knew he was Lynne's cousin. All she had told him over the phone was that she needed to speak to him about a family matter. He had been very happy for her and Libby to see him in his home, a detached property in the Emerson Valley area of Milton Keynes. He was home alone – his wife had gone to see her parents, leaving him to get on with some work.

"I'm in project management," he had explained. "I'm on a bit of a deadline today."

Whether or not he truly was 'prosperous', there was no air of smugness or superiority about him. On the contrary, he came across as remarkably ordinary, if there was such a thing. He'd welcomed them in and made small talk whilst they sat in his kitchen watching him make tea for Aliya, and coffee for Libby and himself.

"So," he said as he sat himself down opposite them, "you want to talk about Lynne? Is she in some sort of trouble? I hope she's all right."

"We'll get to that," Aliya said. "First of all, what can you tell us about your cousin?"

"To be honest, I haven't seen anything of her for years. Not since the funeral. You know about that?"

"This is her parents and brother, right?"

"Yeah. Must be, what? Something like ten years now. Lynne and her brother were back living with their parents after a couple of stints of moving out. You know what they say about the boomerang generation?"

"They keep coming back," Libby supplied.

"Exactly. I don't really know why neither of them had quite managed to fly the nest. Anyway, it seems one weekend the parents were going to Watford for some shopping, and the brother decided to tag along."

"But not Lynne?"

"No. I'd imagine she was a bit old to be going shopping with her parents, or she had other things to do. Anyhow, that afternoon they met a lorry driver who was texting at the wheel. All three died at the scene."

Aliya knew some of this from information supplied by Lynne's neighbour, but it was interesting to get a little more detail.

"That must have been awful for her," Libby said. "How did it affect her?"

"You have to understand, we were never really a close family. Weddings, funerals, the odd big birthday. Even as kids, we didn't see that much of each other. But my recollection of Lynne is that she was a pretty straightforward, normal girl." His expression clouded. "I'd say all that changed the moment her family died."

"You wouldn't expect something like that not to affect her. It must have been pretty traumatic."

"I'm sure it was," said Redding. "Traumatised I would have expected. But to be honest, she became pretty odd more or less overnight. I mean, the family did reach out to her, offering help and support. Remember, she was a young woman in her early twenties, without a great deal of life experience. Yet she refused all offers of help and organised the funeral single handed. Oh, she let people know the arrangements, but she was distant from everyone on the day."

"What about afterwards?" Aliya asked. "Did anyone make contact to see how she was doing?"

"Oh yeah. I know she got a string of invitations from family members afterwards, for meals or to stay with them. Everyone will tell you the same thing. She declined politely but couldn't get off the phone quickly enough."

Aliya privately wondered just how hard anyone had tried. Had they been sincere in wanting to help the bereaved young woman? Or had they just been going through the motions? Aliya herself came from an almost clichéd family background where aunties, uncles and cousins were all quite close and wouldn't take no for an answer if anyone needed support – perhaps to the point of intrusion. A lot of the time, it bugged the hell out of her. But she was grateful to know she had that support network should she ever need it.

She could think of a dozen reasons why Lynne might have behaved the way she did. The trauma of losing her family in an instant. Survivor guilt. Maybe even some sort of fight or flight stress response; only in this case she couldn't really do either.

"Did anyone in particular keep pushing? Try to get her some help?"

"To be honest, I think there's no helping some people. You can't force help on someone who doesn't want to accept it." He looked into his coffee cup. Avoiding her eyes? He took a swig, then looked at her. "But what happened? You still haven't told me."

"Did you know Lynne apparently went abroad last year?"

On the face of it his confusion seemed genuine enough. "Abroad where? And what does 'apparently' mean?"

"That's a no?"

"Yes. I mean, yes, it's a no. I didn't know. Apart from exchanging cards at Christmas, I've had no contact with her at all for years." He paused. "Come to think about it, she didn't send me one last time."

Libby jumped in before Aliya could respond. "That didn't concern you?"

"Honestly? I assumed she'd decided not to bother any more. I was going to keep her on my list for a couple more years..." He shuffled in his seat. "Something *has* happened to her, hasn't it? Has she, you know... done something...? To herself?"

"All I can tell you at the moment, Mr Redding," Aliya said, "is that some bodies have been found. We believe there's a connection to Lynne, but we can't say whether she's a victim at the moment. If that proves to be the case, we would need someone to identify her. Is that something you'd be able to do?"

"Oh my God." He raked his fingers through his hair, messing it up. "But *what*? More than *one* body? But I thought maybe she'd…"

"Killed herself? At present, there's nothing to suggest anything like that, although we can't rule anything out."

"Oh my God," he said again. "She was *murdered*?" He shook his head. "No, no. I understand. You can't say." His gaze wandered upwards, as if perhaps the ceiling, or even the heavens, could provide him with some sort of answers. "But yes. Of course. Of course if you think one of your bodies is Lynne, I can do the identification. It's the least I can do."

Yes, Aliya thought, *it is*.

"Are you her next of kin?" No will had been found so far.

He frowned at the question. "I don't know. It's not something I've ever thought about. My dad was her father's brother, but he died last year. I'm an only child. Her mum had a sister, who had two daughters. I don't know too much about them – if they're all still alive, where they might be living. Shit, I can't even remember Lynne's mother's maiden name. I'm not even sure if I ever knew it. Isn't that dreadful?"

"It's just the way some families are," Libby said. "Especially these days, when people move around. You'd need to check, but I think you might well inherit something."

"Well, that's hardly important right now, is it? Poor Lynne. Let's hope you've got this wrong and she's okay. I mean, if she's abroad…"

The possibility that the whole 'move abroad' might be a fabrication was not something to be shared with anybody for now.

"Just a couple more questions," Aliya said. "I appreciate you never really knew her that well, and haven't seen her for years. But are you aware of anyone who might have wanted to harm her?"

"Well, no. That doesn't mean there wasn't anyone. I just don't know."

"Fair enough. And the second question: would you happen to know if Lynne might be capable of violence? Don't read too much into that, but we have to ask."

He pursed his lips. "Honestly? I can't say I remember her being violent, either as a child, or when she was older. Certainly, at the funeral, she was distant and detached, but I saw no sign of a temper. But again, I can only tell you what little I've seen. I'm not the best person to ask." He looked troubled. "But why would you ask something like that? I thought you were thinking she was a victim. Now it sounds like she might be – what? A murderer?"

"As I said, don't read too much into it." She smiled. "Oh, and one last thing."

She recited the date in August when Donna Mason had gone missing. "I don't suppose you can recall what you were doing that evening?"

"What? Why? My God, you can't think…"

"It's just routine. Could you just answer the question please?"

"Sure." He fumbled with his phone. "It's just as well I've got my whole life on this thing. Just a sec." He did a bit of tapping and swiping on his screen, then shot her a look that was part triumph, part relief. "Yeah, how could I forget? My daughter just got her A level results, and we all went out for a pizza. I guess the restaurant would have a record of the booking if I really need an alibi."

She smiled again. "Hopefully you don't. If you could just tell me which restaurant you went to?"

He duly obliged. She handed him a card, asked him to call her if he thought of anything else. "We'll be in touch."

*

Late in the afternoon, Rachel Sharp phoned Nate for an update. When he'd finished, she sighed.

"That about settles it, Nathan. The Super is going to want to issue a full press statement as soon as Donna's identity is confirmed. I think I can get him to keep some details out of it…"

"At least the freezers, I hope."

"Yes, that'll bowl out the serial time wasters and confessors at least."

"And Wigginton. Just carry on leaving it at Hertfordshire?"

"No, Nathan. People aren't stupid. The locals know there's something significant going on at Hall House. There'll be rumours and gossip. If you look on social media, you'll see that the village Facebook page already has people speculating that it's where our report of 'a number of bodies in a house in Hertfordshire' actually is. You know the press office are being asked about it."

"But we can stonewall them a bit longer."

"To what end? The whole point of keeping it under wraps is in the hope that the killer decides to swing by the house. But we can't suppose he won't notice the chatter. Once Donna's name's out there, the cat'll be truly out of the bag."

He knew she was right.

"Anyhow," she said, her tone a little lighter, "I think you've made pretty good progress. You're going to talk to the gardener, the accountant and the counsellor tomorrow?"

"And we've got Donna's post mortem in the morning. Plus Dr Stoddart's going to take the two bodies out of the older freezer, so it's to be hoped we'll be a step closer to identifying them. We should have a better idea whether Lynne Redding is a victim or a suspect."

His thoughts returned to the issue of press releases. "I suppose there's one thing in favour of releasing Wigginton as the location. If the killer is getting the urge again, or whatever it is that motivates him, that might at least take the wind out of his sails for a while."

15

"I told you, hun," Rosie says. "You can't trust anyone. At least this Paul is likely no more than a harmless do-gooder, but I said that paradise hostel was just pie in the sky."

And Courtney must admit she's disappointed. Maybe she expected too much too soon. All Paul really said was he'd keep his ear to the ground. It could be days, weeks, before he hears anything. Still, she'd somehow hoped he'd maybe drop by and update her. A friendly word wouldn't go amiss, either.

It's not that she sees him romantically, or as some sort of knight in shining armour. He's neither type. But he came across as one of the good guys, someone who saw her as a person and really cared. Maybe he was all talk.

"You're probably right," she says with a sigh. "He just seemed different. After those guys with the hip flask, I didn't ought to trust anyone, I know that. And most of the outreach people seem good-hearted, but it's almost like it's just a job for them, you know?"

"Yeah, that's the trouble. I reckon half of them are in it just to make themselves feel good. They can sweep in, dispense a bit of bounty, then fuck off back to their cosy middle-class lives. They sleep in their comfortable beds and don't give any of us a second thought. Christ, some of them don't even ask my name."

Courtney is grateful to Rosie for adopting her, for being her friend and protector but, just sometimes, her cynicism can be a bit wearing. Then again, she doesn't know exactly how long Rosie has been living like this, but she's pretty sure it's been a lot longer than Courtney.

"Do you think you'll ever get off the streets?" she asks her. "Sometimes you sound like you've no hope at all."

Rosie gives her a look that seems halfway between suspicion and amusement. "Oh, I've got hope, hun. I've got a plan to dig my way out of this shitty life. But it's *my* plan, you know? Believe me, for all the goodie two shoes who come round here pretending to give a shit, the only person you can really rely on is yourself."

Courtney can't help being intrigued. "Is that what you do when you go off during the day? Working on your plan?"

Rosie gives her a sharp look. "That's my business. You're asking a lot of questions all of a sudden."

"Sorry. I just wondered if it could work for me."

Rosie barks a laugh. "I don't think it's your thing. I don't think you'd like it."

And suddenly, Courtney feels sick. She suspects how Rosie might be spending at least part of her day, and she's right. Courtney wouldn't like it. But she's determined not to judge.

"Just suppose," she says, "Paul comes up with something after all. A place to live and a chance to get back on our feet. Would you come with me?"

To her surprise, Rosie's eyes mist. For a moment, she pulls that face that means she's about to say something sarcastic, but if she is, she swallows the comment. Instead she lays a hand on Courtney's arm.

"Not gonna happen, babe," she says, "but yeah, maybe. I'd have a look. No harm in looking, right?"

*

Izzy had been home an hour and was finding it even harder than usual to settle. She knew it was to do with Donna Mason, but it wasn't just her disappearance and her death. It was that group of friends. The 'Gang of Six', DI Seagrave said they called themselves, sort of like the Three Musketeers – all for one and one for all. Okay, so perhaps they'd sort of let her down that last night. They hadn't looked out for her like they should. But any other night and it would have been just a daft story they remembered about the night Donna got herself lost in Brighton and they had to come and rescue her.

The person really to blame for Donna's death had murdered four other women and was still out there.

No, what was really preying on her mind was the idea of six mates who stuck together. Who'd helped Donna through the difficult times surrounding her marriage breakup. Izzy had had that with Bethany, right up until her best friend had started sleeping with her boyfriend behind her back.

It had been a time of momentous change at work for Izzy, seizing the chance to get into CID with both hands, and being thrown in the deep end with a particularly troubling case. Perhaps it had all fogged her brain when it came to other areas of her life. She certainly hadn't been thinking straight.

When she'd first realised what was going on, she'd wanted to make Bethany and Matt pay – Bethany most of all. Her friend had told her Matt was a keeper, but Izzy had never quite seen it that way. There was a lot she liked about being with him, but somehow she'd known there was no long term future in it. It would have petered out anyway. But what Bethany had done was unforgiveable.

She'd wanted to make Bethany pay.

And so she'd decided that, unless and until they had the guts to tell her what was happening between them, she'd carry on as if she didn't know. And that included sleeping with Matt at every opportunity and making damn sure Bethany knew about it.

That lasted a few weeks. Then she realised that the 'arrangement' suited Matt just fine. She imagined the bastard telling Bethany what a chore it was, but the truth was, he'd always had quite the ego. Having two willing women on the go was just the sort of thing he'd get off on.

If Matt seemed to be enjoying it a little too much, meaningless sex for revenge wasn't giving Izzy the satisfaction she'd expected. It only made her feel cheap and dirty. So she'd determined to do what she should have done at the outset. Confront them.

Only doing it by phone or text, even turning up on Bethany's doorstep, didn't seem enough. Instead, she'd hatched a plan that had seemed good in her imagination. She'd got so she knew when they'd be seeing each other and had started... well, some people would have called it stalking.

One night, she'd followed them to a restaurant. She'd sat in her car for a quarter of an hour, then marched inside, brushing off the woman who was supposed to seat diners. She'd found them in a cosy corner, a glass of red wine in front of each of them, and the rest of the bottle on the side. There was a little basket of bread. A wooden board with what looked like interesting artisan butters on it. All very civilised. Izzy had found herself smiling at the absurdity of it all.

Their faces were a picture.

"Iz," Bethany had wheedled, "I, I…"

"Izzy," Matt the liar at least heaved some confidence into his voice. "This isn't—"

"What it seems?" she completed for him. "Still taking me for a fuckwit?"

She'd swept up his glass and tossed the contents in his face. Bethany was still gasping when she got the same treatment. It wasn't enough. Matt was making angry noises, Bethany snivelling and wiping her face with her napkin when Izzy picked up the wine bottle and upended it over her ex-friend's head.

"Enjoy each other," she'd said. "Stay the fuck out of my life."

She'd turned on her heel. The woman from the desk stood there aghast, clearly unsure what to do about this mad woman. With exaggerated calmness, Izzy had opened her bag, pulled out her purse, and extracted a twenty-pound note.

Pressing it into the woman's hand, she'd whispered, "Sorry about the tablecloth. That should cover the laundry."

Yet, instead of feeling free and somehow lighter on her feet, all she'd felt – and still felt – was shame that she'd made such a spectacle of herself. And a deep sadness at the loss of the best and closest friend she'd ever had.

So, for all that the Brighton hen weekend had ended so disastrously for Donna Mason, Izzy envied her that group of friends. People she could rely on, share her troubles with.

She wondered if Bethany was still with Matt. If the relationship was over, could she bring herself to forgive the unforgiveable?

She picked up her phone and scrolled through her contacts. She had blocked Bethany, but she'd never deleted the number from her phone. She could call her. Forget what had happened? She wasn't sure she could ever do that, but maybe forgiveness was possible.

She opened Bethany's contact details and her thumb hovered over the call button. Then she sighed and closed the contact.

She wasn't ready. Maybe one day she would be. But not today.

16

Nate hadn't been looking forward to seeing Dr Stoddart finally getting to work on Donna's cadaver with his array of scalpels, saws, forceps and hammers. He knew pathologists got used to the sights, sounds and odours associated with their trade, and he knew how most of them honoured and respected the dead. It was still a job he couldn't do, and he was glad that, for him, these sorties into their world were a rarity.

"She's thawed out well," Stoddart said when he and Aliya arrived, "and I'm afraid just from a proper visual examination that we can safely say your killer is a particularly nasty piece of work. I'm hoping Donna *is* the most recent victim, because God knows what he might have done to the later ones. The finger and toe amputations might have been the extreme end of the torture, but they weren't all of it."

This man spent his working life in company with the dead, but even he seemed sickened. "There are signs of restraints on the wrists and ankles, so she was probably entirely helpless and vulnerable. I'll show you when we get going, but there are other cuts, there are burns, possibly consistent with cigarettes being stubbed out on her palms, the soles of her feet and her body."

"We're looking at a smoker?"

"Not necessarily. I mean, I'm no expert on these things, but I suppose a certain type of person might enjoy inflicting that sort of pain but otherwise be a lifelong non-smoker."

"I suppose." Nate found himself shuddering at the thought.

"It's safe to say too, even before I start examining her internally, that she suffered some pretty brutal sexual abuse. You'd need to get a psychologist's opinion, but I'm suspecting this individual got more pleasure from the violence and pain than the sex itself."

Soon afterwards, he was beginning his grisly work. Nate made himself watch, experienced enough to appear impassive, human enough to be upset. He glanced at Aliya, a shade paler, but her face set like stone.

Stoddart worked painstakingly but, after an hour and a half, Nate suspected Donna Mason's body had already given up most, if not all, of its most important secrets. A fairly fit and healthy woman in her thirties, her body terribly and agonisingly abused, who had finally died of asphyxia in a freezing cold tomb.

He supposed he could think of worse ways to die. But not very many.

When the pathologist's work was done, and his assistant was finishing up, Nate thanked him, as always, for his thoroughness.

"It's my job," Stoddart said. "Although this is one of those depressing occasions when I almost wish it wasn't."

Nate nodded, seeing the sadness in his eyes. "I know what you mean. But who'd speak for the dead, if you didn't?"

Stoddart nodded. "I know." He shrugged. "Oh, well. I'll let you know about the next stages."

"Nothing else for us, doc?"

"Not on this case for the moment. But there's that other thing you asked me to look at."

He'd almost forgotten. "Have you got time?"

"Sure."

Aliya looked a question at him.

"Head back," he told her. "I won't be long."

The pathologist guided Nate into his office. Nate was always struck by how untidy this space was, compared to the pristine way Stoddart managed his mortuary. The pathologist rummaged amongst papers on his desk and came up with the folder Nate had left with him yesterday.

"So I've looked at that redacted post mortem report you gave me," he said. "This still all seems a bit cloak and dagger."

"I know. Sorry. As I said, strictly speaking, I shouldn't even have it. I don't want to involve you more than necessary, or to compromise you, so it's best you don't know any details about the case."

"So you said. But it means I had to look at the report without any context. You *can* trust me, you know."

He couldn't know how much trust had gone into approaching him at all.

"Just tell me what it's telling you. Please."

"You've read it, presumably, so I won't waste time with the bleeding obvious. The deceased was a white male aged thirty-three, in reasonable health at his time of death. There were a few scrapes and bruises on the body. Blood alcohol content 0.09 per cent, over the legal limit for driving, but probably not falling about drunk. Although there's no hard and fast rule about the effects of alcohol."

"He'd been at his local," Nate said, "so he hadn't driven. And people who knew him said he could hold his drink."

It had also been said at the trial for his murder that he drank for Dutch courage when he was dreading going home.

"Anyhow," Stoddart continued, "cause of death was the result of a single stab wound to the abdomen. The blade hit the abdominal aorta, the largest artery in the abdominal cavity. The results would have been catastrophic. He'd have bled out within about five minutes."

An image of red splashes on white snow swam before Nate's eyes. He blinked rapidly, shaking his head to get rid of the vision.

"Are you okay, Inspector?" Stoddart asked.

"Yeah, yeah," he waved a dismissive but unsteady hand.

"Sure? I can get you some water."

"I'm fine." He was embarrassed. "Sorry."

Stoddart frowned. "Look, I'm not sure what I'm telling you that you don't already know. If I knew more…"

He took a deep breath, steadied himself and gathered his thoughts.

"What can you tell me about the stab wound? Any way of telling how intentional it was?"

"That's really impossible to tell. I suppose it's a slightly odd spot to aim at, if it *was* intended. Also, it seems the blade didn't go in right up to the hilt, but that could say more about how strong the knife wielder was. Not that a lot of force is needed with a sharp blade."

"Anything else?"

"Well, the angle of the incision is a bit interesting, I suppose."

"Interesting? In what way?"

"Well, it was upwards – so almost certainly underarm – at something like forty-five degrees. I wouldn't read too much into it, but I might expect it to be a bit straighter, if it was used by someone standing up. Or slightly downwards, if anything."

Nate stared at him. "You're saying the knife wielder would have been lower than the victim?"

"Assuming it was a normal sized adult, yes. Actually, I'm thinking they might have been on their knees."

"Really?" His pulse quickened. "But... what could that mean? Could the victim have been attacking *them*? Say he'd forced them to their knees and they struck out in self-defence?"

Stoddart paused, evidently weighing the question. "Obviously, nothing's absolutely certain. But yes, it's a possibility."

An ache set in behind his eyes. "No, that can't be right. There was no mention of that in any of the case papers. Surely she..." *Careful.* "...surely the accused would have mentioned it? Why didn't the pathologist mention it?"

"I'm not being funny," Stoddart said awkwardly, "but maybe no one asked. Cause of death was the stab wound and blood loss. So far, so simple."

Except suddenly it wasn't simple at all.

"She pleaded self-defence. There was nothing about her being on her knees. She grabbed the knife to deter him from attacking her, she claimed, and he ran onto it. The jury didn't buy it. But if she was already down..."

"It was a woman then?"

Nate knew his emotions, normally so well controlled, had run away with his tongue, but it was too late to take it back now. He said nothing.

After a moment, Stoddart shrugged. "Well, if she was already down, that might be consistent with a self-defence scenario, yes. But I guess it also undermines the 'ran onto the knife' defence. An angle like that, you'd probably be *deliberately* stabbing upwards. Although ultimately it was bad luck he died."

"Bad luck?"

"I said the wound could have gone a bit deeper. As it turned out, it was just deep enough to reach the aorta, and just in the wrong place. Just a bit less force, or half an inch or so either side, and the result could have been a lot different."

"I don't understand this at all," Nate persisted. "It makes no sense. Surely it's relevant to the prosecution *and* the defence? One side could have pointed to intent, the other to self-defence."

"You've got me," Stoddart admitted. "Again, if only I knew more about the case..."

He chewed his lip, on the verge of being more forthcoming. He found he couldn't do it. "Let's leave it at that for now, doc. I'm really grateful to you for taking the trouble."

"No problem at all. There's one thing, though."

"Which is?"

"Maybe we should be on first name terms, now we're like co-conspirators. Call me Jordan?"

Nate found that he'd like that, and said so. "And call me Nate."

17

While Nate and Aliya were witnessing the horrors of post mortem, other members of the team were tasked with speaking to potential suspects.

For Katie, the knowledge that this case included violence, probably including sexual violence, against women, tugged her emotions in numerous directions: anger and a sick feeling in equal measure. It had been like that ever since, as a still wet behind the ears uniformed PC, a surveillance operation on a slow night had turned into a nightmare.

She'd been partnered with PC Jack 'The Lad' Berry. He seemed to think that women enjoyed banter that bordered on offensive, and unwelcome touchy-feeliness that couldn't quite be described as assault. She hadn't been comfortable about spending hours alone in a car with him, but hadn't known how to object without looking stupid. And, when he'd complained of being bored and said suggestively that they should find something to do with the time, she hadn't called him out. If anything, she supposed she'd gone along with the supposed joke.

Had he taken that as encouragement? All she knew was that it ended with her somehow fighting him off and getting out of the car, frantically adjusting her clothing. Pulling up her knickers. He'd laughed when she'd said she'd report him, saying he'd tell everyone she came on to him. It was her word against his and no one would thank her for shopping a fellow officer.

Her experienced female colleague, somewhat of a mentor, had advised her to drop it, although she'd taken steps to ensure that Katie was never partnered with him again. A year later, he was convicted of raping a vulnerable witness and Katie had known she should come forward to add her own experience to the evidence against him, but had funked that too.

Since then, she'd lived with the fact that, if she'd reported him when she had the chance, maybe that other woman wouldn't have gone through what she did.

The only person she'd told, apart from that colleague, had been her brother, and she'd had a rare glimpse of rage in the normally calm, peace-loving Mick Gray. Given half a chance, he'd have attempted to take Berry apart with his bare hands – and would probably have come off a poor second best. But the last thing she'd needed to see was more testosterone-fuelled bullshit. After that, she'd bottled it up. She'd moved on with her life, but the incident dogged her like a shadow.

The whole thing was probably the reason she'd struggled ever since to form a relationship. There'd been dates – although not for a long time now – but she'd always held something back.

Maybe she needed help from someone like Dr Silas Ross, Lynne Redding's counsellor and the first call for her and Izzy,

Ross had his office at his home in Kings Langley, just twenty-five minutes away down the A41. Katie had grown up in the village, and there was always a hint of nostalgia whenever she had occasion to visit it. Maybe that was part of the reason that the room's faint scent of whisky and cigars called her beloved maternal grandfather to mind.

The room itself had been fitted out with dark, polished wood panelling and bookshelves, and was adorned with framed certificates and a few old-fashioned prints. As for Dr Ross, if Katie had been asked to describe her idea of a stereotypical psychologist, he would probably fit the bill perfectly.

There was more than a touch of the eccentric young fogey about him: salt and pepper hair that looked like he butchered it himself, and then only on high days and holidays, stuck out at every conceivable angle, making Nate Quarrel's unruly thatch look immaculate by comparison. Yet his goatee beard was trimmed to perfection. Round, gold-rimmed spectacles sat on the bridge of his nose. He wore a brown corduroy jacket with leather elbow patches, so wrinkled and threadbare it might have belonged to his granddad, and he'd teamed it with a shirt and shrivelled-up tie that somehow contrived to clash with the jacket and with each other.

He didn't offer them tea or coffee, even though he already had a steaming mug on his desk when Katie and Aliya arrived, but this chimed with his air of slightly absentminded geniality, rather than deliberate rudeness. He sat at his desk, with his visitors perched on chairs opposite him.

"You must know I can't share confidential information about my patients," he said, as soon as Katie explained the reason for their visit.

"I understand," she said, pushing an envelope across the desk. "That's why we've put our request in writing, signed by my Detective Chief Inspector. We feel there's a strong public interest in your cooperating. We'll shortly be announcing the discovery of a number of bodies at a house in Wigginton."

He paused in the act of opening the envelope, his jaw actually dropping. "Oh, but that's where Lyne Redding lives. Dear God, don't tell me it's her house?"

"In confidence, yes, it is. We don't yet know for certain whether Lynne is amongst the dead."

He looked stunned. "But you believe she might be?"

"We're certainly not able to rule it out."

"Dear God," he muttered again. He ripped the envelope open and scanned the contents. "All right. Of course. Ask your questions and I'll do my best to answer."

"Thank you. First of all, we know Lynne suffered with agoraphobia, and we've been told that it started when her parents and brother died."

"That's right. I'm assuming you have an idea what the condition is?"

"I had a look online. As I understand it, it's an anxiety disorder, and the symptoms occur when the person thinks they're in an unsafe environment from which they can't easily escape. On public transport, or in shopping centres, for example."

"Yes, exactly. Different subjects may have different perceptions of what's unsafe. Both genetic and environmental factors might contribute to the condition. Agoraphobia affects about 1.7 per cent of adults, with women about twice as likely to be affected as men. In Lynne's case, simply being outside her home was enough to trigger a panic attack. But you're right about the loss of her family being the catalyst. Stressful or traumatic events such as the death of a parent, or being attacked, are often the start, although the condition often runs in families too."

"Did either of her parents suffer with it?"

"If they did, it must have been mild enough that she was unaware of it. But I suspected that, even before the accident, she'd often suffered a sense of separation anxiety when she was left home alone. After the trauma of losing her parents and her brother, all at the same time, she seemed to feel the need to dissociate herself from her remaining family and the few friends she had. She admitted that she'd always had difficulty forming close relationships at the best of times, and it seemed her small circle of friends had gradually melted away due to her unwillingness to either go out or say why she'd stopped doing so."

Katie hoped that, if she herself had been a part of that circle, she'd have guessed Lynne was struggling in the aftermath of bereavement. She hoped she'd have tried harder to be supportive. But she also knew how people led such busy lives these days. She knew she could go weeks, or even months, without contacting a friend, and they rarely called her in the interim. Neglect was so easy.

"So what would these panic attacks look like?"

"Well," Ross took off his glasses and wiped them on his tie, "during a panic attack, large amounts of adrenaline are released, and that triggers the fight or flight response you're probably familiar with." He replaced the spectacles, warming to his subject. "Usually an attack will have quite an abrupt onset, and it will build to its maximum intensity within ten to fifteen minutes. It rarely lasts longer than half an hour, but the subject may suffer palpitations, shortness of breath, rapid heartbeat, sweating, trembling, dizziness, tightness in the throat, even nausea or vomiting. Many also report a fear of dying, or of losing control of emotions or behaviours."

"And this would have happened every time Lynne tried to go out?"

"The symptoms would occur nearly every time the situation is encountered, so the subject will go to great lengths to avoid putting themselves in those situations. In severe cases, they may become completely unable to leave their home."

"And that was the case with Lynne?"

"I fear so, yes."

"And presumably she couldn't come here. So did you used to visit her for your sessions?"

"Yes. It's not something I like to make a habit of. But with some subjects…"

"And you *were* treating her? Or trying to? How do you treat a thing like that?"

"Well, we'd usually treat it with something called cognitive behavioural therapy, or CBT for short. It's a form of counselling where we gradually expose the patient to the situations or objects they fear. They have to remain in that situation until their anxiety abates; if they leave the situation, then the phobic response won't decrease. It might even get worse."

"And it works?" Izzy asked. "This CBT?"

He smiled. "CBT results in resolution for only about half the people who receive it. But for them, not only the panic attacks, but an ability to return to the situations the patient has been avoiding, can be achieved. But we find that many patients deal better with exposure if they're with a friend they can rely on. As I mentioned, Lynne had more or less isolated herself by the time she came to me. That's possibly why CBT wasn't too successful in her case."

"Did you try anything else?"

"Of course. We tried another technique known as cognitive restructuring, where we coach the subject through a reasoned discussion and try to replace their more irrational and counterproductive beliefs with those that are more factual and beneficial."

Katie held up a hand. "In English, please."

He smiled. "Sorry. Well, there are different ways of doing it. Often, those irrational beliefs amount to a misplaced certainty that if they do a certain thing, it will produce a terrifying outcome. Imagine being invited to visit a zoo and being somehow convinced one of the wild animals will get out and attack you. So the very thought of going to the zoo produces the sort of symptoms I just described."

"Okay…" Katie supposed she could imagine it, just.

"Now imagine that scenario is playing in their mind like a horror film. What we have to do is change the ending. All the animals stay behind bars, and the visit is enjoyable, with treats like ice cream thrown in. Instead of something to fear, a visit to the zoo becomes something to be welcomed."

"But I'm thinking that didn't help Lynne either?"

"She was a particularly extreme case. We also tried relaxation techniques that can be used to prevent the symptoms of anxiety and panic. And we combined those techniques with antidepressants."

Katie had heard no mention of antidepressants being found at the house. "How did that go?"

He looked sad. "Lynne hated the effects of the medication and basically stopped taking it. I'm sorry to admit that none of our interventions – either by themselves, or in combination – proved especially successful with her. More than once, she discontinued the therapy in despair, only to eventually start again. But I don't think I've seen her for at least two years."

"So would you be surprised to hear she apparently made a sudden move abroad about eighteen months ago?"

He stared at her. His smile, when it came, was ironic. "Sergeant, I'd be incredulous if I heard she'd even gone down to the corner shop for a newspaper. But you said 'apparently'?"

"We can't be sure that she did." She watched him take a sip of his coffee, feeling a little thirsty herself. "So after her last withdrawal from treatment, you didn't maintain any form of contact?"

"No. I was sorry, because she was never going to recover without help. Living one's life within four walls must be hellish. I actually hoped that she'd simply lost faith in me and turned to another therapist. But if a patient doesn't wish to continue receiving treatment, that's their right. It wasn't as if she was a danger to anyone else. Anxiety disorders can sometimes go hand in hand with enhanced aggression, but I never saw that in her."

But he was frowning. "You implied there was more than one body. Can you tell me any more?"

"I really can't go into those details. But we're treating the circumstances as suspicious." She knew that was quite an understatement, but it was the form of words agreed for the press statement that was going out at lunchtime.

"Well, it sounds dreadful. Poor Lynne. I suppose the details will emerge when you're ready to release them. In the meantime, is there anything else I can do to help?"

She hesitated. "May I ask you where you were on the night of the 11th of August, around 10pm?" The date and time of Donna Mason's disappearance. The one concrete date they had so far in their timeline. "A Saturday."

He blinked. "Is that when...?" He paused. "Sorry. I'm sure you can't tell me. Let me just check, although I have to say I don't get out much. Most likely, if it was a half-decent day, I'd have pottered around, maybe gone to the shops or for a walk, did a bit in the garden. I'd have cooked myself something in the evening, then either watched TV or read a book." He smiled. "I'm a dull fellow."

He picked up a big desk diary. "Fortunately, this covers last year, as well as this one. "He thumbed through it, then treated them to an even broader smile. "Oh! Actually, I think I'm off the hook, if it's an alibi you're looking for."

"You weren't home alone?"

"Far from it. Believe it or not, I was out on a date for the first and last time since my wife left. I decided to use one of those apps. It didn't go well."

"No?" Katie couldn't say she was surprised.

"We met for dinner in central London, but we didn't last to the pudding, I'm afraid. It was an awkward evening, full of stilted conversation in which I realised how very little interesting conversation I have. She decided she had to go and that there wouldn't be a second date."

"And what time was this?"

"According to my diary, we were to meet at eight-thirty. I can't remember when she decided to call it a night, but with drinks, starters and mains, it couldn't have been much before nine-thirty. If I wasn't still in the restaurant at ten, I'd have been waiting for, or on, the train home."

If he was telling the truth, no way could he have been in Brighton, kidnapping Donna Mason.

"We'd like to check that," Katie said. "Do you have a name and some contact details for your date?"

He consulted his diary again. "It's right here. Julie."

"Surname?"

"Sorry, that's not how it works. But I've a mobile number."

He read it out and Katie and Izzy jotted it down.

"Well," she said, "I'm sorry it didn't work out."

His smile was slightly sad. "That's why I live alone, I fear. That and, as my wife put it, for someone who looked inside people's heads, I'm apparently as nutty as a fruitcake."

She stifled a laugh. "What did she mean by that?"

"I can be a bit dotty. I can't seem to switch off from work, and my mind wanders all over the place. At work, I'm driven by that diary. Outside the office, I can't remember what I'm supposed to be doing, or where. I'd forget to pick her up, come home late for our own dinner parties, double book..." He sighed. "Not what you'd necessarily call bonkers, but it drove her mad. She thought I was very self-centred. I suppose she had a point. I didn't mean to be..."

"Okay," she said, doubting this man could organise a piss-up in a brewery, let alone the series of killings they were investigating. "One last thing, then. Given you've been to Lynne's house, I'd like us to take some DNA samples and fingerprints. Purely so we can eliminate you. Is that okay?"

"Of course."

"I think that's all for the moment," she decided after the samples had been taken. "But we'll be in touch if we need anything else."

Silas Ross inclined his head. "Please do. I liked Lynne. I wish I could have helped her."

18

Ricky found that Postman Pete Savage was a little less eager to talk to him today. It seemed weekends were okay to gossip with cops about an exciting murder, but disrupting his workday routine was not so welcome. Nevertheless, he insisted on coming to the station at the end of his shift, rather than have the police show up on his round.

Ricky was joined by Libby Statham in what he expected would be a short interview. After the preamble, he decided to throw the question at him, out of left field.

"Soo... have you been to Brighton in the last few months? The 11th of August to be precise?"

"What?" Postman Pete looked flabbergasted. "What's that got to do with... I mean, no. Of course not."

"Why 'of course not'?" Libby jumped in. "People do go to Brighton. Especially in the summer."

"Sea and sunshine," said Ricky. "What's not to like? And the 11th was a Saturday. Maybe you had the day off?"

"Look, I didn't go to Brighton. I haven't been there since I was a kid. I hardly ever holiday in the UK these days."

"So can you remember where you were?"

Eye roll. "Can *you*?" Yesterday's cheery fellow was definitely a little grumpier now. Either he was surprisingly easy to needle, or he had reasons for being defensive or evasive.

"Just answer the question, please."

He sighed heavily. "All right, all right. I suppose you're just doing your jobs." He took out his phone. "Let me check my diary." He punched and scrolled, then held the screen so they could see it. "There you go," he said with a note of triumph. "We went to the cinema. Me and the wife and my lad. The new *Fast and Furious*. My son loves that sort of thing."

Ricky inspected the phone. Libby looking over his shoulder. "Have you still got the tickets?"

"Doubt it." He was actually looking worried now. Were they just making him nervous, or had Pete Savage's 'regular guy' persona been a façade all along? "Honestly, though, I don't get it. I thought we were talking about eighteen months ago in Wiggo. Now we're on August in Brighton."

"Did you pay for the cinema tickets by card?" Libby asked helpfully. They hadn't set out to do some sort of good cop/bad cop routine, but that seemed to be how it was working out.

His shoulders sagged in evident relief. "Yeah, I would have. And it'll be on the statement, won't it?"

"And your wife will vouch that you actually went?"

He half-laughed. "I doubt she can remember what she did an hour ago, she's so scatty. She reckons she's so busy her brain is always full. But she'll remember we went to see the film, I'm sure. You really think I need an alibi?" That worried look was back.

"Can you also check what you were doing in May last year?"

"Do I need a lawyer?" He licked his lips. "It sounds like I need a lawyer. I thought I was just helping you."

But he didn't press the matter of the lawyer. He scrolled back through his phone, then smiled. "Depends when in May you're talking about. We went to Dubrovnik for a week. We're big *Game of Thrones* fans, especially my lad. Nothing in my diary otherwise. Like as not we just watched the telly and other normal, boring stuff."

Izzy jotted down the dates of the Savages' Croatian holiday.

"I think we're done for now," Ricky said. "Could you scan that credit card statement and text it to me?"

"Sure, if you like."

"And, if you think of anything that has struck you as odd at the house, give one of us a ring."

*

Lynne Redding's accountant, Adam Downes, had a small suite of offices in Maxted Road, in a big brick and glass block of a building on Hemel Hempstead's Maylands Estate. Katie and Izzy were met in the building's reception by a rake-thin individual, probably about forty, but greying at the temples and thin on top. He had a spring in his step and a friendly smile. Izzy liked him immediately.

"No, no," he said, "I'm afraid I'm not the organ grinder. Adam's with a client. I'm his all-purpose slave, Simon. Simon Younger. He shouldn't be too much longer. Do follow me."

He led them to a lift and they got out on the second floor. Downes's offices appeared not to have the sort of glossy, corporate, over-sleekness Izzy always thought was a bit fake and plastic. The furnishings hadn't quite seen better days yet, but they had some miles on the clock and there was a reassuring sturdiness about them.

"Let me sort you out some coffees," said Simon. "You've chosen the right day. I'm not always in the office, and Adam makes pretty terrible coffee. You won't tell him I said that, will you?"

"Your secret's safe with us," Katie assured him as Izzy stifled a giggle.

He disappeared and returned soon afterwards with two coffees and a couple of little packets of biscuits.

"You're part-time?" Katie asked.

"Three or four days a week, a bit in the office, a bit at home." Simon shrugged. "It's all a bit flexible, to be honest. It suits my lifestyle, and it seems to work for Adam. He's mostly a one man band, but I give him whatever support he needs."

When Downes's office door finally opened, he wasn't quite what Izzy was expecting: he looked not much more than thirty years old, although she wondered if he was older than he looked; a little under six feet tall, casually good looking, with well-cut dark hair and a slim build. Light blue shirt, dark blue tie, dark blue suit trousers. Well-polished shoes.

He said goodbye to a middle-aged woman, and then Simon did the introductions. Downes simply raised an eyebrow and admitted them, Simon following with the tray of coffees, which he placed on the round meeting table to the left of the room. A boring-looking potted plant sat dead centre of the table.

"Want one?" Simon asked his boss.

"Not right now." Downes grinned at him, displaying a set of gleaming, perhaps overly perfect, teeth. "Much more caffeine this side of lunchtime, and I'll be climbing the walls."

"Let me know if you need anything."

Simon closed the door behind him, and Downes invited them to sit at the table. Izzy took in her surroundings. Pale blue walls, upon which hung prints of old racing cars and a photograph of a football team. Izzy fancied she recognised Downes in the front row.

The accountant fiddled with some papers on his desk, then joined them.

"Well," he said carefully, "I didn't expect this today. What's it about?"

"We understand one of your former clients is a Miss Lynne Redding, from Wigginton," Katie said.

Downes nodded, looking awkward. "I can't discuss my clients, or their business," he said. "Sorry, but that's privileged information."

There was a pomposity about him that both irritated and amused Izzy. But she wasn't going to let him get away with that.

"I think you know that's not quite right," she said, before Katie could respond. "Privilege applies to lawyer-client relationships. You're bound by confidentiality, that's true, but it isn't the same thing, is it?"

Annoyance fleeted across his face before he managed to convert it into a boyish grin, holding up his hands. "You got me. It's a fair cop. All right, so it's confidential information. I still can't discuss it."

"Well, we're conducting a murder inquiry," Katie said, "so your cooperation would be much appreciated."

His brow furrowed. "Murder? Not Lynne, surely?"

"It's really not something we can go into at this stage. But we do have some questions relating to her."

"All right. Ask away." He looked flustered. Izzy wasn't going to read too much into that. She knew that a visit from the police, talking about murder, was enough to fluster anybody.

"So she was your client for how long?" Katie asked for starters.

"She engaged me soon after I set this practice up, so four or five years ago."

"And she was a freelance editor?"

"Copy-editor, yes. She wanted someone to make up her accounts, do her tax returns."

"How often did you see her?"

"Couple of times a year usually."

"She came here?"

"No. I always went to her. It was a condition of her taking me on."

"Was that normal for you? Visiting a client?"

"It wasn't *ab*normal." He paused. "Actually, after our first year of working together, she told me she never left the house. She had a severe form of agoraphobia, which meant even trying to go out brought on panic attacks. She never told me any more than that, so I don't know when or how it started."

"Why would she even tell you a thing like that?" Izzy asked. "Surely it wasn't relevant to the work you were doing for her?"

"I don't know why, to be honest. I think I've just got one of those faces. People tell me things."

He smiled, perhaps trying to charm them. Izzy remembered how Matt seemed to find that sort of charm all too easy to exert, especially where women were concerned. But that experience had rendered Izzy immune to such charm; if anything, she was suspicious of it. But there was no doubt that Adam Downes was a good looking guy. She wouldn't be surprised if he saw himself as God's gift, but she also suspected that women in particular might well confide in him.

She imagined Adam Downes and Lynn Redding together. He was probably ten or so years younger than Lynne, who had hardly seen anyone from one week to the next. Had she fallen for a handsome man with a smooth manner and a winning smile? Had their relationship been purely professional?

What would her feelings, her state of mind have been, when she dispensed with his services?

"It was a bit of a shock," he admitted when Katie asked how he'd felt about that. "Not just because it was out of the blue, with no warning. And being dumped by email... not so much as a phone call. But what really surprised me was that she said she was moving abroad for a while." He shook his head. "After what she'd told me about the agoraphobia, here she was, suddenly not just leaving the country but, presumably, getting on a plane, or on Eurostar or a ferry. I could only think she'd somehow got a lot better, but it did seem weird."

"But you thought she might be cured?" Izzy said, making a mental note to find out more about the condition.

"I don't know about that. I looked it up once, and there are treatments. I think I read that maybe one third of sufferers can achieve a complete cure. But Lynne said nothing seemed to be working for her. I'd have thought she might have told me if things were improving." He shrugged. "It was hardly my business though."

"Ever see her in a non-professional capacity?"

"As in socially? As I said, she never left the house."

"But maybe you dropped round there for a chat and a drink sometimes? She must have been lonely, and it seems you were someone she could open up to about her illness..."

"I get what you're saying, but the answer's no. It wouldn't be ethical. Or feel right. I'd have felt I was taking advantage of a vulnerable woman."

She briefly wondered if that was true, and then cautioned herself to try not to project her opinion of Matt onto this man. Again.

"Even just being a friend to her?"

"Even that."

"Fair enough. Are you married, by the way?"

He looked amused. "Is this still a professional interview?"

She felt herself colouring. "What's that supposed to mean?"

Katie shot her a glance, then asked Downes just to answer the question.

"Sorry." He held up his hands again. "Bad joke. I can be a clown when I'm nervous." He looked at Izzy. "My apologies."

"*Are* you nervous?" she pushed back.

"Well, I'm being questioned in a murder inquiry. But no. I'm not married. I was engaged a few years ago, but she died."

"I'm sorry for your loss," she said, hating the way the phrase always felt so meaningless and impersonal.

"Well. It happens."

Katie stepped in again, changing tack. "When you visited Miss Redding, where did you hold your meetings?"

"Always at her kitchen table."

"Did you see any more of the house?"

"I might have used the loo a few times. I didn't have a grand tour, if that's what you're wondering."

"I don't suppose you had access to her online banking, anything like that?"

"No. Why would I?"

"You'd be surprised what people will do. You were handling her finances…"

"I was just doing her accounts and her income tax."

"Anything interesting or unusual in her accounts in the time you worked for her?"

"Such as?" A little too defensive?

"Was there?"

Again, that flash of annoyance, quickly replaced by that winning smile.

"No. All dull and boring. I can dig out some paperwork, if it would help."

Katie appeared to think about it. "It might be useful, thanks. Contact DC Cole when you've got it together."

Izzy passed her card over.

He studied it for a moment. "I've got a Great Aunt Isabel. She's nothing like you, though."

Izzy didn't rise to the obvious flirt this time.

"I'm a bit concerned about Lynne," Adam Downes said when she didn't respond. "Can't you at least tell me if she's all right? I mean, it's pretty obvious from the line of questioning that your murder inquiry's focused on her and the house."

"The last time you spoke to her," Katie said, "was there anything different about her that you noticed? Her manner, her tone, her body language? Something she said?"

102

He shook his head. "We really weren't generally that chatty. She probably told me about the agoraphobia that time just to explain why she couldn't come to me. But mostly, when we weren't talking about the work, it was small talk. I doubt I'd have noticed a bum note, even if there had been one."

He frowned. "Even so, the cold, impersonal way things ended was bizarre. She didn't answer or return my calls, and everything we did to finalise her taxes was done by email. I have to say, I was a bit upset. I wouldn't say we were friends, but I liked her. I half-wondered if I'd managed to upset her. But I kept it professional, did what needed to be done, and then just let it go."

"But her tax return," Katie said. "You got her to sign it, yes?"

"Yep. And posted it back."

"I thought it was all digital now?"

"Yeah, but I still like a signature. I feel more comfortable somehow."

"And it was definitely her handwriting?"

Izzy saw what she was getting at and watched Downes's face.

He frowned again. "Why wouldn't it be?" After a few seconds of silence, he sighed. "Who checks a signature that closely? I'd have no reason to compare it. To be honest, I doubt I'd have even seen the signed form."

"Why not?"

"Well, the way it works is, I get what I need from the client to do the accounts and complete the form, and then I send it to them to make sure they're happy with what it says, and to sign and return it. Unless they have a query, Simon just makes sure it's signed and lets me know so I can make the return online. Then he files the original."

Katie wasn't letting go. "So would Simon check the signature?"

"Why would he? I mean, why wouldn't it be Lynne's?"

"You said the signed returns are retained?"

"Yep. Let me speak to Simon."

He stepped out of the office. He wasn't gone long.

"He's going to dig out her last few tax returns and check the signatures. Shouldn't take him long."

They sat in silence for a minute or two. He looked at Izzy.

"So what exactly is a Trainee Detective?"

She detected no flirting or attempt to charm her in this question. More likely it was just small talk to fill the time.

"It's exactly what it says," she told him.

"And how does that work?"

She gave him a quick overview: the portfolio, the exams, the assessment.

"More exciting than pounding a beat?"

"Sometimes."

"Not today?"

She found herself smiling. "I couldn't possibly comment."

"I'm wounded." But his eyes were twinkling.

She didn't respond. She thought there was no harm in establishing a rapport with a witness, but this was getting a bit *too* informal. Especially in front of her boss.

As if reading her mind, Katie cut in. "Can I just ask where you were around 10pm on the night of Saturday the 11th of August?"

His smile faded. "Why? What happened then?"

"If you could just answer the question?"

"Of course." He took out his phone and started tapping. He exuded the air of a man trying not to look flustered. Izzy didn't read too much into that. It wasn't an uncommon response to the police asking about your whereabouts.

"Ah, yes," he said, "the 11th. That was the day I drove down to Southampton for lunch with friends. I went back to their place for coffee and then drove home."

The fact that Southampton and Brighton were both on the south coast, albeit sixty-odd miles apart, wasn't lost on Izzy.

"Where's home?"

"Berkhamsted. Gravel Path."

"When did you leave Southampton, and when did you get home?"

"What's this about?" When Katie didn't respond, his eyes searched the ceiling for answers. "Well, I would probably have headed for home around six. It's a couple of hours, so I'd have been back maybe around eight."

"Can anyone verify that?"

"What, the getting home bit? Do I need an alibi?" Again, Katie said nothing. "Look," Downes said, "as far as I know, the answer's no. But what happened on the 11th?"

Simon knocked and entered.

"I've got Miss Redding's last three signed returns here," he said.

He put them on the table side by side. Each copy was stapled, and he'd folded the pages back so the signature pages were presented.

"That's the latest." He indicated the one on the right.

Simon remained standing while the other three studied them.

"All look the same to me," said Simon.

"I'm not so sure, to be honest," Downes said.

"Nor me," said Izzy.

If Katie thought the same, she wasn't saying so. She simply nodded encouragement at Izzy. "Go on."

She allowed her gaze to shift from one signature to the other, studying them until she was sure.

"Well," she said finally, "the first two, the signatures look like most people's. A bit dashed off."

"Exactly," Downes agreed. "The last one looks a bit more… what's the word?"

She looked at him and their eyes met. "Practised?"

"Yes. More painstaking. Oh, but why forge a signature on a tax return?"

"You said Lynne sent you what you needed to do the accounts and the return," Katie said. "How complicated is it?"

"Not complicated at all. Pretty well just invoices and receipts for income and expenditure, and there's never masses of it. I know she had a system for keeping the papers together. To be honest, she could easily have done it all herself, but she said she preferred to have someone professional on the case." He looked from Katie to Izzy. "I don't get it. You're thinking someone forged that last return?"

"We'd like to take these away," Katie said. Downes looked minded to protest. "I know it's confidential and all that, but it's important."

"I could make you copies," Simon offered.

"No," Katie said firmly, "I want the originals. And we'll need someone to take fingerprints from both of you for elimination."

"Fair enough," Downes said, evidently not prepared to argue. "Simon, can you find an envelope large enough for these?"

His PA went off in search of one.

"By the way," Katie said, "did Simon ever visit Lynne's home? Maybe to drop something off or pick something up?"

"Never. Especially once I knew about the agoraphobia. I didn't think extra people descending on her was a good idea. It was only ever me."

As they headed back to the station in Katie's car, passing more industrial buildings on either side of Swallowdale Lane, Katie asked Izzy for her thinking on today's interviews.

"Interesting. Dr Ross seems a bit of a bumbler, doesn't he? Could he carry off what we think happened at that house? Or was he only showing us what he thought would make us least likely to suspect him? It strikes me that a psychologist would know what buttons to press."

"And what did you make of Downes?"

"Not sure really. At first, to be honest, I didn't much like him. I thought he was a bit of a creep, actually, and then there was that flirty stuff."

Katie raised an eyebrow. "You thought he was hitting on you?"

"Maybe, maybe not. Some guys can't help themselves, even if they're not really interested."

"He didn't flirt with me." She pouted, then grinned. It was a grin that didn't reach her eyes. "Can't compete with you, obviously."

Izzy felt herself blushing again. "Leave it out."

"You're right, though. He's a type that..." She shook her head, as if shaking off a bad memory. "So what about that alibi of his?"

"I think it's a bit flimsy. Brighton's close enough to Southampton for him to have made a bit of a detour, snatched Donna, and taken her back to Wigginton. Or maybe, he'd have taken her home in his car and transferred her to Lynne Redding's house in his Handyman Steve van the next day."

"I agree. When we spoke to DI Seagrave in Brighton yesterday, we talked about CCTV footage from the city centre the night Donna disappeared. I'll speak to him again and ask him to check for Adam Downes's car, as well as vans that might be Handyman Steve's." She crossed a roundabout onto Queensway, industrial buildings giving way to residential properties. "Do you think he could be our man, then?"

She considered it. "He's got the charm, the gift of the gab. White collar job. You could say he's not that organised and relies on the PA – Simon – to keep him on the rails, but maybe that's not the case and he just needs someone to do all the admin stuff. So, yeah. He's got a few of the traits you might find in a psychopath. Or a narcissist. You know, I've read up on this stuff and I still don't know exactly what the difference is." She shrugged. "None of that necessarily puts him in the frame, of course. And he *did* spot that signature discrepancy."

"True. Although he might have guessed we'd want an expert to look at those documents anyway. Voluntarily flagging it up looks like the action of an innocent man, but maybe that was calculated. Either way, if that signature really is forged, it doesn't look good for Lynne, does it?"

"Not great," Izzy agreed. "She's been a bit of a Schrödinger's cat from day one for me. Either alive and living on the continent, just as everyone was meant to believe – maybe for purely innocent reasons, or maybe because she had a hand in five murders."

"Or...?"

"Or dead in one of those freezers." Izzy sighed. "To be honest, that's what I've thought right from the start, and if that signature *is* forged, it clinches it for me. Whoever killed those women, I'm thinking they started with Lynne, and they've been maintaining the fiction that she's alive ever since, so they can keep her house as their private torture chamber and body store."

"I think so too," Katie agreed. "And, once the story hits the news, he's going to know we've found out about it – if he doesn't already suspect as much." She looked troubled. "I wonder what he'll do then."

19

By the time Nate's afternoon briefing kicked off, a press release had been issued and the media feeding frenzy had begun. The story was all over the news websites and trending on social media. Only the barest of details had been released, with no mention of the basement or freezers, but multiple bodies were more than enough to spark the tabloids' love of alliteration. 'Hertfordshire House of Horrors' was already threatening to stick.

Within an hour, Wigginton had been under media siege. By tomorrow, Nate would wager that all manner of locals, regardless of whether they'd known Lynne Redding, or anything about her, or her house, or even anything about the street it stood on, would be on the TV, dishing out their opinions in exchange for thirty seconds of fame.

There was talk already of a vigil being arranged, a protest against violence against women. By all accounts, Superintendent Taylor was under significant pressure from his superiors for a quick breakthrough.

"Ricky," Nate said, "did you get a chance to speak to the company that supplied those two newer freezers?"

"Yes, guv. As you know, they were ordered and supplied, apparently by Lynne Redding, in February and July. They emailed me the paperwork, for what it's worth."

"Did you manage to speak to the drivers who delivered them?"

"Yeah. As it happens, they were both delivered by the same driver."

"And he remembers the jobs?"

"He's not gonna forget. Seems it was a two-man job, and manhandling the freezers into the basement was a nightmare. His sidekick almost put his back out with the second one."

"And there was already one freezer there when they delivered the first of the two?" Nate checked.

"Yep. He thought it was hilarious. He thought two freezers was a bit enthusiastic, but when he was back there, delivering a third..."

"So they thought it odd. Not suspicious though?"

"Oh, they'd had a good old laugh about it. Stocking up for a siege or an apocalypse... yeah, they even joked about storing bodies in them, but a joke was all it was. The driver said you saw all sorts, and it was none of his business how many appliances people had." He shrugged. "To be honest, guv, I'd probably be exactly the same."

"Did he remember who took delivery? Did he see Lynne?"

"No, guv. It was a man. And yeah, he called himself Steve. It definitely sounds like the guy we know about. Well, alleged handyman, I suppose. Fits the description we have, right down to the Watford cap."

"He was wearing it indoors?" Katie sounded incredulous.

"Maybe he's a huge fan."

"Accent?"

"Yeah, West Country again."

Nate made a note on the Wall. All of the people so far known to be contacts of Lynne's had been spoken to now, and their images, were there: Adam Downes; Silas Ross; Pete Savage; and Steve Redding.

"There's no doubt now, is there?" he said. "Whether Steve exists in his own right, or is one of these people in disguise, he's our prime suspect."

"Guv," Katie said, "any merit in adding the neighbours – the Carltons – to our list?"

"Go on."

"Well, apart from the freezer delivery guys, they're the only ones who've actually seen Handyman Steve. And they had that note that they can't now produce. Maybe they're working as a team. The husband, Mike, lets in the freezer men in his Steve disguise, and that's the description they give to us."

"Fair point," said Rachel Sharp. "Although, even if we add them, none of the names we have so far is yet what I'd call a compelling suspect at this stage. I know we need to do some more digging. But they're only suspects at all if we buy the idea that Handyman Steve isn't real. But what if he *is*? Word of a reclusive woman living alone finds the wrong ears. He parks outside the house, waits until the coast is clear, then sneaks up and rings the doorbell. She answers and he forces his way in."

"He tortures Lynne for her passwords so he can take control of her email, her finances," said Nate. "He drops the note through the Carltons' letter box, establishing Lynne's absence and his own occasional presence."

"Exactly," said Rachel, nodding. "Now he's got the house to himself. He sees the chest freezer and, as Izzy suggested, sees a way of preserving Lynne's body, and subsequent victims, as the ultimate trophies."

"*Or* he's still real and Lynne is in on it," Aliya suggested. "Her cousin had never seen signs of violence in her, but she was clearly pretty troubled. Who knows what direction that might have taken?"

"Not sure I buy that, guv," said Ricky. "The woman never set foot outside the house, even if she was faking some of the phobia."

"And fooling a psychiatrist," Katie added.

"That too. So how's she met this bogus handyman? I've seen my fair share of online dating sites, but none where you can find your perfect psycho accomplice."

A ripple of laughter went round the room.

"*Or* Lynne's still in on it and one of those faces on the wall is turning up in disguise," Aliya persisted.

"That's just bonkers, though," Ricky said. "Why go through all that pretence of Lynne going abroad and there being a mythical handyman? She could carry on living there, and her accomplice would have a legit reason for coming and going. She's dead, mark my words."

"We'll know soon enough whether Lynne is a victim or not," Nate said, sensing things were about to get heated – Aliya was directing a hard stare at Ricky, clearly unimpressed by the 'bonkers' jibe. "If she is, then we're as sure as we can be that she'd be in that older freezer, and Dr Stoddart is defrosting those two bodies even as we speak. Once they're separated, we can get a proper look at the faces."

"Sophie," he said. "How are we doing with known local sex offenders?"

"Well," she said, "there's the ones we're already familiar with and quite a few more in neighbouring counties. I'm assuming we can discount the paedophiles – I don't see that fitting with what we're looking at here. There's the flashers, of course, but again, unless they got away with stuff between those activities and the start of the Hall House murders, it seems a jump."

"I'm inclined to agree," he said. "What about some more violent stuff? Rape, especially."

"Yes, some of those were actually in prison for at least some of the time we're interested in. For the others, I've spoken to people who know them. We should follow it up, of course, but for my money none of them really chimes with what little we know about this guy, guv. Or accepted wisdom on serial killers, come to that."

Nate knew what she meant. He doubted if anyone would argue that they were looking at for a psychopath. Not all psychopaths became serial killers, but serial killers usually seemed to display psychopathic traits: not valuing human life, callousness towards their victims – especially sexually motivated serial killers. A total lack of empathy, remorse, or guilt. In other words, it was 'all about them'.

"But they could get good at hiding it, right?" said Ricky.

"They could," Nate agreed. "We know behavioural problems can begin – the seeds of their motivation sown – when the killer is quite young. They'll have found their impulses and behaviours hard to control, but taken no responsibility for their actions, trying to shift the blame onto others, and learning how to do that well. So they grow up thinking the world of themselves, but they can learn to project a different face to the outside world."

"Ted Bundy in the States was deceitful, manipulative and charming," Izzy said. "He had people fooled for years."

"How likely do we think he is to have a white collar job?" Katie said. "Izzy mentioned that in the car earlier in connection with Adam Downes."

"I wouldn't get too hung up on that," Rachel said. "One of the ways some serial killers get away with it is certainly by being organised, meticulous planners. Some are actually pretty stupid and chaotic, but I don't think that's our guy. But organised and meticulous doesn't automatically mean he has to be an office worker or a manager."

"Pete Savage must be quite well organised, doing his postman round," Ricky chipped in. "He comes across as Joe Regular, and I bet he's well liked by the people he meets when he's out delivering. For all we know, he could be manipulating them."

"We need to know more about the victims," said Aliya. "It'll be interesting to see what they have in common. If there's a type he goes for, as such."

"It's not all about type, though," Izzy said. "I was looking on the Internet last night. I read this article that said victim selection is really based on three factors. What were they?" She started ticking off on her fingers. "Availability, vulnerability, and what was the third? Oh, yeah, desirability. So availability is all about the lifestyle of the victim, or their circumstances that allow the killer access to them."

"The only circumstances we're sure of," Rachel said, "are that Donna had had a few drinks, was lost, and was asking for directions. But then I guess that might have been all that was needed to make her available."

"Let's hold that thought," Nate said. "As we identify other victims, we might see a pattern. What else was on your list, Izzy? Vulnerability?"

"Yes, that's about how susceptible the victim is to attack. Donna was lost, anxious to find her mates, and maybe tipsy enough for her guard to be down. A charming white knight offers to show her the way…"

It sounded all too plausible to Nate.

"And desirability?"

"Yeah, that is to do with the appeal of the victim, related to the killer's motivation."

"So we're back to type," Ricky said. "He fancies them, or they look like his mum?"

"Could be," Izzy acknowledged. "But it can be quite complex. Race, gender, ethnicity, age, and other preferences can play a part. I know there's that cliché about psychopaths and their mothers, but they might not have to look like her. It could be their voice, how they speak, a mannerism, what they wear…"

"All we know for sure at the moment is they're all white women," Nate said. "But I agree with Aliya. We might see more of a pattern as we ID the victims. Still, that's useful, Izzy. But let's think about the freezers again. I get that he might have been storing the bodies as trophies, but he killed them by locking them in alive. Maybe that's a part of his mind set."

"Maybe he's recreating something from his past?" Katie suggested. "And it mightn't even be about freezers specifically. Maybe death in the cold, or in a confined space is what floats his boat."

Nate's head was starting to ache. He would take some paracetamol later. But at least part of him was encouraged; he had no doubt that some of the keys to the killer's psyche, even his identity, had come out in the discussion. But what were they?

At the same time, all-too-familiar frustration and fear of failure were beginning to gnaw at him again. There was a killer out there. Five women had been murdered in horrific circumstances on his watch, undetected, and there could be little doubt there would eventually be more if he wasn't stopped.

20

DI Quarrel had told everyone to call it a day, and Izzy was thinking about packing up, when her phone rang.

"DC Cole? It's Adam Downes. From Maxted Road? Lynne Redding's accountant?"

Like she'd have forgotten him and his flirty ultra-smoothness.

"Mr Downes. What can I do for you?"

"It's that paperwork I promised you. Look, sorry it's so late in the day, but it's been one of those afternoons..."

"Have you got it together?"

"Yeah. Are you still at the station? Only I'm actually in the town centre now."

It looked like she wasn't going home quite yet.

"Yes, just about, if you want to drop it in."

He paused for a beat. "Ah. Thing is, that's what I meant to do but, well, to be honest, I needed a loo, so I dropped into The Market Arms."

"Too much information, thank you. So how long do you think you'll be?"

The pub was in Waterhouse Street, only two minutes' walk from the police station.

"Ah," he said again. "See, I don't like just using pub loos and not spending any money, so I thought I'd just have a quick drink, then I thought, I'm not going to feel much like cooking when I get home. So, since I'm here, I'm treating myself to a bite. I suppose I should have swung by the station first, but I wonder if you'd mind awfully picking that stuff up from here?"

She did her best to keep the irritation out of her voice. "Yes, okay."

"In fact, you're welcome to join me, although you probably won't have time."

Annoyance prickled her. This had 'orchestrated' written all over it. Cheeky, presumptuous sod. What game did he think was playing?

"I don't think so," she said.

"I suppose it would be inappropriate?"

"Yes. It would be."

"Sorry. Stupid."

The apology sounded genuine, but she half-suspected that was all part of the charm. More likely he'd expected her to jump at the chance and was more disappointed than remorseful.

"Thanks, though. I'll just pick up the paperwork and leave you to it."

And yet...

She wondered if spending a few minutes with this man in an informal situation wasn't a bad idea. His guard might be down, and if she played it right, he might just let something slip.

Always supposing he was involved in the murders

"Actually, I guess you could order me a latte, and I'll pay you for it. I was about to grab a coffee anyway." A quick coffee she'd paid for herself? What could be the harm?

"Only if you're sure."

"So long as we're clear I'm just collecting papers. It's not a social thing. Okay?"

"Of course. How long will you be?"

"More than five minutes, less than ten."

"Okay. I'll be the one with the rolled up copy of *The Times* and the yellow carnation."

"I think I might recognise you." But she found herself grinning. *Get a fucking grip, Iz.*

She hadn't ventured into Hemel much prior to her attachment to the CID. Her rare shopping expeditions tended to be to Milton Keynes. Since she'd been working at Combe Street, she'd passed the pub a few times but never actually been inside.

She found the place fairly quiet. Adam Downes had tucked himself away in a corner. He waved as she walked in.

"Hi," he said, jumping up to pull out a chair for her. A charming, old-fashioned gesture, or more of his smoothness? He had a pint in front of him, maybe a quarter already drunk. She sincerely hoped he didn't have any more. She'd hate to have to go all police on him and remind him that he still had to drive home.

He pushed a cup towards her. "One latte, as requested."

She fumbled in her bag for her purse. "I'll pay you."

"It seems ridiculous. It's only a couple of quid."

"I know, I know." But she placed three pound coins on the table in front of him. He shrugged and slipped them in his pocket.

They fell silent.

"I should have just left this at the desk," he said finally, handing an envelope over. "It would have been much simpler, and less awkward."

And it did feel awkward. Maybe this hadn't been such a good idea. But she was here now. She might as well keep it light and see what, if anything, she could get out of him.

"It's fine, really. Good to get away from the station for ten minutes."

"I'm guessing it's all a bit frantic with a murder case?"

"Yeah. Not that I can say much about it of course."

"God, no. Especially with me being a potential suspect." He grimaced. "I caught the lunchtime news. Bodies in a house at Wigginton?"

Fishing?

She stirred her coffee and went for small talk. "So how's your day been?"

He rolled his eyes. "Dull. Accountancy seemed like a good idea when I was starting out, and it certainly pays the bills, but I don't know. I'm not sure it's really me."

"No?"

"Let's just say it doesn't make my pulse quicken. The thought of doing it for the rest of my life…"

"Don't then," she said, without thinking.

"I know. You're right, of course."

"Life's too short." Here was a chance to engage with him, gain his confidence.

He sighed. "Thing is, I'm at that awkward stage where I'm a bit too settled and committed to just chuck it in without a Plan B. Not that I know what I'd fancy instead." He took a swig of beer. "How about you? Did you always want to be a cop?"

"Not always. I wanted to be a unicorn when I was little, apparently."

"You should have done that."

She laughed. "Then I went through the ballerina and showjumper stages. In my early teens I wanted to be Beyoncé for a while, although you really don't want to hear me sing."

"Not even karaoke?"

"Oh, I've been known to. Probably sounds like a cat being murdered. But yeah, for some reason the police was a career idea that stuck. I wanted to make a difference, I guess. Once I was in, I realised what I really wanted was to be a detective."

And suddenly she was telling him all about her.

"And here you are." Another sip. "And does your husband or partner mind you working long hours?"

"There's no one like that," she said. "Not for about a year now."

"So he *did* mind?"

But that was a share too far.

"Well," he said. "I think that's sad. And, if I may say so, a waste." Back to smooth again.

"No more than doing a job you find boring."

"Ouch." He winced exaggeratedly. "Touché."

Time to take charge of this conversation, she decided.

"But there's more to life than working, right? What does Adam Downes do when he's not putting figures on a spreadsheet, or whatever accountants do?"

He shrugged. "Not a lot, to be honest with you. I guess I've been a bit rudderless since my fiancée died. I don't really have any hobbies. Watch a bit of football sometimes…"

That grabbed her attention. "Watford?"

"Guilty. Well, they're the local team, aren't they? My dad used to be a big fan, but he doesn't go any more. I only go now and again."

"And when you go, are you like a proper supporter?" She hoped she sounded casual. "You know, scarf, shirt, hat? All that?"

"Is that what proper supporting is?" He looked amused. "Wearing all the gear?"

She wondered what he was smiling about. The banality of the question? Or did he know only too well what she was fishing for? Maybe a little more subtlety was called for.

"But you do have friends," she said. "The ones in Southampton, for example?"

"Yeah, and after Cherry died, family and friends really rallied round. But that only lasts so long. They've got their own lives, and I guess I wasn't much fun to be around back then."

"Can I ask what happened to her?" Not so subtle then. "Tell me if you don't want to talk about it," she added.

He sighed. "It's fine," he said. "Thing is, Cherry and me were chalk and cheese. They say opposites attract, right? I was all about sober suits and work. But she loved outdoor stuff with a bit of adventure in the mix. She loved trying new things. Climbing, abseiling, wild swimming. I tagged along a couple of times, but it really wasn't for me. But it didn't matter, you know? When we were together, it was good, and our differences meant we had different things to talk about, if you know what I mean?"

He paused and took a deep, shuddery breath. The haunted look in his eyes didn't look fake. Izzy felt suddenly uncomfortable, like an intruder. Or a voyeur.

"If she was happy doing what she was doing, that was good enough for me," he continued. "Just once, I really didn't like the sound of something and asked her not to do it." His voice faltered. "Begged, actually."

"What was it?"

"Caving in Wales. I didn't like the sound of her going underground, and I vaguely knew it could be dangerous. Then I made the mistake of checking it out online. I still remember the stats. One hundred and thirty-six deaths over the last hundred-odd years. Forty-seven deaths by drowning alone. It doesn't sound a lot, but…"

Izzy was surprised the numbers were that low. About one a year. That wasn't what she might consider a dangerous sport. She had a cousin up north who was into caving, and she'd mentioned that the numbers of regular cavers, to say nothing of those who went on organised courses, amounted to tens of thousands every year.

Still, she sensed that this could be an important glimpse into Adam Downes's psyche.

"So what happened? In Wales, I mean."

"Well, no one could ever tell Cherry what to do, and we had quite a row about it. She was going with a couple of friends, and there was no way she was pulling out."

"So she went?"

"Yes. And they found a pocket of foul air. Her friends were lucky. She wasn't."

Izzy's human side was moved by a mixture of horror and sympathy. Yet even now, the detective in her was analysing what he was telling her. An image of a naked woman, trapped inside a freezer, flashed through her mind.

"So she died in a cold, confined space?"

As soon as the words were out, she realised how clumsy and obvious they must sound if Downes *was* the killer. How off-key, even if he wasn't.

But he showed no sign of either reaction.

"Yes. That was one of the reasons I was opposed to her doing it in the first place. I've always been a little claustrophobic myself." He looked haunted. "Can we talk about something else?"

"I'm sorry," said Izzy. "I guess detectives are naturally nosy. I didn't mean to upset you."

"Forget it. Look, I know you can't talk about the case, but I'm not stupid. Whatever's happened. I'm one of the few people to have spent time with Lynne Redding. So if you're trying to see what makes me tick…"

She made a show of checking her watch. "I should be heading back." She drained her cup.

He looked disappointed. "Already? Only I was about to say I understand and it's okay."

Again she couldn't decide if he was sincere or playing her. Maybe letting her know he was on to her and enjoying it.

"Yeah, well. Murders don't solve themselves."

"Look," he said, "maybe I'm being inappropriate again but, when it *is* solved – when I'm not a potential suspect – maybe we could meet up properly? Have a meal? Talk about the meaning of waste, and how to stop doing it?"

She pushed his envelope into her bag, stood up and flashed him a smile. "Maybe I'll think about it." Two could play that game, if it *was* a game. "When the case is closed, obviously."

"Obviously." He smiled. "This was nice. I'll be seeing you, Isabel."

"Izzy," she corrected automatically.

"Izzy." He appeared to try it on for size. "I like it. Call me when I'm off the hook."

21

Nate arrived home to an empty house. Laura was back on night shift. He put *Sam's Town* by The Killers on to fill the silence.

After a less hectic working day, he might have relaxed by cooking something from scratch, but tonight he was too weary to put the thought or the effort into it. He rummaged through the options in the freezer and settled for a pizza. Not a great option, but minimum effort.

Once it was in the oven, he took a glass of wine to his office and uncovered his private murder wall. Arguably, what Jordan Stoddart had told him today changed nothing. Yet it could change everything.

His grandparents, the nearest thing to parents he'd ever really known, had told him the truth about his parents – or their version of it – when they'd deemed him old enough to hear it. He'd always been surprised, looking back, that it hadn't unlocked his repressed memories of his father's death, but they'd remained sealed away in whatever recess of his mind they'd retreated to.

They'd told him nothing inconsistent with either what was in the public domain or what was in the case file he'd illicitly obtained. His mother had been a drinker with an uncontrollable temper who'd made his father's life hell until she'd finally gone too far and stabbed him in a rage in front of their son.

His mother, Sandra Bowman, when he'd finally spoken to her last year, had given him a different version. He'd come at her in a drunken rage in the kitchen. She, terrified, had picked up a knife she'd just been using to try and warn him off. Somehow he'd run onto the blade.

She'd tried to persuade him that his grandparents were blinded to that truth. Philip Bowman had been their little boy, and he could do no wrong. Nate's grandfather had connections in the local police and doubtless hadn't been opposed to using them to ensure all the bias in the case went one way.

Although Nate had agreed to take a look at the case – and, having done so, had kept that promise against his better judgement – he'd never seriously expected to find anything that challenged the verdict or came close to changing his mind. Apart from Laura, his grandparents were the only people he had ever truly trusted.

And yet a piece of information from the post mortem report that Nate thought was at least relevant hadn't gone any further. Hadn't gone anywhere. Why?

Even if the police and the prosecution had missed it, or even deliberately ignored it, all the evidence would have been shared with the defence. Had they missed it too? Surely that strained credibility too far.

He sipped his wine and sighed. He knew what he had to do. Had known from the moment the doc – Jordan – the name still felt unfamiliar – had first raised the issue.

The phone rang several times, and he was almost resigned to it going to voicemail when she picked up.

"Mum?" It felt alien on his lips. "Sandra? It's me, Nathan."

"*Nathan?* Oh, God, how lovely to hear from you! How are you? How's Laura?"

Anyone would think he was in the habit of making social calls to the woman he'd hated for most of his life.

"I need to ask you something."

"Of course, love."

Whatever Yorkshire accent he'd once had, it had softened to the point that it had all but vanished, along with the name Nathan Bowman. People with a good ear could pick out the faintest twang. Hers, on the other hand, was as strong as it presumably always had been. But the 'love' irked him. Just as she didn't get to be called 'Mum', so she didn't get to call him 'love'.

"It's about your case."

"You looked at it?" There was eagerness in her voice, and something else. Tension?

"I said I would. I still don't know what you expected me to find. But there's one thing I don't understand."

"What's that, love?"

Stop calling me that!

"I got an expert opinion on Dad's post mortem report. There were no surprises. Except the angle of the stab wound. It's not what you'd expect if you'd actually attacked him, nor even if it was like you said and you'd been trying to keep him at bay when he ran onto the knife."

"No?"

"No. The blade went upwards at an angle, like an awkward underarm thrust. My expert reckons the person holding the knife could have been quite low down. Maybe on their knees."

"Really? Well, maybe. It's all a bit hazy now." It sounded evasive.

"*Hazy?* Seriously? I'm supposed to be the one with the repressed memory. It seems one possible explanation is that you were on your knees, being attacked, and you struck out in self-defence, or maybe, like you say, you were trying to make him back off. Whatever. Before you get your hopes up, I'm not buying it."

"Of course not." A hint of bitterness. "So why did you bother to call?"

"Because it might have helped your case, and it doesn't seem to have got so much as one mention in court. How do you explain that?"

When she didn't answer immediately, he ploughed on. "All right, let's say Granddad really did have influence with the police. Or that it just wasn't in their interests, or the prosecution's, to risk their nice tidy case by lifting that stone. But what about your own brief? It could have helped you. Introduced a shadow of a doubt, maybe."

"Ah, well. I couldn't afford much in the way of a defence. The man I got was pretty useless, and I think even he thought I was guilty. Maybe he missed it."

"But it wasn't even in the story you told the court. You could have said he forced you to your knees, if that's what happened.

But you didn't. You said nothing to suggest you weren't on your feet when the blade went into him."

He sighed. There had been the ghost of a suspicion at the back of his mind, something else that he was unwilling to confront, and nothing in this conversation was making it go away.

"Well," he said after more silence from her, "maybe for some reason you were holding the knife low at a funny angle when you stabbed him."

"I didn't stab him."

"No, he ran onto the knife. Right."

"I wish *you* could remember," she said. "I mean," she ploughed on hastily, "I don't want you to relive that horror, of course I don't, but you were the only other person there. If you could only recall how it was…"

"Yes, but I can't."

"And there are no ways it might be retrieved? I mean, I've read up on it. You'd expect me to."

"And so have I, Sandra. Even hypnosis runs the risk of just implanting false memories."

"But there's a theory that certain sounds, sights, even smells, can trigger memories that are buried deep inside. Or places…"

"Places? You mean the old house?"

"If we went back here? The familiarity after all this time?" There was a desperate pleading in her voice. "Maybe you'd remember something?"

"I doubt it."

"But couldn't we try?"

He glanced at his watch. He was in danger of burnt pizza.

"I've got to go," he said.

"Can you at least think about it?"

"Okay," he said. "I've got a big case on right now, but when things quieten down, I'll think about it."

"You promise?"

He drew a deep breath. "I said I would, didn't I? You do not get to extract promises from me."

"Sorry, love. Didn't mean to push."

"And please. Don't keep calling me 'love'."

22

Wigginton was now well and truly on the map for all the wrong reasons: all the national newspapers, including the front pages of most of the red tops; and prominence on national radio and TV news. The likeness of Handyman Steve was also out there.

The media spotlight was never the ideal environment for conducting an investigation, not least because it caused a spike in calls from the public. There were, to be fair, well-meaning calls from people who hoped they could help. Then there were the nonsense calls from members of the public with theories about the case.

And the confessors.

Nate thanked God most of the detail, including the freezers, the restraints, the mutilations and the fact that the bodies were naked, wasn't in the public domain. At least the kids who'd first discovered the bodies seemed to have kept their mouths shut, probably because they didn't want to broadcast their break-in. But, as a result, when asked to describe what they'd done to the victims, none of the bogus confessors came even close to what had actually happened.

With the explosion of anger that such a thing could have happened came the usual advice about what women ought to be doing to keep themselves safe: not dressing 'provocatively', not being out alone after dark, downloading apps that could help family and friends track their movements…

"Isn't that just typical?" he overheard Katie saying as he got himself a coffee from the machine near the main office. "We're not the problem, but we're the ones who have to be constrained."

"Yeah," said Aliya with feeling. "Next we'll have morality police telling women how to dress and behave modestly. Sound familiar?"

"It does," Katie agreed. "That truth is, the problem is men who do violence to women. They're the ones who should change their behaviour. Maybe it's men who shouldn't be allowed out after dark, and we women can get on with our lives without fear."

"That's just ridiculous, Sarge," Ricky protested. "I mean, don't get me wrong. I hate these bastards as much as you do, but some sort of curfew on *all* blokes, just to keep the few bad apples off the street? That's way over the top."

"You just don't get it, do you?" snapped Katie.

"I do actually. But that's not the answer. I mean, it's not like the risks are gonna go away overnight. All I'm saying is, maybe it makes sense for women to take a few precautions."

"Ricky, you're a nice guy, but you have no idea." Katie spoke more calmly, but Nate detected an edge beneath the surface. There was a fury she was barely containing. It was a side of her she rarely showed. "You have no idea how exhausting it is as a woman to be constantly on guard. A stranger asks you the time and you hope that's all he wants. You're walking home after dark and you see a guy coming the other way. Do you cross the road, just in case? If you do, will that signal that you're nervous and provoke something?"

"Choosing an outfit for a night out," he heard Izzy say. "Thinking through the logistics of the evening. Not wanting to send out the wrong signals in the wrong place. Not feeling you can wear what you like, where you like."

"Getting unwelcome attention and wondering where it'll end," added Aliya.

"Being scared absolutely shitless," said Katie, with real heat. "Like..." her voice cracked. "Like those poor bloody women at Hall House must have felt."

"Yeah, well," Ricky tried to laugh off the hostility. "I'm scared shitless myself now. Three scary ladies. I've got calls to make."

Although it was true that she'd been backed by pretty much every woman on the team, Nate wondered if some bad experience lay behind Katie's rare display of anger.

He felt conflicted about the issue. Everyone on his team knew that the sort of 'boys' club banter' that used to be tolerated was not going to be accepted on his watch. And he completely agreed that it was men who needed to change their ways, including the decent majority actively calling out offensive behaviour whenever they witnessed it. He also entirely refuted any notion that women who didn't take all the responsibility for making sure they weren't raped or murdered had themselves to blame.

Yet, with a serial murderer only one of the predators at large, he couldn't help worrying about Laura, and all the women he cared about, and wishing he could protect them all – and, since he plainly couldn't do that, he did want them to stay safe. He didn't know what the right answer was.

Meanwhile, Wigginton, already ankle deep in reporters, had a candlelit vigil descending on it this evening. It would need to be policed, which would compromise the number of bodies on the ground and impact resourcing for the investigation.

At least the message from the Chief Constable was that soft policing was the watchword. The last thing she wanted to see on the news was scenes of women, protesting against violence to women by men, being manhandled by male police officers.

Nate knew that all he could do to help was catch the killer, taking at least one more predator off the streets. With that in mind, he went with Aliya to the mortuary to see the two bodies from the older freezer – now thawed and separated – and to observe the first of those post mortems.

"I'm starting with the woman who was at the bottom of the freezer," Jordan Stoddart said. "This one, at least, we'll have no problem identifying."

There was no doubt at all now that the first woman to die at Hall House had been its owner. Nate had seen enough photographs of Lynne Redding to recognise her. It confirmed once and for all that she hadn't gone abroad. Just as in life, she hadn't gone anywhere. A woman who rarely set foot outside her door had probably paid with her life just for opening it to the wrong person.

The pathologist's examination revealed no material differences from the injuries inflicted on Donna Mason: beatings, sexual violence, amputation of fingers and toes. No cigarette burns, but he had already observed that these were present on the other victim in that freezer.

"I can only suppose that the burns are a refinement," he said, "although we can hardly say Lynne got off lightly in comparison. You mentioned that Lynne might have been tortured for things like passwords. Obviously I have no way of knowing. But it's clear that a lot of it, and especially in the later victims, was violence for its own sake. Because he could. Because he had the power."

"When will you do the second post mortem, Jordan?"

"This afternoon. I'll take a break for lunch and to write this one up first, then I'll give you a time. I take it you'd like photos of her now?"

"Yes please. The face and any distinguishing marks you can see. Anything that might be on a missing person report or database."

Aliya was quiet on the way back to the station, and Nate could tell she was deep in thought.

"Guv," she said finally, "I've just been doing some sums."

"Yes?"

"Well, now we know for sure Lynne's the first victim, it's most likely she was killed around the time she supposedly went abroad – so May last year, right?"

"Yep."

"And we know Donna was taken in August this year. That's fifteen months, and we think she's the fourth victim after Lynne. So about three months, three weeks between victims. On average."

"So…" he saw where she was going. "You reckon he'll be looking to strike again maybe late November? In about a month?"

"At the latest, guv. But obviously we haven't got that much of a pattern to go on until we know who the other victims are. What we do know is, the urge to kill often comes in shorter and shorter intervals. Knock a month off that estimate, and he could be getting that urge right now."

He stopped walking, running through the sums in his own head. "I agree," he said. "Although, once he realises he can't use Hall House any more, that might slow him down."

"It might," she agreed. "If he can help himself."

He couldn't fault her logic. "Quite. Well, that's just dandy. It means we might have no time at all to catch this bastard before he does it again."

*

Nate hadn't been back long when a rather pleased-looking Ricky James walked into his office.

"A couple of little developments, guv. First of all, the van Handyman Steve is supposed to be using."

Nate looked at him. "You've got something?"

"I think so. Me and some uniforms have been checking out CCTV cameras in and around Wiggo, looking at vans. We know this Steve character, or whatever his real name is, apparently has one. But up to now, it's all been a bit unguided, because there are a hell of a lot of vans out there. Except now we have not only a rough idea when Lynn went off the radar, but we also know precisely when Donna disappeared and was presumably brought to Lynne's house."

Now he had Nate's full attention. "You've been focusing on footage around those times?"

"Exactly, guv. And it's quite interesting. I mean, there are vans that you just see all the time, kidnaps or not. But we found just this one old, white Bedford van that first crops up at a time that would work for Lynne, and again on the night Donna went missing."

"Interesting. Could be a coincidence though. Only *those* times?"

Ricky puffed his cheeks out. "I can't say that for sure, but here's the thing. See, we've checked out the van with DVLA, and it turns out it's registered to Lynne Redding."

Nate stared at him. "Say that again."

"This van we're interested in. The registered owner is Lynne Redding, from Wigginton."

"But that's ridiculous. Lynne never went anywhere. The neighbours said she didn't have a car, and didn't her cousin say she never learned to drive?"

"So I'm told, guv, so we checked that too. And yeah, she's never held a licence. But, to be honest, it's not difficult to register a vehicle to a third party. But there's more."

"Go on."

"Katie's guy in Brighton has footage from around the time Donna was taken. Most of their focus has been on trying to spot Donna going off with someone, but they've been reviewing it to look for anybody resembling Steve in the vicinity. So we fed him the vehicle reg, and wouldn't you know?"

"They found it around Brighton at that time on that date."

Suddenly Nate was more energised, more positive. He knew this revelation didn't mean an arrest was imminent, but it was perhaps the first time since this investigation had started that there was anything really useful to follow-up.

"Can you make out the driver in any of the footage?"

"I left the guys doing enlargement and enhancement, so we'll have some pics for you soon. But yeah, he looks like the description of Handyman Steve."

"Any passengers?"

"Sorry, no. Always on his own in what we've found so far. If any of the women are in the van, they're in the back, or maybe out of sight on the back seats. But I'd bet the farm on this being Steve and his van."

"Let's put out an order for all cars to watch out for it. And track down the previous owner. See if they remember who they sold it to."

"Will do," Ricky said. "You know, registering to Lynne seems twisted. But better than fake plates. I bet he sticks to the speed limits, too, when he uses it. Never runs a red light..."

"Mind you, he might not fancy going out in that van again, now he knows Hall House is compromised. Not only won't he be going back there, but most likely wherever he stashes the van when it's not in use is where it'll stay until he thinks he can safely dispose of it.

"You never know. But yeah, I'd never be surprised if it turned up burned out somewhere."

"Nor me. But he might make a mistake. If and when he decides to pick up where he left off, he's either got to use that, or his own vehicle, or something else. This is great work, Ricky, well done. Anything else?"

"There is, guv." Ricky looked pleased with himself. "I got hold of Pete Savage's wife, just to verify his alibis. It turns out they're not together."

"Really? I thought they went on holiday together in May, around the time Lynne was meant to have gone away, and then they were at the cinema together the day Donna was taken."

"She's confirmed all that. Seems their son is disabled, and that's put a strain on the relationship. So they've been living apart for about six months – Pete's in a bedsit for now – and seeing how that goes. But they still do things as a family."

"I guess it doesn't make much difference really."

"Well, yes and no, guv. She happened to mention the actual timing of the film. She couldn't swear, but she said it was a late afternoon, rather than evening, showing. Sophie had a word with the cinema, and it sounds like it would have finished about six-thirty. She says he normally drops her and the kid home, but doesn't go in. So he could go and get his van, and drive down to Brighton. Two to two and a half hours? He could have been there by nine-thirty, and been on the prowl around the time Donna was lost and asking for directions to the next bar. As for the holiday, we don't know precisely when the killer took control of Hall House, do we?"

"That's true," agreed Nate. "You've been busy."

"He sort of lied to us, guv."

"Only by what he *didn't* mention. He could argue that we didn't ask for those details."

"We could bring him in and really give him a hard time."

"We could. I'm just not sure we've got anywhere near enough to justify that." Nate pondered. "But have a chat with him. Feed back what his wife said and ask him to account for his movements after he dropped them. Gently express surprise that he didn't mention his living arrangements to us. See what he says."

"Will do."

"And we've got that clever software. Get someone to fiddle with the picture we have of Savage and see what he'd look like with a beard, long hair, glasses and a cap. See how it compares to the artist's image of Handyman Steve."

"On it, guv. Although I reckon you or me could look like him by the time you put all that on."

"Still, it's worth a try. Of course, there's one positive, if it's him."

"What's that, guv?"

"Even if he gets the urge to kill again, he's not going to start bringing his victims home, is he? I think if you were holding and torturing someone in a bedsit, somebody would notice."

23

The text had been waiting for Izzy when she'd taken her phone off charge this morning. The battery had died again by the time she'd got home, and she'd plugged it in and not got around to looking at it again until after she got up. Adam Downes had sent his message late last night:

Good talking to you. I meant what I said about meeting up when the case is over. Unless you've jailed me, obvs lol.
Adam Downes.

She was still fuming. It tied in exactly with her first impressions of the man. Thinking that, with his charm and good looks, he could get away with anything.

Even murder?

He'd not denied that Lynne Redding had opened up to him about her phobia. She might have been isolated and reclusive, but that didn't automatically mean she wouldn't crave male company. Had Adam reeled her in, gained her trust, and then pounced?

In terms of what she knew about serial killers – and she knew her research had only touched the surface – he certainly ticked quite a few boxes. He appeared to have no criminal record, juvenile or other, but that didn't mean he didn't have a few undetected crimes – maybe even undetected murders – under his belt.

She'd been in two minds whether to tell anyone about their pub meeting, but the text had settled it. She'd asked Katie for a private word, and now they were seated in a colourless meeting room.

"You shouldn't have done it, Izzy. Meeting up alone with someone connected to the case. If we do have cause to arrest him, and it gets into he said-she said, he can make claims about that conversation that are completely uncorroborated."

"I know." Izzy knew she was blushing. "I knew it at the time, but it was late and I kidded myself if I could get his guard down, he might give something away."

"Yeah, well," Katie said. "He seems to fancy you, that much is obvious, so you might have had a point, but for two things. One, I'm less than convinced the sort of person you profiled yesterday *would* let his guard down. Anything a psychopath told you would not necessarily be true, and would be all about serving their needs. Am I right?"

Izzy nodded glumly.

"And two," Katie went on, "anything useful he did tell you, he could simply deny, and there were no witnesses to that conversation."

She paused until Izzy was about to speak, but then she held up a hand, silencing her. But her expression had softened.

"Look, I get it. You're young, you're ambitious, you're in a hurry to prove yourself. You're a woman, which is still a tougher gig than it ought to be. I've been there. Just think before you act. You admit you wondered at the time whether it was a good idea. You've got great instincts. Listen to them."

"Does DI Quarrel need to know?"

"I think he's got enough on his plate, and this really isn't that important. Might be worth seeing what more there is about the fiancée's death, though."

"It's already on my to do list."

"Good. By the way, for what it's worth, I've been contacted by a suspect too."

"Really? Who?"

"Dr Ross. Lynne's psychologist? He gave me a call. Said it was obvious from the news that we're hunting a serial killer, and asked me if we're using a psychological profiler. I declined to discuss how we're handling the case, but he offered his services. Thought he might have some valuable insights."

Izzy digested this. "You know, I'd do something like that, if I was the killer. Try and get inside the investigation. It'd help me keep a step ahead of the law, and I could feed you nonsense that would lead us away from me. And, as we've said before, that absent-minded professor look could just be a sham."

"His date on the 11th of August checked out though."

Izzy waggled her hand. "Well, she – Julie – confirmed the date took place. She couldn't be sure what time she pulled the plug – although I agree, even if it was early, it would have made it tight for him to get to Brighton." She frowned. "Although being dumped might have provoked our killer into taking revenge on some other poor woman."

"Maybe."

"So what are you going to do?"

"Oh, I'm gonna play along. I reported it to Nate – DI Quarrel – and he thought it was a good idea to take him up on it. Bottom line is, those insights might actually be valuable. I want you to come along. Between the two of us, I'm hoping we'll be able to tell if he's bullshitting."

"Or actively trying to mislead us?"

"That too. After the late morning briefing, I'll get back to him and set it up."

*

Nate was pleased to be able to offer at least a little good news when the team assembled. The mortuary photograph on the Wall of the woman assumed – for the moment – to be victim number two had been replaced with the image of a thin-faced woman, her dark hair shot through with grey. A smile that didn't quite seem to reach the eyes. And it now had a name beneath it.

"Angela Andrews," he told the assembled team. "Originally from Northamptonshire, but last seen in the red light district in Luton."

"Luton?" Katie echoed. "That's a bit closer to home."

"Indeed." Probably less than a dozen miles up the M1.

"She was a sex worker?"

"Yes. It seems a couple of the other girls she was particularly friendly with reported her missing. It sounds like she was a nice girl from a nice family, living in a quiet little town who made some bad choices, found herself with a drugs problem that got out of hand and landed her in a financial crisis."

It was too common a story. It was almost as if some people found themselves at some sort of crossroads. A fork in the road where the Angela Andrews of this world might have turned right instead of left and might now be living a different, happier, more normal life.

But Angela had taken that left turn instead and found herself on a road with no exits that had led her from a quiet Northamptonshire town to a Luton estate where she earned a meagre living shagging and giving blowjobs to strangers in their cars.

Nate knew it was a dangerous trade, never knowing if a client would turn violent. If this was the night she'd get herself killed.

"She was thirty-one years old when her friends reported her missing in November last year," he said.

It seemed some of the girls on her patch looked out for each other. Suddenly, there was no sign of Angela. They thought maybe she'd had one fix too many and was either sick, or had even died, but her pimp insisted he hadn't seen her either.

"By all accounts he was pretty angry she wasn't working. He thought maybe she'd gone back to her family."

"But she hadn't?" Rachel Sharp asked.

He shook his head. "I spoke to the lead officer in her missing persons case myself. Apparently, family and friends had tried to reach out to her, more than once. Maybe she was ashamed of the life she was leading, but it's clear she cut herself off from them all, one by one. In the end, they lost contact with her altogether. They didn't even know she was in Luton, but she'd given one of the other girls a contact number for her parents, just in case. The girl called them, but they hadn't heard from her in ages. So she reported it to the police."

"And it was taken seriously?" Aliya wanted to know, a slight note of scepticism in her voice.

"Seems so, yes. I know we sometimes hear reports of sex workers being treated as less important but, as luck would have it, there's a female officer who checks on the girls from time to time, so they went to her. She quickly became concerned something bad had happened to Angela, and she persuaded her bosses to launch a missing person case. When we circulated her photo, it happened to land on the right desk."

"And their inquiry... do we know what they looked at?" asked Rachel.

"Unsurprisingly, some suspicion fell on the pimp, and another working theory was that maybe she'd got in the wrong car with the wrong client. But there was never any actual evidence for either hypothesis."

"The file's still open?"

"Yes, but the feeling up to today was that perhaps she'd simply woken up one morning and realised the truth about the man who'd been giving her shelter – one tiny room – with enough food to keep her alive, and enough drugs to feed her habit. Enough to keep her dependent and working. Obviously he was pocketing most of her earnings."

"God, I hate those bastards," Ricky James muttered loudly enough for the whole room to hear.

Nate couldn't disagree. It was a depressingly familiar story that his colleagues who dealt with vice had heard way too many times. So many sex workers deluded themselves that the men who lived off their earnings cared about them. Yet the women took all the risks, got to have their bodies used and abused, while their so-called boyfriends just pocketed the money.

"Me too," he acknowledged. "But it's pretty clear now that she was kidnapped," he said, "and taken to Wigginton. We know the rest."

"So in fact it seems we're looking at three completely different victim types," said Katie. "An agoraphobic woman held captive in her own home, a divorcee taken on a hen weekend, and a drug-addicted sex worker." She looked past Nate at the board. "Interesting. You might entice a prostitute into a vehicle relatively easily. So why Donna? Why Brighton?"

"It's possible we can discount Lynne to some extent," Nate said. "I still think the motivation there was the house, plus the fact that she could be made to disappear without arousing undue suspicion. But as for Angela and Donna, I agree. Why them in particular? And why those locations?"

"How about this, sir," Izzy ventured. "We think he's got it in for women in general – gets his kicks from torturing and killing them, and who they are doesn't matter. The 'type' is that they're females who are accessible, vulnerable and desirable. So he's got this setup where he can use Lynne's house as a killing base, but he's too smart to bunch all his victims together geographically. He figures someone might notice. So he's spreading it around. Different locations, different forces. If he's careful, women will go missing, but no one will link them."

"Especially someone like Angela," Katie added thoughtfully. "Okay, in this case, she was reported missing and the police took it seriously. But there's a perception out there that it won't be like that. That, even if they get reported, it won't get followed up. A prostitute, a drug user? Just another statistic."

"For all we know, he's just sticking pins in a map," Aliya said.

"I think there's a lot in all that," Nate said, "but let's see what the next twenty-four hours will bring. If we can ID the last two victims as quickly as the first three, then surely we'll either see a pattern or be confident that there *is* no pattern."

"Another day." Katie looked and sounded as frustrated as he felt. "Another day, and who knows where this animal is? Who he's got eyes on? He might already have someone." She grimaced. "He could be torturing them right now."

He nodded, sharing her sense of impotent horror. "He might," he agreed. "He could. Aliya did some calculations that suggest he might well be getting the urge to kill right now. So let's keep ourselves updated about women who've gone missing recently, and keep updating. Meanwhile we need to find out more about *all* the victims, and see if it helps. Even if we seriously doubt that it will."

Because, if it was really the case that nothing connected the victims in a way that might point to the killer, then all they could hope was that he made a mistake, or they got a break that owed more to luck than detective work.

And the body count could continue to mount until that breakthrough came.

If it came at all.

The team listened to other reports and updates.

"Okay," Nate said afterwards. "So this afternoon, Katie, can you take Aliya to Luton? Make contact with the cops there, especially the one who knows the working girls. See if you can talk to the ones who were friends with Angela. They're more likely to open up to women. I want to know all there is about her and the days before and after she went missing. Had there been anything, anything at all, unusual going on at the time?"

"As soon as we break up here," Katie said, scribbling a note. "Oh, but I've arranged for me and Izzy to see Dr Ross now."

"I'll take that meeting," Nate decided. "Izzy, you're with me. Let's see what so-called insights the good doctor has to offer."

24

DS Jamila Ahmed had spent a lot of time over the past few years on gaining the trust of many of the women who worked in Luton's sex industry. She'd been happy enough to meet Katie and Aliya on the outskirts of the estate where Angela Andrews had plied her trade, on condition that they did nothing that risked undermining that trust.

They met outside a tired-looking café – an old-fashioned greasy spoon in a small row of shops – and Jamila led them inside and bought coffees for Katie, builders' tea for Aliya and a herbal tea for herself.

They found a large table away from the window and prying ears.

"A couple of the girls who were closest to Angela are joining us," she checked her watch, "in about fifteen minutes. It's probably worth telling you a little about my patch."

Katie had taken an immediate liking to her friendly but no-nonsense approach.

"Please," she said. "Background and context are always good."

"First thing to say," Jamila said. "Luton's a really great town. Oh, the closure of the Vauxhall car plant in 2002 hit the economy hard, but it's still got an awful lot of positives. There are some lovely areas to live, some decent parks, good transport links. It's also one of the most populous – and diverse – towns in the country not to have city status. But yes, we do have some pretty bad places, as well as the good ones. In some real hotspot areas, the sex trade, and the drug abuse that goes with it, can make residents' lives a total misery."

"And it damages many vulnerable women?" Aliya suggested.

"Exactly. They're often victims of sexual exploitation due to their vulnerabilities, or they can even be victims of modern day slavery."

"So how do you tackle it?"

Jamila sighed. "We've made it our priority to identify the buyers and traffickers, rather than coming down hard on the woman. They're victims of the sex trade, and we try to keep them safe. We also identify and close down properties used for prostitution."

"We've closed down a couple in our area over the last ten years," Katie said. "Not many though."

"It's a bit like whacking a mole. Close one brothel, successfully prosecute one pimp, and a new problem will pop up the next day. You know what it's like."

"But, as you say, the sex workers are often vulnerable and exploited," Aliya said. "You've got initiatives to help them?"

"Of course. There's partnerships and strategies, and we work with the women, if they'll let us, to offer a way out, and try to give them a chance of a better life. We also work hard on prevention. But all forces have finite resources, and we're no different." She shrugged. "We do the best we can."

"And you knew Angela personally?" Katie asked.

"Yes, a couple of us did. You get to know most of the girls if you put the work in. It's so sad when they describe their pimp as their boyfriend. Angela did that. You think, what kind of boyfriend would have you out giving blowjobs in alleys and then take the money for themselves?"

"You say Angela fell into that category?"

"Angela was basically a nice person, terribly exploited, and we've never been able to lay a glove on the creep who controlled her and a number of other girls. She often talked about going home to her family, but talk was all it ever was. She was always saying she just needed to get herself straight first, and of course she never did. It was pretty clear she was ashamed of what she'd become."

"And these girls we're meeting? They're happy to talk to us?"

"Yes, although they're a bit jumpy about being seen talking to the police."

"Even plain clothes?" said Aliya.

Jamila laughed. "Look in the mirror, mate. You guys don't exactly blend in, and people round here can spot a cop a mile off." She smiled, evidently reading their faces. "Don't worry. You'll be fine. But look, I've held off telling them Angela's dead, as you asked on the phone, but they're not stupid. They've guessed and they're a bit cut up, so go easy on them."

"Of course."

Portia and Trina arrived a few minutes later. Jamila did quick introductions, and orders were taken.

Aliya went to the counter to order. While Katie waited for her to return, she surreptitiously studied the two newcomers. Both looked to her as if they'd aged beyond their years, and they were too thin under their cheap and skimpy attire. Dark roots were beginning to show through Portia's blonde hair and Trina's over-bright red. What Jamila had told her about the local sex trade echoed back and she felt a wave of sadness wash over her.

Orders taken, Aliya rejoined them and, with gentle prompting from Jamila, the women began to open up, talking in quiet voices.

"The thing about our business," Trina was saying, "you've got to try and be tough. Ange never really was. She didn't really belong, and some of the more brutal bastards could see that. We tried to keep an eye out for her, me and Portia, but what can you do?"

"I thought one day she'd either get herself killed or, if she could do it, she'd get the hell out of here," Portia said. "Maybe try and make it right with her friends and family and get clean."

"You said she was different," Katie said, "and that the nastier clients saw it. So did they single her out?"

"Sometimes," Trina said. "But, to be fair, even most of them know not to go too far. If you hurt a girl so she can't work, there can be repercussions, you know? But Ange still did get hurt a few times."

"So what did you think when she disappeared? How did you come to miss her?"

"We just stopped seeing her around. We was worried. Anyhow, she gave me her mum's number one time, after she took a bit of a pasting. She said they didn't really get on, but I should have it just in case something happened to her. So, I rang, hoping she'd done it – gone home, I mean. But they hadn't heard from her in ages."

"How did they respond when you called?"

"Well, obvs I wasn't gonna tell them what she was doing for a living. Not for me to do that. But the funny thing is, considering she said there was this big split, you could tell they were worried out of their minds about her. You know what? All that about them not getting on? She just didn't want them knowing what she'd sunk to."

"So did you do anything else?" Katie probed. "To try and find what had happened to her, I mean?"

The two women exchanged a glance.

"I think we both knew something was wrong then didn't we, Trine?" Portia said.

"Yeah, like someone had put her in hospital or worse. So I went and spoke to her old man. I mean, he'd know, right? So I asked him where she was, but all he could talk about was how she'd be in trouble when he saw her."

"You didn't think he'd done anything to her himself?" Aliya asked.

"His meal ticket?" Portia scoffed. "You're kidding."

"I think he hit her a few times," Trina said, "but nothing bad enough to stop her working."

"So you exhausted your own inquiries?" said Katie. "And then you went to the police? That was quite brave, I'd imagine?"

"Yeah, well," Trina said, "Jamila and her girls are great, as cops go. Like, yeah, if word got back, we'd be in trouble. Same as this meet-up."

She paused and the table fell silent as teas and coffees, and food for Portia and Trina arrived. As soon as the waitress retreated, Trina began to speak again, while adding mustard and ketchup to her bacon roll.

"Anyhow, it was the right thing to do. I mean, we're not tarts with hearts or any of that bollocks, but she was a bit of a mate and someone had to look out for her."

"Looks like we didn't do much of a job," Portia said. A tear slid down her face, tracking heavily applied mascara. "She's dead, isn't she?"

"Can I ask you not to say anything?" Katie said. "Until it's been on the news. Her family are being informed, but—"

"No worries," Trina said.

"Thanks."

"I assume you spoke to the other girls when she went missing?" Aliya asked.

"Yeah. Anyone who knew her, anyway."

"And do you or anyone else remember anything strange or unusual from that time?"

"I asked that before," Jamila said mildly.

"Yeah," Portia chuckled around a mouthful, "I'll tell you the same I told her. We see so much weird stuff in our line of work, even that seems more like normal and usual."

Katie liked the way she'd turned the question around, but that thought spawned another.

"What about the opposite?" she asked.

"How do you mean?"

"Well," she had a horrible feeling that she was about to make an idiot of herself, "what about someone so normal and usual that *they* were the strange and unusual ones?"

Trina rolled her eyes. "You've lost me, love."

"No," Portia said, "I get it." She took another bite from her roll and chewed, seeming to give the question serious thought.

"Well," she said finally, "there was that nice, oldish guy who came around a couple of times. Remember, Trine? Talked to a few of us, but didn't seem to be after, you know, our services?"

"Yeah, yeah," Trina was nodding now. "Oh, him. He wasn't *that* old, was he? But yeah, I couldn't decide if he was a do-gooder wanting to save us, or what he was."

"You mean he was religious?" asked Aliya.

145

"I dunno about that. No, he was just a nice guy. Didn't seem to want nothing." She looked at the detectives. "I mean, most of our punters are all right. It's business, right? They want something, we want their money. Some seem just lonely. Some you just can't fathom. So long as they're polite and don't get rough or nothing..." She stared at a point somewhere beyond Aliya's shoulder. "But yeah, that guy. He wasn't a punter at all. I don't know what he was. Maybe he was writing a book. But he did talk to Ange a couple of times, I think."

A waitress clearing a table dropped something and it smashed noisily on the tiled floor. A ragged cheer went up from a group of young men in a corner. She curtsied and called out for a dustpan and brush.

"And this was when?" Katie asked.

"Oh," Portia said, "I dunno. But I suppose it might not have been long before she went missing."

"That's right," Trina agreed. She glanced at Portia, then at Jamila, to whom this was obviously news. "Sorry," she said. "Didn't think it was important."

"And did he speak to either of you?" Katie pressed.

"Not Porsh," Trina said. "Me though, yeah. Not much, mind. Asked if I was okay and did I have somewhere to stay. Yeah, that's right, must have been October, November, and it was getting cold. You know it's funny. I remember thinking later, if most people came asking things like that, I'd tell them to piss off, but – I dunno. He really seemed to care, know what I mean? Just like one person to another."

"Have you seen him since?"

"No. He came a few times and that was it." She looked at Portia. "That's right, yeah?"

Portia nodded.

"I don't suppose he mentioned his name?"

"Oh..." Trina's brow furrowed.

"Mark?" Portia suggested. "No, not Mark. Martin, that was it, wasn't it?"

"Not Steve?" Katie knew she sounded slightly disappointed.

"No," Trina said. "Definitely Martin."

"Can you remember what he looked like?" Aliya jumped in.

"Yeah. Bit scruffy actually. Lot of bushy hair, bushy beard, scruffy clothes."

"Glasses," Portia reminded her.

"Oh, yeah."

Katie's pulse was racing. "Grey hair?"

"No, a funny sort of ginger."

"In what way funny?"

Trina frowned again. "Not quite a proper colour is the best I can explain. Almost like it came out of a bottle."

"I don't suppose he wore anything on his head?"

"Now you got me," Trina said. "It's amazing I remembered what I did. Not sure."

"No," Portia said, "I think she's right. There was a baseball cap. Wasn't there?"

Trina shrugged.

"Did he have an accent?"

"Scouse, maybe. Some sort of Northern, anyway."

"Not West Country?"

"Like Cornish? Don't think so."

Aliya opened her bag and pulled out the likeness of Steve, self-proclaimed handyman to Lynne Redding. Being a pencil drawing, the hair colour didn't matter much.

"Could this be him?"

The two women stared.

"What do you reckon, Trine?" Portia asked her friend.

"Yeah, maybe. Yeah, could be."

It wasn't the most glowing affirmation, but Katie wondered how clearly *she*'d remember someone she'd met only fleetingly a year ago.

"Think carefully," she said. "You reckon you saw Martin around close to the time Angela went missing? Can you pinpoint the last time you actually saw her?"

"I could work it out."

"Did you see him then?"

"I'm pretty sure not," Trina said.

"No one said, if they did," Portia agreed.

There wasn't much else they remembered that added to what they'd said.

"Keep the picture," Katie said. "Show it to anyone who might have seen him if he'd been in the area that night."

"You're kidding, right? That's your job."

"She's right," Jamila said. "They start acting like some sort of police informants and they can get into all sorts of trouble. Give me the picture and we'll make copies and show it around ourselves."

"Sorry," Katie said. "But can we give you cards, just in case you think of anything later?"

"Sure," Trina said.

Driving back across country, eschewing the M1 at this time of day, Aliya voiced what Katie was thinking. "It's really him, isn't it? Steve. Clever bastard. Changes his hair colour – either dyes it, or he has wigs – and uses different names, accents. Lots of hair, a beard…"

"Glasses, a cap."

"DCI Sharp is right, isn't she? It's all fake."

"Portia described him as old," Katie said, gazing out of the window as they passed fields that would be bright yellow with oilseed rape come the spring.

"Old-*ish*."

"Yes. But Trina didn't seem so sure. The truth is, he could be someone we know nothing about, or someone we've spoken to, hiding in plain sight."

"Whoever he is," said Aliya, "those two thought he was trustworthy. What's the betting Donna Mason trusted him when she got herself lost in Brighton?"

25

When Ricky had contacted Pete Savage in the morning, he'd been out on his round. As usual, he'd opted to come into the station to answer what Ricky had described as 'a few more questions'.

The guv had favoured a soft approach, just clarifying the man's movements the night Donna had been snatched from Brighton. Ricky thought it was probably a long shot, but he didn't like what Savage hadn't told them. Maybe he'd have a satisfactory story. Or maybe he'd unravel.

Maybe this was Ricky's time to shine.

Savage took his seat in the interview room, nodded to Sophie Monahan, and then fixed Ricky with a hard stare.

"So what is it now?" he said irritably. "Only I keep asking if I need a lawyer, you keep saying it's routine, and here we are again."

"You're not under arrest, Mr Savage," Ricky said with a smile. "Obviously, you can decline to answer any questions without representation. That's your right." He leaned back in his seat. "Is there someone we can call? Or would you prefer the duty solicitor?"

Savage drummed his fingers on the table. "Nah," he decided, "let's get on with it. I can stop if I don't like where it's going, right?"

"Of course, you can, sir," Sophie said.

"Right. So what's the problem?"

"So you told us that, on the 11th of August, you went with your wife and son to the cinema," Ricky said.

"I did. I checked my credit card statement to make sure it was that day."

"Yes, but you implied that it was in the evening. According to your wife, it was more like late afternoon. What's more, she can't vouch for what you did with the rest of the day, because you're not living in the family home any more."

"Frankly," Sophie said, "we're surprised you never mentioned any of that to us."

"Why would I? I couldn't remember the film times. And it *was* part of the evening, wasn't it? As for the rest, that's private."

"Not in a murder case, sir," Ricky said, keeping his tone pleasant. "See, we're not thinking you *lied* to us. But put yourself in our shoes. It looks a bit, what's that phrase?"

"Economical with the truth?" Sophie suggested.

"That's the one." Ricky leaned forward. "Look, Mr Savage, all we're doing is trying to eliminate you from our inquiries, and that's not easy if you keep important information from us. If we can't eliminate you, we'd have to treat you as…" he turned to Sophie, "what do we call it, PC Monahan?"

"A person of interest, DC James."

"Exactly. So, Mr Savage, I'll ask you again to account for all your movements on that evening. Ideally with some way of corroborating it."

Pete Savage's gaze switched from Ricky to Sophie and back again as his cheeks reddened. He stared at the table. Took a sip from the glass of water he'd been provided with.

"Look," he said finally. "Okay, look, all it is… See, I don't know what my wife told you, but our lad's disabled. He means the world to us, both of us, and you'd think it'd unite us. And it has done. But it's been so hard lately, and we keep snapping at each other and rowing. So we agreed we needed some space."

He sighed. "We're not splitting up. At least, I hope not. We just thought a bit of a break would make sure we don't. So I've moved out. My shitty little room isn't ideal, but it's worth it if we can sort things out."

Ricky personally doubted trial separations could solve anything, but he hadn't come across anything quite like this before.

"But you still go out together as a family?"

"When we take our son out for treats, we do it together, keep it as normal as we can. It's not like we can't get on. It's just…"

He shook his head. His eyes were misted with tears.

"Okay. I hope it works out, I really do. But we have a problem, because that Saturday in August is really important. So you dropped your wife and son home after the film, but you didn't go in?"

"No."

"So you what? Went back to your bedsit? Did anyone see you?"

He looked absolutely stricken now. "No. I didn't go back to the bedsit. Not right away."

Ricky glanced at Sophie, then focused once more on Savage. "So help us out. Please."

"All right. But I'd appreciate it if my wife doesn't hear. I've got this friend..."

"A woman?" Sophie raised an eyebrow.

"Yeah, but not like that. She's another postie, and we're just mates. She's a good listener and, like I say, it's a tough time right now. Since I moved out, we've met up a few times, just for a drink and a chat, you know?"

"So that Saturday?" Ricky prompted.

"After I dropped Paula and Joe off..." It was the first time he'd used their names. "I felt a bit down, being on my own. So I rang her up, and she was in – she's divorced. So I picked up a bottle of wine and took it round."

"And..."

"Nothing happened, all right? She's just a friend I can talk to. But my wife might get the wrong idea."

"And you left...?"

"I dunno, maybe eleven? I didn't keep a note. I didn't think I'd need to."

"How often do you see this friend?"

"As I say, she's another postie."

"But socially?"

"There's no regular date, if that's what you mean."

"And is there anything else you haven't told us that might be important? Because none of us wants to be in here again, clarifying things."

"There's nothing."

"All right, for now. We'll need to speak to your friend."

*

The day was running down. Nate stood alone in the briefing room, staring at the Wall of Death, hoping against hope that something would jump out at him – a connection they'd overlooked, something they'd missed. There was no shortage of information, and no shortage of names associated with the case. None of it shone any light in the darkness.

Yet somehow, Nate had the strongest feeling that the answers were somewhere on this board. Everyone known to have an association with Lynne Redding was there, and that had to be the key.

It had all started with the house. Nate even wondered if Lynne being a vulnerable woman alone might have been a bonus for the killer. If the house's potential as a base for torture and murder would have been all it took for him to have moved in, taken control, and create the 'going abroad' fiction.

On the plus side, they now had three named victims, and the remaining two – presumed to be victims three and four – were sufficiently thawed for Jordan Stoddart to have sent over photographs of their faces. They'd been circulated, and Nate hoped they'd have as much luck identifying them as they had with the others.

Katie's sortie into Luton had at least shown that Handyman Steve – or someone posing as a handyman called Steve – had to be the killer. Different name, different coloured hair, even different accent. CCTV in Brighton had drawn a blank, but Nate would bet he was there, too, when Donna Mason was taken.

The nagging question persisted. Who was Steve really? An actual handyman who really had been engaged by Lynne? A suspect they hadn't identified yet? Or one of the faces already on the Wall?

The board also now included images of Pete Savage, Silas Ross, Adam Downes and Mike Carlton, manipulated to add Steve's beard, hair, glasses and cap. As Nate had feared, they all looked much alike. The disguise, if that was what it was, so completely concealed the men underneath that all that remained were four identikits.

Pete Savage's 'friend' was called Sarah Rogers, and had confirmed the postman's story about his visit back in August. Although she couldn't recall the exact date, she agreed that he'd taken his family to see *Fast and Furious* beforehand. Sophie Monahan's instinct was that she wouldn't mind being more than friends, but she had been insistent that friends were all they were, and that he genuinely loved his wife.

That left his and Izzy's visit to Dr Ross. It had been a waste of time. Either the psychiatrist took them for fools, or he just wanted a chance to show off. Certainly, he seemed disappointed that Katie hadn't come. Maybe he fancied her.

If Ross was the killer, fishing to find out what they knew, held some water, then any probing he'd done had been vanishingly subtle – and Nate thought he'd have been sorely disappointed.

The fact was, nothing he told them added anything significant to what Izzy had already shared with the team. It was, she said afterwards, all textbook stuff. He could have got most of it from the same sources Izzy had consulted.

He knew he should go home. That staring at the board would get him nowhere. It might even be that some distance from it would somehow allow the missing pieces of the puzzle to come into focus.

Yet tonight he was reluctant to return to an empty house. Laura was still on nights, but normally he was quite content with his own company. Tonight, though, he feared his thoughts turning to his mother, and to his father's death. Sometimes he wished, that night he'd come home to find her having tea with Laura, he'd followed his first instinct and thrown her out. Instead, he'd allowed himself to make a promise, and following it through had raised questions. Questions he wasn't sure he wanted the answers to, but it was a Pandora's box he had opened now.

He sincerely doubted whether returning to the scene of the crime would restore his lost memories, or turn the tentative bridge between him and his mother into a real mother-son bond.

Yet he knew in his heart that he'd go there anyway. He wouldn't be able to help himself.

26

Courtney sits alone on her usual wall, savouring the cup of hot soup she's been given by one of the kind souls who support the homeless.

"Hiya," says a voice beside her. Paul sniffs the air. "That smells great. Tomato, right?"

"Paul!" She realises how pleased she is to see him. But then there are so few friendly faces in her life that she's always pathetically delighted to see one.

"Hello," she says a little more shyly. She sips her soup. "How are you?"

"I'm good, thanks. Sorry I haven't been around for a bit. But look, I've been looking for you."

She feels her eyebrows lifting. "Yeah?"

He grins. "Yeah. Remember I said I'd keep an eye out for somewhere that could get you off the streets. Somewhere safe where maybe you could start rebuilding your life?"

She does remember. She was beginning to think Rosie was right. That maybe he was just another bleeding heart, all talk. Most likely he still is. Or maybe some of her friend's world-weary cynicism is starting to rub off on her.

"I remember," she says.

"Good." He looks excited now. "Well, thing is, I've just this minute got word about a new hostel. It's a little out of town. But let's be honest, you don't belong here, Courtney, I can see that. And this place... it sounds nice. It's for women like you who just need a bit of help getting back on their feet. It's got rooms now, but not many, and they reckon it'll fill up fast – not just Watford homeless, but from surrounding towns too. But I reckon I can get you in, if you're quick."

The tiniest warning bell sounds somewhere in her mind. People being nice to her may be in short supply, but Rosie's drummed into her the need to watch for danger signs.

Even so, in out of the cold and damp. A room of her own, with a door she could close on the world and feel safe. A proper, soft bed.

Just the thought makes her heart ache with yearning.

"But I can't afford any rent."

"They don't charge any. It's a charity. You get a room and three meals a day. They'll help you find work and, when you're earning, you contribute what you can reasonably afford, and then they help you transition to a place of your own. What do you think?"

Another thing Rosie has drummed into her is to beware of things that sound too good to be true, because they usually are. But still. A charity… and this does sound like the sort of thing people who want to do some good might chip into.

"I don't know…"

He strokes his beard. "I'd hate you to miss out on this, Courtney. I could take you there right now. My car's just up the road."

He's so reassuring, like an animated, slightly moth-eaten old teddy bear. There's another bell tinkling in the recesses of her mind. Not Rosie this time, but her mum, warning little Courtney not to accept lifts from strangers. But she likes him and, surely, if he was up to no good and just pretending to be a nice guy, he'd try to present a less scruffy exterior.

Still she hesitates.

"Would there be room for my friend too?" she asks. "Rosie?"

He frowns fleetingly, appears to consider it, then nods. "I'm sure there would but, again, we need to be quick. Where is she?"

"I'm not sure. She'll be here later though…"

"Tell you what, then. Why don't we go now, get you booked in, and persuade them to save a place for Rosie. Then we can come back for her later, surprise her."

It sounds like a plan. She reckons that, after all the help and support her friend has given her, it'll be nice to repay some of it. She looks at this friendly, generous man, with his kind eyes, and she smiles.

"Okay, then," she says. "Thank you, Paul. You're a star."

*

Izzy had left the station with the case still buzzing in her mind, but also conscious that she was exhausted. She had also realised, on her way home, that her body was craving something different and healthier than the zap-in-the-microwave ready meals that had become her staple in the past few days. So she came off the A41 one junction early and slipped into Tesco, where she found a bag of salad, some tomatoes and half a cucumber. A jar of olives, some roasted chicken pieces and a packet of bake-at-home rolls completed her meal plan.

Indoors, she changed straight into pyjamas and dressing gown – even though it wasn't long after 9pm – and started arranging her salad while the oven was baking. She'd closed her eyes to the inviting and opened bottle of white in the fridge door and had decided to opt for a pot of tea. She was just opening the packet of rolls when the doorbell rang.

Sighing, and wondering who might be calling at this time of night, she padded into her tiny entrance hall and squinted into the spyglass. The face she saw was as familiar as it was unwelcome.

The face of betrayal.

The scene she'd made with Bethany and Matt at the restaurant hadn't quite been the end of her dealings with them. There were odds and sods of Matt's at her home to get rid of. She'd toyed with simply binning the lot, or giving them back damaged. In the end, she simply dumped them in a heap on his doorstep.

Bethany had at least attempted to get in touch a few times, tearful voicemails with apologies and excuses. Izzy blocked her on her phone and on social media and, when she turned up at Izzy's door a couple of times, she told her to fuck off.

In spite of everything though, Izzy couldn't quite stop missing her. Lately, her thoughts had even been turning to forgiveness.

But not tonight.

Izzy's first instinct was simply to ignore her, to put some loud music on and get on with preparing her meal.

"Iz?" Bethany wailed from outside. "I know you're in there. Please let me in, hun. I need you!"

The downright bare faced fucking cheek was so staggering that Izzy opened to door without thinking.

Bethany's face was blotchy and puffy-eyed with crying. But whatever the source of the tears, Izzy didn't want to know. She was tired and hungry, and all she felt right now was the kind of anger you can only feel when someone you love has hurt and deceived you.

"Oh," she said, her voice oozing sarcasm. "You *need* me? Well, why didn't you say? *Hun?*"

"Can I come in?" The hope in Bethany's eyes suggested the sarcasm had been wasted.

"Ooh, let me think." She made a show of doing so. "Er... no."

She made to close the door, but Bethany had already inserted a foot.

"*Please*, Iz. It's Matt. He dumped me. He's been cheating on me."

Izzy felt the laughter bubbling out of her. "Well, fuck. Who'd have thought *that?*"

"I know, I know." Tears streamed down her face. "He's a shit. I'm so, so, sorry, Iz. I know I never should have done it. I can't explain. It was like... I dunno, I was under his spell or something. I'd never felt that way. I—"

"Yeah? Well, you *did* do it, Beth, and that's that. Now get your foot out my door or, so help me, I'll slam it anyway."

"Please..."

Izzy pulled the door back as if she was about to slam it hard. Once, seeing Bethany so broken would have hurt her heart, yet now, at this moment, her heart was impervious. She wasn't cruel by nature, but now her rage was rising, the urge to *be* cruel seemed to trump everything else. She almost *wanted* to slam the door on that foot. To break it.

"Last warning."

Bethany withdrew her foot. "Everything's wrong," she snivelled. "Even my car—"

"Now fuck off, Bethany," Izzy spat. "Fuck off and don't come back, you hear me?"

27

If Nate felt they were getting little in the way of breaks, the one thing he couldn't complain about was the speed with which victims were being identified. Two sets of photographs had been circulated to the usual agencies yesterday evening. This morning, the woman who had been at the top of the final freezer – the one they were assuming was victim number four – had a name.

Thirty-four-year-old Kimberley Wade had become known to the charity workers who did their best for Manchester's homeless population. They knew she'd appreciated what they tried to do. A bit of food, a hot drink, maybe clothes and some bedding. Shelter, when there are spaces available. A young woman with a big shopping bag that contained all her meagre possessions. A few square feet to contain all she had to show for her thirty-four years on the planet.

One woman in particular served coffee and sandwiches to people like Kimberley from a mobile café. Kimberley had opened up to her a bit, and Alice had learned something of her story.

Once she'd had a life. She had a job. A home. Nothing special. Hand to mouth living, really. What a former Prime Minister would have described as Just About Managing. She'd never had much luck with relationships, so she only had herself to rely on. When the job had gone, eviction from her home had followed, and somehow everything else had slipped away from there.

It seemed she had a regular spot, where she would sit down, her plastic mug placed where people could see it. She admitted to Alice that she'd perfected a look halfway between humble and pathetic. People would drop a few coins in the mug. Maybe the odd note, on a good day.

Then, some time in June, a couple of other homeless people who vaguely knew Kimberley noticed she wasn't around any more. Not that they necessarily saw her as 'missing'. They assumed she'd moved on, maybe got herself into a hostel. But Alice on the coffee van had an uneasy feeling.

"So she poked about," Nate told the hastily assembled team. "She badgered the police, and Kimberley went on a missing persons file. Alice had taken a selfie with Kimberley, and she cropped it for the file. It's the one we're seeing on my screen. I don't think there was much of an inquiry to be honest. One minute she was there, the next she was gone."

"Manchester, though," Katie said. "And we thought Brighton was a bit of a jaunt. He really is spreading it around, isn't he? And why those places? Random or significant?"

Izzy raised a hand.

"Guv, it might be irrelevant, but we do know serial killers often target homeless people. There are cases here, in the US, all over. The theory is that they're nigh on invisible. No one notices them, no one cares when they're not around."

"Same as sex workers, really," Ricky said.

"Well, not really," Izzy persisted. "As we've seen with Angela Andrews, she was missed and people did care. And she had a life, however shitty, in Luton. The homeless can be a bit more 'here today, gone tomorrow', either because a local programme gets them off the street, or they simply move on. We're actually lucky this lady got worried, and we can see her concerns weren't top of the priorities list."

"What's your point, Izzy?" Nate prompted.

"Okay, so it's likely our killer's local enough for Wigginton to make sense logistically. He's clever enough to want to spread his victims around, so he starts in the red light district in Luton – with Angela. But let's say he realises – maybe he even reads about it, like I did – that the homeless are a better bet than sex workers."

"I don't think we can assume that with just one victim," Nate said mildly.

"Hear me out, sir. If – yes, it might be a big 'if', but *if* he decides to target homeless people, where better than the bigger concentrations? Manchester's certainly one such place. And you know what's another? Brighton."

"Hang on, though," Ricky said. "Donna Mason wasn't homeless or a sex worker."

"No," Izzy agreed, "but suppose he goes to Brighton looking for a homeless woman. Maybe he'd been down earlier and targeted a specific woman. But for some reason his plan doesn't work out. Did you say Kimberley went missing from Manchester in June, guv?"

"Yes." Nate was all attention.

"Just two months before he's in Brighton. That's quite a short interval. Like Aliya said, the urges are getting stronger. And now he's all dressed up, nowhere to go, and impatient for his next kill. And there's Donna, simply asking the wrong person for directions at the wrong time."

"And you're sure Brighton has a high homeless density?" Katie asked.

"I checked again on my phone, just before the briefing. It's about one in every sixty-nine of the population. That's the equivalent of about a thousand people in a big Premier League stadium crowd. It's not insignificant."

"It's not," Nate agreed. He tapped another picture on the wall. The dead woman would have been pretty in life, with blonde hair that hadn't come out of a bottle. Physically different again from the others. "I'd really like an identity for victim number three, and to see how she fits in with your hypothesis, Izzy." But his gut told him she might just be on to something. "I take it there's a list of the highest homeless populations?"

"Yes, guv."

"Then let's target them with this last picture and ask them to focus on missing people from the homeless communities. Get them to show it to the homeless charities too. It might boost our chances of getting a name."

"What about all the calls we're getting in response to the artist's image, guv?" asked Sophie Monahan. The sketch had received a good response from the public, and every contact was being followed up. None had taken them any further forward so far, but the task was monumental.

"Good idea, Sophie. Can we prioritise sightings in locations with high homeless densities? Get the list off Izzy?"

While he had been speaking, a uniformed officer had slipped in at the back and had been slowly but purposefully making his way down the side of the room towards the front. When Nate paused, he raised a hand and stepped forward.

"Sir, sorry to interrupt, but call handlers thought you'd want to know. It's about your killer."

"He's giving himself up," joked Ricky.

Nate gave him a look that said humour wasn't appreciated. "What about him?"

"Apparently, two women have walked into the police station at Watford, saying they recognise him."

Nate was faintly irritated by the interruption. Just another sighting.

"Pass the details to DC Monahan," he said.

"Sorry, sir," the uniform persisted, "but I think this one's a bit different. They think he tried to abduct one of them last night."

*

Nate had been anxious to go to Watford to meet the two new witnesses, but he was also due at Kimberley Wade's post mortem. He'd toyed with making Katie go and take a sick bucket with her, but he wanted her in on the interview too. In the end, Rachel Sharp had agreed to attend the post mortem. Aliya would accompany her for consistency.

Watford Police Station was in the ironically named Shady Lane. Within forty minutes of the briefing being interrupted, Nate, Katie and Izzy sat opposite two women in what he'd been assured was the least horrible interview room. Coffee and a plate of biscuits had been organised.

On the way, Izzy had confirmed that Watford was not in the top ten towns and cities for homeless populations, but was certainly in the top forty.

"Less far afield than Brighton or Manchester, too," Katie had observed, "and back in Hertfordshire."

If that seemed to weaken Izzy's theory about victim selection, the news that these two women were homeless themselves made them sit up and take notice.

For now, the women had volunteered only their first names. Rosie was tall and formidable with hair that looked as if someone had slept in it. Courtney was more slight and mouselike. Neither seemed overly comfortable with their surroundings, and Nate wondered how much courage it might have taken them to come in here at all.

"First of all," he said, "thank you for coming in. I understand you've got some information about a man we've been looking for?"

"That's right." Rosie pushed a tabloid newspaper, one of the free ones that came out daily, across the table. It was open at a page bearing the story about the 'Wigginton House of Horrors', with the likeness of the man police were anxious to talk to.

"You're lucky I spotted it," she said. "I always try to pick up one of these if I can. It's something to read, and sticking them inside your clothes at night helps to keep warm. I recognised him straight away."

"And you had an encounter with him last night?"

"Well, yeah. He was trying to get Courtney here into his car. She would have gone with him, too, if I hadn't seen what was going on."

Nate turned his attention to Courtney. "He was trying to force you into his car?"

If Rosie exuded a degree of confidence, then her friend was the opposite. She looked nervous and awkward.

"Not force, no. I'd have quite happily gone, he was so convincing. I can't believe how stupid I was."

"So talk us through what happened."

"What would he have done to me?" She looked and sounded distressed. "He'd have killed me, I know, but what else?"

"I can't go into that," he said gently. "If you can just tell us what happened?"

"If I hadn't seen the paper, we would probably have chalked it down to experience," Rosie said. "But now I'm thinking she's had a narrow escape."

On the face of it, she had.

Katie reached out and nudged the plate of biscuits towards Courtney.

"Take your time," she said. "But you were ready to go with him? So how did you come to meet him?"

Courtney helped herself to two chocolate biscuits and set them beside her coffee mug.

"Okay," she said. "He called himself Paul. He'd come and spoken to me couple of times around town. Brought me coffee and pastries, that sort of thing, but he seemed different. Not trying it on, and not quite like the usual outreach people either."

"Different how?" asked Nate.

"Well, he seemed really interested in me as a person and said he was trying to make a difference to homeless people. I honestly thought he was a really nice guy. He seemed... I don't know. Cuddly. Does that sound stupid?"

"He used to *cuddle* you?" Katie said. Too sharply.

"No, no. He never laid a hand on me. Perfect gentleman. He was like a cuddly, hairy bear, that's all."

"But that changed last night?" Nate asked.

"Not at first. He came to me with a story about a new hostel opening up. Out of town, but he didn't say where, not that I really know the area. Said it was a charity trying to get people like me back on their feet, and that he thought he could get me in. He said he could get Rosie in, too, but I needed to go with him straight away before it was full up." She bit off a piece of biscuit and nibbled it before continuing. "Believe it or not, I'm not a total idiot, but he completely took me in."

"Where was he parked?" Nate was hoping there might be CCTV cameras.

"They didn't get as far as the car," said Rosie. "I saw them walking along together, and I've been on the streets long enough to know that, unless you're so desperate that you're thinking of turning tricks, you don't just go off with a bloke. So I go up to them, just to make sure everything's okay. Just, you know, 'who's your friend?'."

"And that's when he changed," said Courtney. "I mean, if he really meant to get us both into some hostel, you'd have thought he'd be pleased to see her. But you could see that her turning up wasn't part of his plan at all, and that he was pretty angry about it."

"He became aggressive?" asked Katie.

"Not exactly. It was more the look on his face and the way he tensed up."

"He looked like he wouldn't mind hitting me, I reckon," Rosie said. "But instead, he just made some lame excuse and shot off."

"Lame excuse?"

"Yeah. Really ridiculous. Said he just remembered he had to be somewhere. And that was him gone."

"After all that about how important it was we went to the hostel there and then," Courtney added.

"Tell the truth," said Rosie, "until I saw the picture in the paper I thought he was just some sort of pervert. Just another opportunistic predator. It happens. It's not something I would have reported to the police. But now it looks like you're wanting to talk to him in connection with – what is it – five murders?"

"And was that the first time you'd seen him, Rosie?" Katie asked.

"Yeah. Seems like he's only started sniffing around in the last few days, and for some reason he picked out Courtney. I mean, she's quite new to it all, and maybe he had a nose for that. You know, women who aren't that sure of themselves. Anyhow, I'm betting that new hostel doesn't even exist."

"We can check it out," said Nate. "But you could well be right. It could be just a story to lure Courtney into that car."

"We'll get you to make formal statements, if that's okay," said Katie. "But for now, can you tell us a bit more about him? What colour were his hair and beard?"

"Sort of a non-descript brown, I'd say," said Courtney. She looked at her friend. "Do you think so?"

Rosie nodded.

"I don't suppose he was wearing a cap, by any chance?"

"Yeah," Rosie volunteered. "Baseball cap. Mostly black or dark blue, I think, with some sort of badge."

"Yeah, yeah," Courtney agreed. "A badge. Red and yellow, I want to say, but it's not like I took that much notice."

"Watford?" Nate suggested. "The football club?"

"No good asking me," said Courtney. "I know absolutely nothing about football."

"Nor me," said Rosie. "But now I think about it, I think I've seen a few caps like it. And it's the local team, right?"

After the two women had given their statements and departed, the detectives headed back to Hemel and assembled in Nate's office. Rosie had an old, basic pay as you go mobile, and they had the number in case they needed to contact them again.

It hadn't taken long to check out the hostel 'Paul' had dangled in front of Courtney, and indeed there were no new hostels opening up in the area.

"The local force are checking out CCTV around the town centre," Nate said. "We need to keep on at them about that. If only we can pick him up, either with Courtney or somewhere around where she says he was with her, then maybe we can track him to his vehicle and follow its movements from there."

"And we do know the registration number of that van he's been using," Katie added. "I know we suspected he'd have stopped using it, but we can't be sure."

"Get Ricky to liaise." He looked from one to the other. "Any other ideas?"

"We're still thin on suspects, aren't we? But you just sense that none of their alibis is as robust as they might be. We should find out where they were tonight and see if there's CCTV near their homes that could help us track their movements. Run their vehicles through ANPR. Maybe talk to their neighbours in case they happened to see them going out?"

"All good ideas," Nate said. No blinding flashes of inspiration, but often it was the good, solid police work that got results. "Can you get that organised?"

He frowned. "Izzy, you're quiet."

"Oh, yeah. Sorry, guv. I was just thinking. It sounds like he targeted Courtney at least a few days ago and he's almost groomed her, planning this move."

"Agreed."

"So the fact that Hall House is discovered isn't stopping him. What's more, he's been thwarted, hasn't he?"

Nate saw where she was going.

"We were speculating that he might have gone to Brighton intent on picking up a prostitute or homeless woman? That maybe it didn't work out and, in his frustration, he grabbed Donna Mason at random?"

"Because he'd have been too hyped up to wait," Izzy agreed. "So, after last night's disappointment, I guess he could scout out a new victim and start cultivating her, just as he seems to have done with Courtney. That would be the way of the meticulous planner."

"But you don't think so?" Nate's stomach was churning again.

"I think, just like in Brighton – if we're right about that – the sense of anti-climax will be enormous. He won't be able to wait, to regroup."

"So you think he could already have his next victim?" Katie said.

It was a question that didn't really need an answer, because it was all too plausible.

"Okay," Nate said wearily. "We'd better see if any local women didn't make it home last night."

"How local?" Katie looked as sick as he felt.

"How do I know?" He thought for a moment. "All right. He could have struck in Watford, of course. Otherwise, we have to assume he's living somewhere within reach of Wigginton. So let's liaise with Thames Valley and see what comes up between Watford and Aylesbury. But alert other local forces too. Because right now we're chasing a shadow in the dark. Again."

28

She tests the restraints again, but finds nothing but resistance. Attempts to cry out behind the gag, knowing it is futile. It's all she can do, and she knows it's hopeless, and might incur punishment.

What form that might take, she doesn't even want to think about. And, of course, the more she tries not to think about it, the more her imagination dwells on it. All that has happened to her so far could be a picnic, compared to the possibilities she has glimpsed.

She's already losing track of time in this dimly lit place, wherever and whatever it is. She's pretty sure it was only last night that a day she hadn't thought could get any worse had abruptly descended into the stuff of her darkest nightmares. She'd regained consciousness to find herself here, gagged and secured to this bed, with no idea how long she'd been out. Soon after, she'd heard the door handle turn and the pain and horror had started.

Afterwards, that leather tool roll, with its ominous dark stains, had been opened and shown to her whilst, in matter-of-fact tones, she'd been told she was now property, to be disposed of in any way considered fit. That she was operating on a reward and punishment system.

The punishment for disobedience or defiance lay in that roll of tools.

The reward for absolute compliance was that she might not get the punishment.

And she wonders if there's anything she won't do to reap that reward.

The worst of it is, no matter how ridiculous the notion may be, no matter that sole responsibility for her predicament lies with the person – or maybe people – doing this to her, she feels it is somehow her fault, some karma she has called down upon herself.

She wonders if she has been missed yet. If anyone is looking for her. If there is any hope at all that they might find her.

Footsteps on the stairs, halting outside the door. The sound of the handle turning. Cold sweat bathing her as her stomach knots with terror.

He is coming.

*

Izzy wondered if anyone had noticed how quiet and distracted she had been a couple of times today. It had been a really good day so far, with her being involved and contributing ideas that were helping to drive and shape the investigation.

It was when she was left to her own thoughts that she kept coming back to last night's altercation with Bethany. It was ironic that, up until her doorbell had rung, Izzy had been dwelling more and more on how and when she might ever be able to forgive her old friend. But, whatever script she might have been writing in her head, Bethany had fluffed her lines badly.

Yes, she'd apologised again, but really it had been all about her.

Her problems, her heartbreak.

Even so, Izzy had been amazed at the intensity of her own hurt and anger in response.

Perhaps it was a good thing that she'd been out, away from the office, and spending a fruitless time going door-to-door chatting to Adam Downes's neighbours.

The whole exercise had been like walking a precarious tightrope: it wouldn't do to imply that Adam was under any sort of suspicion, yet at the same time, they needed to know about the movements of Lynne Redding's accountant, last night and at other key points in the investigation. It had involved quite a bit of dancing around and asking generic questions that seemed to be about all the neighbours, rather than just one in particular.

And Adam Downes wouldn't have been her choice to be asking questions about.

She wished she'd never agreed to meet him in the pub. The funny thing was, he wasn't quite her type, and she still thought he was too smooth, too self-assured. Yet there had seemed to be a vulnerability there when he spoke of his dead fiancée.

That didn't mean her death hadn't triggered a thought process that had led onto a killing career.

He'd also seemed genuinely willing to listen to her and not just talk about himself, like so many blokes did. Was that all part of a psychopath's manipulative charm? The dinner invitation, the text after their brief meeting, had seemed presumptuous and had annoyed her. Yet at the same time she had to admit to herself that she couldn't quite dislike him nearly as much as she should.

Back at the station, she dumped her bag on her desk, powered up her computer, and popped into the ladies'. She was washing her hands when Libby Statham came in.

"Any luck with Downes's neighbours?" Libby asked her.

"Bit of a busted flush, to be honest. It was probably always a bit of a long shot. Any developments here that you know of?"

"As a matter of fact there are."

"Really? Anything big?"

"Could be," said Libby. "You know we've been checking to see if anyone went missing last night?"

"Someone did?" Her pulse quickened

"Yeah. I've just told the guv. I came up with a hit in Aylesbury Vale."

"Aylesbury again? Where those kids came from? The ones who first found the bodies?"

"Yes, but I wouldn't read too much into that. This woman came from a village called Cheddington. Not far from you, I think?"

"I know it." Bethany's face, tear-streaked, mascara running, and contorted with misery, came into Izzy's mind again. "An old friend of mine lives there."

"I spoke to Natalie Chen – you remember, she helped us pick up those kids? Well, it seems a twenty-five-year-old woman didn't turn up for work today, and her colleagues haven't been able to contact her. They tried the next of kin they had on record, her parents, and to make a long story short, no one knows where she is, and no one can get hold of her."

"She's not simply sick at home?"

Libby shook her head. "No. Her mum has a spare key and she's checked. She's not there and neither is her car. That's why she contacted us. Apparently it's entirely out of character for her to simply not show up, so she was worried. Of course, it's too early to assume that she's been taken…"

"But what we know about our killer makes it all the more urgent that she's found."

Libby shrugged. "Who knows, though? Maybe she met someone hot last night, and is having mad passionate sex with him even as we speak. Just because things are out of character, doesn't mean they're never going to do it."

But Izzy knew they were both thinking the same thing, no matter how much they wanted to hope that there was a simple explanation for this young woman's apparent disappearance.

And, almost from nowhere, Izzy felt a knot tightening in her stomach as a hideous, but surely ridiculous, thought entered her head.

"And you say the guv knows?"

"Yeah." Libby's forehead creased with concern. "You all right, Iz?"

"Yeah. Just thinking." There was one question she hadn't asked, one piece of information Libby hadn't supplied. She didn't want to know. She badly needed to know. There was a panicky fluttering in her chest but she tried to keep her tone casual. "This missing woman. I take it she has a name?"

*

Nate had barely returned from Rachel Sharp's office, where he'd been updating her and, in return, hearing about Kimberley Walsh's post mortem – virtually identical to the others in its conclusions – when Izzy Cole knocked on his door.

She was white-faced and crying, and it didn't take long to find out why.

The young woman missing from Cheddington was twenty-five-year-old Bethany Kerr. While Nate was talking to Izzy, Bethany's car had been found, broken down and abandoned on a grass verge by a roundabout just outside Tring.

It didn't look good.

But what also didn't look good was that she was Izzy's erstwhile best friend. That they'd fallen out over a man. That there had been an altercation outside Izzy's flat last night.

Now Katie had joined them in his office, the door closed. So far, only these three knew that Izzy might well have been the last person to have seen Bethany.

"I'll have to speak to DI Lara Moseley at Thames Valley," he said. "She's leading on Bethany's missing person case apparently, and I can't rule out the possibility that she'll treat you as a suspect, Izzy. In the meantime, I'm not sure you should be anywhere near the case."

She didn't look surprised. But she still looked disappointed. "Look, sir, I completely get why we have to go through the motions. In normal circumstances, I'd probably suspect me too. But these are not normal circumstances and you know and I know we're wasting our time here. There's a serial killer out there who's snatching women. We should, all of us, be putting our time and energy into catching him. Because if we find the killer, then most likely we'll find Bethany. And, with respect, the clock is ticking."

Everything he knew about Izzy led him to agree with her. Yet he also knew she was an intelligent young woman with a sharp mind. She knew how the police worked, and would likely have assumed that everything she had told them would have come out anyway. Nate's copper's mind reminded him that coming clean was the best policy for diverting suspicion.

She looked hurt, almost as if she'd read his mind

"If you really don't believe me," she said, "the parking area for our flats is covered by CCTV cameras, and I'm pretty sure they're working. You'll see my car arriving home. Bethany arriving later. Bethany leaving alone… and no more sign of me until I leave for work this morning."

He made eye contact with Katie, who smiled.

"Okay," he said, relieved. "We'll look at that footage. If that's what it shows, it's good enough for me. Hopefully, it will be good enough for DI Moseley."

"Thanks, guv. I do get it, really."

"Look," he said. "You need to keep calm. Thames Valley are trying to get hold of Bethany's boyfriend—"

"*Ex*-boyfriend. Matt."

"At the moment, they're not sure where he is either. Maybe she called him when her car broke down. He picked her up, they made up, and they're together somewhere. He had the day off work booked today. Maybe they've gone off somewhere and neither of them are answering their phones because… well, you see where I'm going."

She frowned, a little more hope entering her eyes. "I suppose it's possible. He was quite happy carrying on with me when he started seeing Bethany, so he's hardly Mr Monogamy."

"Your ex sounds an absolute charmer by the way," Katie said.

"That's exactly what he is. A bastard, but a charming one." She still looked doubtful. "I still don't get it. You said her car broke down. And she just waltzes off with Matt and leaves it there?"

It was bothering Nate too. "I must admit that's odd. It seems Bethany had breakdown cover – the documentation was in her glove box. So why wouldn't she have simply dialled for help and sat tight?"

"The breakdown service had no record of a call from her?" Izzy asked.

"Apparently not. And that location isn't a flat spot for signals. Had her phone's battery died? But then how would she call Matt? Unless she walked into Tring and found a payphone. But then why not call the breakdown from there?"

"She was in a state," Izzy said. "I guess maybe Matt was the first person who popped into her head. I'd already given her the brush off. Now I think about it, I do remember her starting to say something about her car. Maybe she was trying to *tell* me it was on the blink." She grimaced. "I wasn't interested, and I wasn't listening. I didn't let her finish. If I'd not been so angry, if I'd handled it differently, maybe we wouldn't be having this conversation."

"You were hardly to know," Katie said. "But actually... what was she even doing there?" Katie wondered. "If she was going home from yours to Cheddington, it makes no sense."

Izzy looked thoughtful.

"Well," she said, "it's no more than a mile from Tring Tesco, which would still have been open. Unless she's changed, her go-to comfort when she's upset is wine and chocolate. Maybe she decided to pick something up." She shook her head. "No, that's not right. If you're coming from Tring, the roundabout is after Tesco. So maybe she was heading for her parents in Berkhamsted for some tea and sympathy."

"If she was, she hadn't phoned ahead to warn them," Katie said.

"The state she was in, maybe she just would have wanted to get there."

"Okay," Nate said, making a decision. "It seems to me we have two possibilities. Either Bethany's probably somewhere with this Matt, or somewhere else, licking her wounds – obviously DI Moseley is checking with local hotels as well as hospitals, just in case..."

"Or the killer has her," Izzy finished for him, her face crumpling again.

"And we'll pursue that possibility our end," he said. "But I still think you're maybe too close to the case, Izzy."

Her face crumpled. "Please don't take me off it, guv. I didn't hurt her, but this is still partly my fault. I turned her away."

He hesitated. "All right. Provided the CCTV around your flats ties in with what you said, and DI Moseley is happy. She'll probably want to see you, though. In the meantime, let's get on with our job. We're already looking at CCTV between Watford and Aylesbury last night," Nate said, "checking for any sign of Handyman Steve's van or any of the suspects' cars. We should make sure that includes any cameras around where Bethany's car was found."

"I'll double check whether Ricky has enough pairs of hands for all that," Katie said. "But we still can't be sure what's happened here. Maybe she phoned for a taxi, or found a bus, if such things exist in the evening, in that neck of the woods."

"Can you check out the bus services, and the local taxi firms, Izzy?" Nate said.

"We should," agreed Izzy. "But what's more interesting is that someone coming from Watford – the opposite direction to Bethany – could have spotted the car on the verge. Maybe she was standing by it, looking helpless or, like we said, maybe she'd gone to find a phone."

"Yes," Katie said. "If this is our guy, and he's desperate and frustrated after failing to grab Courtney, I can only think of one reason he'd have been heading that way."

Nate thought they made a good point, and he was impressed that Izzy seemed still to be thinking clearly. "The road to Wigginton comes off that roundabout, too, and we've been thinking he could be quite local. What if, after the scare with Rosie, he got the hell out of Watford, he was headed home. Bethany just happened to be in the wrong place at the wrong time."

"And now he's got her." Horror and desperation were raw in Izzy's voice. "Chances are she's still alive – for now. But he could be doing Christ knows what to her even as we speak."

"Trust me, Izzy," he said, "I'm going to do everything I possibly can to find this man – and Bethany if he has her – before it's too late."

"And so am I," she said. "I ignored her when she was trying to tell me she had car trouble, and she might have walked straight into the arms of a maniac. I've got to make it right. I've just got to."

29

Just about everyone who'd had a part to play in the case had been gathered, crowded into the briefing room, which was abuzz with the news that a local woman was missing, and that she was feared to be in the hands of the killer. Even a contingent of Tring officers, who'd helped with door to door inquiries, were there, including Izzy's former colleague, PC Chris Harrison.

Izzy's relationship with Bethany Kerr was now known to close colleagues, but not to the wider team. For now.

If the killer really did have Bethany, where was he holding her?

"There only seem to be two possibilities," Nate said. "Either at his own home, or he has another place. The latter seems unlikely, or why go to all that trouble with Hall House?"

"Unless it's not the ideal base for his activities," Aliya suggested. "But safer than his own house."

"Maybe," he conceded. "Okay, so all our main suspects have been questioned about their movements last night, and we've asked around the neighbours again to see if they saw or heard anything suspicious. I know we've drawn a blank again, but what are your instincts? Anyone? Did you pick up any shiftiness, any anxiety? Any sign that someone was hiding something?"

No one had anything to offer. He knew he was clutching at straws, but the last time he'd felt such dread was last year, when a killer seemed to be striking at will, and Nate's team were powerless to stem the tide. His frustration bubbled over.

"Frankly, I'm more than ready to break some doors down."

"Let's not all start putting vests on and going all Bruce Willis just yet," Rachel said mildly.

He took a breath. Forced himself to calm. "You know what I mean," he said.

"We need a warrant to enter someone's home, or at least reasonable cause. I'm not sure 'shiftiness' or 'signs of hiding something' would cut it."

"What about reasonable belief that a crime is in commission? Or a life in danger?"

She shook her head. "It won't do. Look, we're especially interested in Downes and Ross, yes?"

"They're our strongest suspects, for what it's worth, yes."

"Well, we have two choices. Get warrants—"

"That takes time."

"Or ask them if they'll agree to a voluntary search."

Neither option appealed. "Boss, getting a search warrant will take time Bethany might not have. If we can persuade the court to issue it at all. And asking permission tips our hand. If he's got her there, he might refuse and then kill her quickly. If he welcomes us in for the grand tour, it could be that he's holding her somewhere else and he's laughing at us."

It was Harrison who raised his hand.

"Sir," he said, "I've been thinking. This is sure to be nothing, but…"

"Let's hear it." Perhaps there were still straws to be grasped, after all.

"Well. It's what you said about a second home. I mean, it's not exactly that, but I was part of the house to house around Hall House. We were told to include Mr and Mrs Carlton next door, even though they're sort of suspects, so it wouldn't look odd. The husband wasn't there, but we spoke to Sharon Carlton."

"What did she say?"

"Well, this isn't so much about her. I knew she liked to gossip, but honestly… Anyhow, she happened to ask if we'd managed to ask the local postie – Pete? – what he'd seen at the house. We said we couldn't discuss the case, but then she starts off about how hard everything is for him. His disabled son. His mum going into a home…"

Nate looked at him. "His mother's gone into a home? Recently?"

"Last couple of months. Dementia. The dad's been gone a few years."

"You said this was about second homes. Do you know if she had a house? Or what's become of it?"

"She did mention that, sir," Harrison said. "Apparently he's waiting for probate before he can put it on the market."

Nate settled his gaze on Ricky. "Did he not mention it? Did his wife?"

"No, guv. Maybe they didn't think it relevant."

"Okay. Maybe it isn't. But can we try and find out where that house is? Discreetly though. It could be yet another complete dead end but, if it isn't, we don't want to spook him into moving Bethany or worse."

That also could take time.

"Meanwhile, Katie. Dr Ross is keen on sharing his knowledge of serial killer behaviour with us. Why don't you go and see him, play up to it? But go in with your eyes and ears open. Don't compromise the rules." He glanced at Rachel Sharp, who looked about to intervene, then shrugged and nodded. "I'll be just round the corner with..." He thought about it. "Ricky, and Libby, in case she's there."

"And me, sir," Izzy said.

"Okay. If – and only if – we think it's genuinely possible he's got Bethany there, we'll go in."

"And what about Adam Downes?" Katie asked. "I think Izzy has a bit of a rapport with him."

Nate hesitated, wondering if that was such a good idea. She was emotionally invested in saving Bethany, and Katie had mentioned Downes's flirting with her and persuading him to meet her in a pub.

Izzy must have sensed his hesitation. "I'm up for it, guv. Same deal as DS Gray. Eyes and ears, and straight out if anything seems amiss."

He didn't want to be seen not trusting her on this, and she obviously knew to be careful.

"It would have to be after he gets home from work, I guess. And then we'd need a reason to call in that wouldn't spook him – if he's the killer, I mean."

"Actually," Katie said, "that paperwork he gave us is apparently no help to the investigation. We might as well return it. Does that sound a good enough excuse?"

"Sounds like a plan," Izzy said.

30

Katie's car turned the corner ahead of Nate's Volvo, drove up and pulled in in front of him. He got out, walked up and got in beside her.

"Well?" he demanded.

She turned to him, wide-eyed and gaping.

"I can officially confirm that he's the most boring man I've ever met," she said, "and yes, he's clearly taken a shine to me. Unsubtle questions about my marital status, what I like to do with my free time. I thought at any moment he was going to ask me out, but he didn't. Although I wouldn't rule out a phone call."

This wasn't really what Nate was interested in, but she was on a roll.

"He's certainly full of himself, too," she went on. "Pompous, as well as dull. No new insights into serial killers, though. But," she evidently sensed his impatience, "Bethany's not there."

"You're sure?"

"Oh, yeah. I said it was an interesting-looking house, and he insisted in giving me the tour. I've seen every bloody room, including the loft."

"Please don't tell me you let him lure you into his loft?"

"Well, it was the only place left he could have been holding her, Nate. It would have been a bit pointless missing it out. All I had to ask was what the storage up there was like and he was whipping the ladder down and urging me to take a look. I just climbed up and stuck my head in. Let's face it, if he was going to attack a copper who was there by appointment – whose colleagues doubtless knew she was there – he could have done it any time."

"Nothing up there?"

"Just the usual junk. And not a chest freezer in sight, by the way."

"And no indication that he has other property?"

"I got him into a nice little chat about holidays and holiday homes, but he didn't bite, and I had no sense he was holding back. Although I'm no expert at reading psychopaths."

"Okay. So we've tracked down Pete Savage's mum's house – I got a call from Sophie while we were waiting for you. She had to negotiate some data protection obstacles, but she managed it."

"Where is it?"

"Warner's End. A small cul de sac. And it's detached. Sophie found it on one of the property websites and even a floor plan. It has a cellar, believe it or not. Seems his mother went into the home just before the bodies were discovered at Hall House. If Postman Pete is the killer, he could almost have taken it as a sign."

"Are we going to take a look?"

"Straight away, I think. Oh, and I had a word with DCI Sharp. She's sanctioned our use of Colin."

*

Sergeant Colin Webster had an unusual skill for a copper. He had a set of lock picks and had been on a course to learn how to use them.

Most of the time when those skills were deployed, it had been to help out people who'd managed to lock themselves out of their homes, but this was a rare occasion when showing off his talents assumed rather more seriousness.

"The boss doesn't really like this, Colin," Nate told him when he arrived, "but she agrees we're running out of options. Ideally, we want to be in and out with no one the wiser. If we're challenged or, more important, if Bethany is in there, we're going to say we thought we heard a faint cry for help and believed a life might be in danger. She and I will take the responsibility. You just have to get us in."

Colin surveyed the door. "Pretty straightforward lock, by the look of it. Not that much of a challenge, to be honest." He sounded almost disappointed.

In less than two minutes, he was pushing the door open.

The house was still furnished, but had that empty house feel about it as Nate stepped into the hall. He paused to slip on booties and gloves, knowing his colleagues would do likewise. Full crime scene suits would cause too much excitement amongst any watching neighbour. As it was, some busybody might be calling the police at this very moment.

"Let's get on with this," he said when they were all inside with the front door shut. "Katie, Libby, Ricky, check upstairs. Be sure to get into the loft. The rest of us will do downstairs and check out the cellar."

They made short shrift of the ground floor rooms and, judging by sounds overhead, the same could be said for the four bedrooms and the bathrooms. Sophie had sent him the floor plan and the door to the cellar was quickly located, but was locked.

Before he could stop her, Izzy stepped right up to the door. "Hello?" she called. "Bethany?"

As he silenced her with a finger to his lips, he thought he heard indistinct sounds. They exchanged glances. Her eyes were wide, and he found that his mouth was dry. Somehow, a local postman who liked a bit of gossip simply hadn't chimed with his image of a well-organised, high functioning, psychopathic killer – even though he knew better than to make assumptions or apply stereotypes.

The lock took Colin a little longer than the front door. But not much longer. The door opened into darkness. Nate fumbled around inside for a light switch, then Izzy located one on the wall outside. The cellar was illuminated to reveal some racks of wine, a few packing cases, a cobwebbed snooker table, a couple of chairs, and some piles of magazines and newspapers. Rather a lot of papers.

All was silent.

"It looks like a fire hazard," Colin said. "But I mean, I'm no expert, but it really doesn't look like a serial killer's lair."

The sounds started again, a rustling. Nate even fancied he heard a muffled cry.

"Let's go down," he said.

At first, there seemed nothing to see, and it was hard to pinpoint the sounds. Izzy went to investigate behind a stack of packing cases.

And she let out a scream.

Nate rushed to her side. "What?"

She laughed shakily and pointed a finger. "Sorry, guv. Rats."

He looked where she was pointing just in time to see a sleek rodent scurrying out of sight.

"Typical," he said. "Mice and rats love empty houses when the temperature drops. Ideal shelter for them to nest and breed. They just need to find damaged pipework, drains or gaps in brickwork where they can get in."

"They don't like disturbances much, though, do they, sir?" Colin remarked.

He sighed. "No, they don't. I suspect this place hasn't seen much traffic since Pete Savage's mother moved out. Didn't his wife say he was waiting for probate before he can put it on the market?"

"Yeah," Izzy agreed. "We're not going to find anything here, are we?"

Sounds from upstairs had suggested that a loft ladder was being pulled down. By the time they had emerged from the cellar and climbed the stairs, Ricky was putting the ladder away again.

"All the usual loft crap, guv," he said. "Any luck downstairs?"

Nate shook his head, disappointed. "Nothing. Damn. I'd really hoped this might be our break."

"All down to Izzy then," Ricky said. "Looks like it's this Downes guy, or it's some random nutter after all."

31

Back at the station, the team had regrouped. It was time for Izzy to make contact with Adam Downes.

For her, this wasn't just another chance to shine, to repay the guv's faith in her. It was personal too. Having yoyo'd between loathing and liking Adam, between empathising with him and wondering if he might actually be serial killer material, she now found herself having to play a part with him whilst being torn apart by worry for Bethany and fearing he might really be responsible.

Yet, instead of making her nervous, it somehow made her all the more determined.

And, with Dr Ross and Pete Savage apparently so far amounting to nought, she found herself almost hoping Adam Downes was their man. If he wasn't, if their suspects list was exhausted, then they would have to face the real possibility that Bethany was in the hands of someone unknown.

She was picking up her phone when DCI Quarrel called her name from the doorway. In the corridor, he asked her if she'd spoken to Downes yet.

"Just about to, guv."

"I've just had a call from DI Moseley at Thames Valley. She's satisfied you're in the clear for Bethany's disappearance, but she's still treating it as a missing person case her end and you're still the last person to have seen her. So she'd like you to go over to Aylesbury for a chat about how Bethany was when you saw her, anything you know about her that the Aylesbury team doesn't know."

"What, now?" She knew she was rolling her eyes.

He held up his hands. "I know, I know, but she's got a job to do too. And wouldn't it be great if Bethany turned up safe after all? So play nice. Set up that visit to Adam Downes before you go. If he seems evasive, I'm going round there with Colin, whether the boss likes it or not."

She returned to her desk and, cursing under her breath, dialled Adam's number, noting that she was down to two battery bars already. She really must do something about her phone when this case was over.

He picked up just as it was about to go to voicemail.

"Mr Downes, Adam? It's Izzy. DC Izzy Cole?"

"Izzy!" He sounded surprised and pleased. "To what do I owe the pleasure?"

"Oh, nothing much. It's just about that paperwork you gave me. We've done with it. I could drop it off, but I'm just about to head off to Aylesbury for a meeting, and then I've got other stuff. Maybe I could bring them to your house later?"

"That'd be great," he said, sounding even more pleased. "I could rustle up something to eat, if you fancy."

"No, no," she said quickly. "I'm only dropping off papers. Maybe a coffee."

"Actually, there was something I wanted to talk to you about. Oh, but damn."

"What's up?"

"Actually, I was going to ring you about that paperwork. Simon was saying he could do with that stuff quite urgently. I've no idea why, and if you still needed it, he'd have to wait. But when you bring it round, I think I should really run it straight over to him."

The plan was unravelling already.

"Not even time for a quick coffee?"

"Sorry. Maybe another time?" he added, sounding hopeful.

"He's working at home today?" she asked.

"Yep."

"Where does he live?"

"Wilstone? I don't know if you've come across it?"

It was about three miles from her own home.

"I know it. Look, I practically pass that way on my way back from Aylesbury. Well," she amended, "I could. Suppose I drop the paperwork with Simon? But there's a couple of other things

I'd just like to check with you, so I could still come on to you, if that's okay."

She had no idea what that 'couple of things' might be, but they'd come to her. The village of Wilstone wasn't much of a detour, and a chat with Simon might even supply some useful insights into his boss.

"What time are you home?"

"About six?"

"Perfect."

She checked her watch. She supposed that, if Bethany really was at Adam's, nothing could be happening to her while he was at work. Nor while Izzy was there. Yet his enthusiasm for Izzy's visit suggested either that, even if he was holding Bethany, it wasn't in his home. Unless he was very confident indeed that Izzy wouldn't see or hear anything.

Or Bethany was already dead.

The thought made her swallow hard.

"Let me have your address," she made her tone light, "and Simon's."

*

DI Lara Moseley was friendly and professional. She understood Izzy's concern, and that of her team, but she was still keeping an open mind about what may have happened to Bethany.

"It wouldn't be the first time we've begun to fear the worst and then someone turns up alive and well and wondering what the fuss was about," she said. "If Bethany was as distraught as you say, who's to say she hasn't simply turned off her phone, and now she's sleeping it off at a mate's place?"

"I don't know what mate that might be, ma'am," Izzy insisted. "Unless she's made new friends since our falling out."

"Maybe she has."

That hurt. "A mate who doesn't listen to the news?"

"Not everyone does, Izzy. I know it must seem like a faint hope, with you so worried, but it's still a hope. Hang on to it."

Feeling that the meeting had served no other purpose than to waste her time, she checked her watch when she was back in the car. Getting on for 5.45pm. By the time she'd dropped those papers off at Simon's and asked some questions, she'd get to Adam's home soon after he returned.

She'd promised to keep Katie up to date with her movements so, as she drove away, she asked the hands free to call Katie. The car's computer told her in its schoolmarmish voice that the number could not be found, and she realised with annoyance that the phone's battery had really given up the ghost this time. She shrugged mentally. When she was leaving Simon, she could just ask to borrow his phone to call in.

She made a left at a roundabout onto the Lower Icknield Way and followed the winding road, passing a popular farm shop before turning off for the little village of Wilstone. She hadn't set foot in it very often, but had gone one time with DI Quarrel to interview a witness. She remembered him telling her that perhaps the village's greatest claim to fame – or notoriety – was that in 1751 it had seen the last ducking to death in England of a person suspected of witchcraft, some sixteen years after it was outlawed.

Simon Younger's house was semi-detached, but set on a corner with a wide frontage. Above the front door, a concrete slab proclaimed that the property had been built in 1833.

His face, when he opened the door, suggested mild bemusement. Certainly not guilt or fear.

"Good afternoon," she said. "I don't know if you remember me?" She held up her warrant card. "DC Cole. *Acting* DC Cole."

His face folded into a smile. "Of course. You came to see Adam at the office. What can I do for you?"

"I'm really sorry to disturb you," she said. "I've got some papers Mr Downes let me have, and he said you were the best person to return them to." She held up the envelope.

"Thanks. I should have made copies before letting Adam give them to you, but he seemed in a hurry. And now I really could do with them."

She handed them over.

"Thanks," he said again. "Was that it?"

"Actually," she said, "I wouldn't mind a quick word about Adam's movements, just to straighten a couple of things out."

"Sure." He shrugged. "Not certain how much help I can be, but you never know. I hope you're not going to ask me anything I'd feel awkward about though."

"Such as?"

He smiled. "I'll know it when I hear it."

"So may I come in?"

He glanced up and down the street. She imagined that, in a small village, there were always busybodies to worry about, if that sort of thing bothered you. At least she wasn't in uniform.

Apparently satisfied, he stepped aside and waved her in.

"I'm just about to make a coffee," he said, "if you fancy one."

*

Nate was beginning to feel useless. All the team were checking and re-checking things. So far, they seemed to be coming up empty handed, but at least they were doing something. Nate was just holding his breath – hoping for the best, but fearing the very worst.

He'd be glad when Katie got the call to confirm that Izzy was on her way to Adam Downes's home, so he could repeat the process of what Ricky called 'hiding around the corner' until she emerged to say whether anything there had aroused her suspicions. He was beginning to feel that it would prove yet another dead end. If so, he feared that Bethany Kerr might become just one more person whose name occasionally cropped up on local news, but who may never be seen again.

Unless a lucky break came out of left field. And, right now, he wasn't sure he set much store by luck.

There was a casual tapping on his open door. He looked up to see the smiling face of Shauna O'Connell. No ponytail today, her hair hanging loose. Another designer suit, this time in a silvery grey, twinned with a pink top with sequins.

"Can I trouble you, DI Quarrel?"

He beckoned her in, noting the sheets of paper she held.

"If you've got the name of the killer on there, you can trouble me all you like."

She shrugged as she sat down. "Well, now. That might be a bit of a tall order. But I do have something you might care to check out."

"Have a seat."

She did so. "Here's the thing. We've been going through all of Lynne Redding's emails with a fine-tooth comb, just in case there was anything new. But, to be honest, none of them have been telling us anything we weren't aware of. Until we recovered some deleted stuff and found this one from Adam Downes."

"Downes?" Was this the breakthrough? Maybe Izzy's visit wouldn't be necessary.

She was holding the paperwork out to him. He tried not to snatch it.

He looked at the email she'd brought him, read it through again. Looked at her.

"My God," he said. "We missed that, didn't we?"

"Yes," she said. "We all did."

32

Simon Younger's front door opened straight into a good-sized sitting room, kitted out almost exclusively with Ikea-style furniture. No artwork on the walls, no photographs. Lynne Redding's house, with no one there except for five bodies in the basement, and the occasional serial killer visit, had felt more lived in.

Doors led off right and left. Beside the closed right-hand door sat a desk and chair. A laptop stood open on the desk, a wire tray beside it containing a slim stack of papers. Simon was either a minimalist, a neat freak, or just exceedingly well organised.

He led her past the bottom of some stairs and into a kitchen that looked somewhat tired and outdated. At least this was a little untidy, so the place wasn't totally lacking in soul.

"So, coffee?" Simon said cheerfully. "I've got one of those fancy machines. Not one of those rubbish ones where everything tastes like axle oil…"

She smiled. "A latte, if you can." She didn't especially want one but, if Simon was loyal to his boss, keeping the conversation casual might help loosen his tongue.

She waited with her hands in her pockets while he fiddled with the machine, popping a pod in and getting it going.

"You live here alone?" she asked.

"Yeah." He shrugged. "I'm not a settling down guy."

"Big place for just—"

"Just a PA?" He looked amused.

"I was going to say just one person."

"Sure. But I bet you're really wondering how I can afford it." He smiled. "No offence taken. The fact is, I've had the high-powered corporate jobs, but it was too much of a rat race for me. All that greasy pole stuff, slave to the company. The bonuses were good though. Enough to buy this house, put some cash in the bank for a rainy day. What I do now is enough for most of my needs, and I don't have anyone breathing down my neck."

"So you're pretty much your own boss now? I mean, it sounds like you come and go as you please."

"True. We don't actually see that much of each other. When you saw us both in the office the other day, it was one of those rare occasions." He put his hands in his pockets, mirroring her own stance. "So how can I help, anyway?"

"Well," she said, keeping it casual, "it's really just routine. You probably know we're trying to eliminate a few people who knew Lynne Redding from some inquiries."

"Yeah, I was asked about that, and I wasn't much help, I'm afraid. I'm not in the office all the time and Adam gets out and about a bit. And most of the dates were a bit vague."

In all cases except Donna's – which was in any case a Saturday – the precise date and time the women had been taken was uncertain, although there were ranges of dates between sightings and them being noticed as missing.

"Fair enough," she said, "although I'm guessing you still do communicate all the time. I don't suppose there was anything unusual in Adam's behaviour around those times? Any reason to think he wasn't where he was supposed to be?"

"As in something that made me think he was off killing people, for instance?" He chuckled as he set her coffee in front of her. "I read the news, Constable. It's pretty obvious Lynne's house is the one where you found all those bodies. But you can't think Adam…"

"As I said, we're honestly just covering bases. That's why *I*'m here, just a lowly DC."

"Well, I don't know that I can help you, much as I'd like to. We're colleagues, not mates. From what he tells me, working or falling asleep in front of the telly at home are his main hobbies."

He painted a sad picture. But was it a picture of a man whose life had gone largely on hold when the woman he loved had died? Or a picture fed to Simon by a man eager to conceal his real activities?"

192

"Look," he said, "I really do wish I could be more use to you. I already told your colleagues what work commitments he had for the dates you're interested in, but if you're asking me to vouch for him – well, I can't, can I? As for his behaviour..." He appeared to consider it. "Honestly? He was just Adam."

She'd known it was a long shot. Katie had thought it was worth a try. Sometimes things unremembered first time around suddenly shook loose.

But she supposed, if Adam wasn't eliminated, then he was still in play as a possible suspect. Nothing was really pointing at him, but nothing was pointing away, either. Although she understood that rather more would be needed to obtain a search warrant, all she really wanted to do was go in with all guns blazing. To know one way or the other if he was holding Bethany.

But she had to admit defeat here. She sipped her coffee. "Oh, well. I just hoped the dates, and maybe the reasons you weren't in, might jog your memory about Adam's movements and we could rule him out once and for all."

He took his own coffee from the machine.

"I suppose I can show you the office calendar for what it's worth. If you like."

It seemed pointless, but she supposed the history of detection was riddled with pointless exercises leading to breakthroughs.

"Why not?" she said.

*

Nate had grabbed Katie, and they and Shauna O'Connell were in his office.

"First up," he said, "where's Izzy?"

"Still at Aylesbury, I assume. She said she'd call when she was leaving, so we'd be ready to move once she was on her way to Adam Downes."

"Well, get her back. There's been a development. It's probably nothing, but we need to look at it before she goes over to Adam Downes."

"What's going on?"

He briefly introduced Shauna before inviting her to share the email she'd turned up.

"It's from Adam Downes to Lynne Redding," she told them. "Same old, same old, talking about paperwork. Only here there's something for her to sign – I mean physically sign, not an e-signature – and papers to collect. He can't get over to her because he has wall-to-wall meetings, so would she mind if his assistant drops by?"

"Simon Younger?" Katie checked.

Shauna nodded. "That's the one."

Katie looked at her. "And did she mind?"

"We found her reply, double-deleted just like Downes's, and she said it would be fine."

"So suddenly we have someone who's been to the house we weren't aware of," Nate said. "But the strange thing is, Downes said he'd never been there. He didn't want Lynne to have a new visitor to contend with."

"That is odd," said Katie. "Do we think maybe he just forgot?"

"He was pretty definite. Anyway, I'd like to know a bit more about Simon Younger."

Katie chewed her lip. "Izzy's actually going to see him after she finishes at Aylesbury. She's dropping those papers off to him. She thought doing Downes a favour would help put him at his ease. Oh, but what if Simon Younger *did* go round there? It doesn't mean..." She shook her head. "I don't know what it means. But I'll get on to Izzy now. Get her straight back here. Unless you want her to go to Younger's anyway? Try to work it into conversation?"

"No," he said. "We've got a whole new variable, so let's do a bit more digging before anyone talks to him."

She took out her phone and speed-dialled a number. After a few moments, she left a voicemail asking Izzy to call her straight back and ended the call.

"She's either not answering, or she's turned her phone off," she said. "I hope DI Moseley isn't giving her too hard a time."

"She won't be on her way to Younger already?"

"No, she was going to let me know when she was leaving Aylesbury nick and again when she was leaving Simon's, so we could have everything in place at Adam Downes's." She put her phone on the table. "So what are we thinking?"

"I think there are three possibilities," he told her. "Like you say, it's most likely nothing – Downes genuinely forgot Simon had been to Lynne's and it's all no big deal anyway. *Or* they're both killers, working as a team. Or – and you're going to have to help me out here, Shauna," he looked over at the technical expert, "maybe Simon is able to get into his boss's email. He sent that email to Lynne and then deleted it and her reply at that end."

"He probably double deleted it at Downes's end too," she said.

"Well, we don't have time to speculate. Where did Izzy say Simon lived?"

"Wilstone," Katie supplied. "I should have asked for the address."

"It hardly seemed relevant then," he said, "but we need it now. Plus what car he drives. We ought to check if that car is on CCTV footage anywhere and any time we're interested in."

"I suppose it could explain why there was no trace of the van, nor Downes's car around Watford last night," Katie admitted. "Or anywhere near where Bethany's car was found, or in between. I'll get Ricky and Sophie to get on all that right away."

"You've met him, Katie. What were your impressions?"

"I didn't really see that much of him. But we do know Simon pretty much runs Downes's life, so that ticks the 'well-organised' box, if we're making him a person of interest. Plus he's only part-time and works flexibly." She looked thoughtful. "I suppose, hypothetically, he could seem to be carrying on his normal life, doing his job, and no one would know if he was in Wigginton, using kidnapped women as his playthings until he decided it was time to lock them in a freezer."

"Okay," Nate said. "Get everyone available digging out everything we can find on Simon Younger, and quickly.

Anything on police computers, anything of interest on the Internet. Any other questions will occur to us as we go along."

"I can do some Internet stuff too, if it'd help," Shauna said. "I might have some search techniques that will turn up some extra material."

"Yes please. And, Katie, once you've spoken to the team, try Izzy again. I don't want her going anywhere near Simon Younger until we know a lot more about him."

*

Every muscle in Bethany's body seemed to be aching, and she needed to pee. He'd warned her what would happen if she pissed the bed.

If she made any noise.

She tried to calm the terror that was constant. In the time she'd been held here, her state of mind seemed to have swung like a pendulum between the outskirts of sanity, barely holding on, and acknowledging that – for all her situation seemed horrendous – her imagination was capable of inflicting further torture on her.

Each time he'd come to her, the abuse, the wanton infliction of pain, had been punctuated with his rants about women in general – all of them whores – and one who he considered the biggest whore of them all. Alone, with nothing to do except think and try to hang onto her sanity, she'd tried to piece the fragments together. She'd even felt some sympathy for the child he'd been – could see how the seeds had been sown that would grow into a monster.

It didn't stop her hating him with all her might. She wasn't a naturally violent person, but she'd fight to protect herself and people she cared about. A memory flashed through her mind of her and Izzy in the school playground, side by side, facing up to the bullies. Her own fist lashing out and catching Hannah Scott full on the nose. The gush of blood. She'd been threatened with suspension for that, but her parents had been proud of her for standing up for herself, and the bullies had left them alone afterwards.

If the chance came to save herself, she'd do whatever it took. She thought she could even kill. But all that seemed a forlorn hope.

Yet she told herself she *had* hope. Hope that she would be found. That maybe this sadistic maniac would tire of her and let her go, dumping her somewhere, maybe in countryside, a few miles from the nearest houses, but alive.

Those positive moments were fleeting and few. She'd had one a few minutes ago when she'd heard the doorbell ring. Whoever had been at the door, they must be inside the house now, because she could hear voices downstairs.

If it was the police, looking for her, why weren't they searching the place?

And how would they find her, when even *she* didn't know where she was?

She tensed as another possibility came to her. Perhaps her abductor had a partner, another man who would be coming up to rape her any time soon.

Maybe he was selling her on the dark web. She didn't know much about it, but she was pretty sure there wasn't anything you couldn't get there. For all she knew, she was being advertised on a website. Men could pay money, come round here and do whatever they liked to her.

She listened, straining her ears to catch words, and failed to make anything out, save for one thing. It sounded like a man talking to a woman.

*

Simon Younger had woken up his laptop and pulled up a calendar. Izzy stood at his shoulder, giving him dates associated with abductions, and he was double checking the relevant periods.

"Well, I really can't see Adam as your man," he said finally. "I knew you were barking up the wrong tree. See, nothing remarkable in Adam's diary at any of those times. A few client meetings, as you've seen. And yes, I was mostly out of the office. A bit of leave, some sickness, a family emergency…"

"Talk me through all that," Izzy suggested. If Adam was the meticulous killer they were looking for, he could work better around Simon's planned absences than random illnesses and emergencies.

He frowned. "What do you mean?"

"Oh, you know. What you did with the leave? What was wrong with you when you were sick. That family emergency."

He stood up, eyes narrowing. "I thought this was about Adam?"

"It is. But context is useful. You want to help Adam, right?"

"Yes. I don't see *how* it helps."

"It's just procedure."

For a moment she thought he might kick back and become uncooperative. Then the tension seemed to go out of him.

"Fair enough. Let me think." He looked ceilingwards. "Well, not much help, to be honest. The sickness would have been migraines. I get these cluster migraines, which go on and on, and all I can do is lie down in a darkened room. It's often days. Then the holidays. I take time off sometimes, to recharge my batteries, but I don't go anywhere. I sit in the garden and read if it's a nice day. Daytime TV if it's cold or wet."

"No hobbies?"

"Nothing exciting, no."

"And you said there was a family emergency?"

"Yes, sort of."

He looked fleetingly shifty. Was he a leg-swinger, making up illnesses to get out of work? Taking advantage of his working pattern and his boss's trust?

"What 'sort of' family emergency?"

He looked sheepish. "Okay, you got me. Look, that's what I told Adam. It wasn't strictly true. Tell the truth, I was feeling awkward about keep being off with migraines, so I made up a different excuse."

"So you basically lied?"

A mild flash of irritation. "With respect, surely the point is, I wasn't around. So whatever your issue with those dates is, I'm afraid I can't help."

"Sorry," she said. She thought a touch of self-deprecation wouldn't go amiss.

"In fact, though," he said, looking at the calendar again, "if Adam *was* getting up to anything untoward, dates when I wasn't working would have been a bit convenient, wouldn't they?" He half-laughed. "But come on. Adam's no killer. I'd know."

But why would he? By his own admission, he and his boss didn't know each other that well. Had he been charmed and manipulated too?

As she and the rest of the team had flailed around for concrete leads, Izzy had had the nagging feeling that they were missing something. Was this it? She felt as if one missing puzzle piece was right under her nose.

Adam looked like the strongest suspect they had, yet she felt none of the thrill of the chase. Was that because she needed that missing puzzle piece to be really convinced?

Or because, despite the ways he'd managed to irritate her, despite her suspicions that he wasn't so different to Matt, she rather liked him?

"So what now?" Simon pressed. "Surely you won't be arresting Adam?"

Whether he was being loyal to his boss or simply enjoying a rare bit of excitement in his life, she wasn't about to engage with him on that. She couldn't think of anything else to ask him. No doubt something would occur to her halfway back to Hemel.

"I think that'll do for now," she said.

He raised an eyebrow. "No card in case I think of anything?"

She reached into her bag, fished out a card and offered it to him.

As he reached for it, something made a loud thud upstairs.

33

Bethany had noticed the lamp earlier and, in a ridiculous moment when she'd been able to think of anything other than her predicament, she'd reflected on how it looked like an accident waiting to happen. Tall and spindly, without much centre of gravity, it reminded her of one she'd had at her parents' home when she was growing up. There was always a glass of water by her bed, and she'd reached for it in the dark and sent the lamp flying. He dad had rushed in in his PJs, bleary eyed and confused, and given her a telling off she hadn't really thought she deserved.

Whoever was downstairs, friend or foe, she'd known she had to at least try to attract attention. And that, if she was going to do that, she needed to think fast.

She'd almost given up rocking the bed when it finally thumped against the tatty bedside cabinet. The thump was just enough to topple the lamp, which crashed to the floor. But her triumph at getting it to fall was almost immediately replaced by terror. What if the person downstairs didn't think anything of the noise, or even didn't hear it? What if they really were an accomplice or, as she'd also feared, a 'customer'?

One thing was certain. Her captor would guess what she'd been trying to do, and there was sure to be a punishment. She whimpered as she imagined him opening up his tool roll. What might he select?

What might he do with it?

She fancied the crash had caused only the minutest lull in the conversation downstairs, and then it continued as if nothing had happened. So whatever would result from what she'd just done, it had been a pointless gesture.

Despair washed over her. It was as if any glimmer of hope she'd been harbouring had been extinguished. No one was coming.

Maybe making him angry was the best she could do. Angry enough to kill her quickly. At least the torture wouldn't be prolonged.

*

"What was that?" Izzy said.

Simon blinked. "What was what?"

"Didn't you hear it? Sounded like something toppled over upstairs."

He chuckled. "What's that damn cat done this time?"

"You've got a cat?"

"Yeah. Pampered bugger's even got his own room."

"You shut him in?"

"Well, yeah, when I'm working. Otherwise he'll just be seeking endless attention."

She glanced around the room. Not a trace of cat, not even a water bowl. But then Simon was clearly a neat freak. Maybe it even extended to the cat.

"Don't you want to check on it?" she suggested.

"I'll see you out first. She can wait." He moved towards the door, laying a hand upon the handle.

"She? I thought you said 'he'?"

"Did I?" He looked blank.

"Must be my ears." She affected a shrug.

Suddenly she just wanted to get out of there, because, like the tumblers of a lock, things seemed to be clicking into place. Had she and the team been looking at the puzzle from the wrong angle?

She cursed the dud battery in her phone and the time she would waste rousing a neighbour and persuading them to let her use theirs. Because suddenly, using Simon's was not a good idea.

"I'll be off then," she said.

He smiled, let go the door handle, and moved to block her way. "I don't think so."

What had given her away? Something in her eyes? A slight tremor in her voice? The tensioning of her shoulders?

She tried to heave some authority into her voice. "What do you mean, you don't think so? Step aside, please."

"Can't do that. Why'd you come here? Alone?"

"My team know where I am," she said evenly.

"Yes, but you left. By the time they come looking, they won't find a trace. Of you, or…" He glanced ceilingwards. "Tell, me, was it just my slip up over the cat's gender? That and whatever that whore upstairs did to make a racket?"

He wanted to talk. Good. It would give her time to decide what to do. She could try to fight her way out, or she could run back into the house and try to find a weapon. Make some sort of a stand. Maybe her bosses would wonder where she'd got to and come looking for her.

"That was the clincher," she agreed. "But I think it was already at the back of my mind that your working arrangement with Adam wasn't just convenient for him, if he was the killer. A day off here, a 'migraine' there… why wouldn't he take it at face value?"

"He had no idea I was looking for whores," he giggled. "Whores just like *her*. At first, it was actual whores, but the ones before I set up in Wigginton had shown me all women are the same. So easily broken. Even Anthea."

"Anthea?"

"I owe her everything. The promotions, the bonuses. My nest egg. Anyone looking from the outside would see that rare thing: a predatory female using a younger, junior male colleague. But I was doing the using. By the time I'd finished with her, there was nothing she wouldn't do for me."

"But when you moved on to Wigginton and took over Lynne's house… you didn't stick to prostitutes, did you?"

"I realised the homeless ones were better… well, who's going to miss them? The last two, though. The ones I wanted got away and I had to improvise. Donna. Now Bethany…"

And there were her suspicions confirmed. She glanced into the too-neat kitchen, everything put away. He'd be on her while she was rummaging in drawers for a knife, for anything.

"Anyway," he said. "That's enough time wasting. As it is, you've fucked everything up for me. I might not have time to clean up enough here after all. I might have to do a runner. I have plans if I do. But that's not going to be your problem."

He took a step towards her. "Why don't we make this easy? Go back into the kitchen."

If that was where he wanted her, that was the last place she was going. She let her shoulders sag, as if accepting her fate, then stepped forward and shoved him hard, slamming him against the door, before kicking him in the balls. He squealed with pain as she wheeled away and hared towards the stairs.

"You fucking whore!" he bellowed. "Come back!"

As she hurtled up the stairs, two at a time, she could hear him gasping in pain as he came after her.

And now she realised that this wasn't just about saving herself. Even if she could somehow get away, he could kill Bethany quickly before she could get help. Before he made good his own escape.

Izzy knew she didn't just have to fight for herself. She had to fight for both of them. And that meant getting to Bethany.

She ran along the corridor, throwing open doors. The first on the left opened into an unremarkable bathroom. On the right was a bedroom, and then what looked like a library. At the end of the landing was an opening onto a little passageway. She thought it must lead to the end of the house that sat on that corner, furthest from the attached neighbours. If Bethany *was* here, surely that was where she'd find her.

She heard Simon hit the top of the stairs behind her, but she daren't look back.

Beyond the little passageway, the landing widened again. Here it was quite dark, the only natural light coming from the passageway itself. It was as if she had fallen down Alice's rabbit hole, or emerged from the back of a wardrobe, into a sinister, shadowy world.

Here, two doors led off – one to the right and one straight ahead, both closed. She pushed open and glanced through the right-hand door, her blood running cold as she took in the chest freezer that stood humming in the middle of the room, the shelves holding cardboard boxes, neatly arranged, the sturdy kitchen-style chairs and the small, waist-high table. A tool roll lay open – *weapons!* – but he was too close, practically breathing down her neck, and she had to get to Bethany.

She ran on to the other room, turned the door handle, and walked into a scene from Hell.

The room was small and narrow, poorly lit, with the curtains drawn across a single, small window. The ceiling pitched down on one side. There was a small bedside cabinet and another kitchen-style chair. A broken lamp, perhaps the source of the noise she'd heard recently, lay on the floor beside the cabinet.

The bed took up most of the space, and Izzy only had eyes for the naked figure bound to it. Bethany's eyes were wide and she was making sounds behind her gag.

Izzy went to her. "It's me," she said as Simon clattered in behind her. Without a second thought, she rose and spun in one movement, striking out at the hand that held the syringe. He'd been about to plunge it into her neck. The syringe flew from his hand, clattering on the floor, and she went after it. He grabbed her by the shoulder and she struck him in the face with an elbow, shaking him off.

Whatever was in the syringe, she doubted she'd be able to pick it up and use it on him. He was too close. So she stamped her boot heel down on it, smashing it, and turned, prepared to fight for her life and Bethany's.

He laughed. "Seriously?"

She took a fighting stance. She'd done the self-defence classes, but never used the training in anger, and now she really didn't fancy her chances. She needed a weapon. The chair was probably too heavy. That broken lamp! She hurled herself towards him, then dropped and rolled across the floor, grabbing a sizeable shard and rising fast.

He'd closed the ground rapidly, and she slashed at him, a sudden recklessness coming over her.

"Come on then," she panted. "Come on, you bastard."

And he did come. The shard of broken lamp grazed his arm as his fist swung, connecting hard with the side of her face and causing her to stagger. He grabbed her right arm, pushing her back, slamming it into the wall behind her. Her makeshift blade fell from her grasp as he swung her round again, slamming her against a side wall. Then he threw her to the floor, dropped to his knees and straddled her, hands upon her throat.

Her fingers scrabbled against his, trying to prise them off as her airway closed. When this failed, she felt around on the floor in case the broken lamp shard was in reach, but it wasn't. She could hear a dull pulse in her head, as well as muffled screams from Bethany. The world was turning grey, pinpricks of light exploding in her vision as her lungs fought for air that wouldn't come.

"I was going to put you both in the freezer," he said, his voice straining with exertion. "I've never done two live ones together. I know I haven't got much time, but it would have been fun to listen to the two of you. Both of you in the cold and dark, trying to get out. With both of you using up the air, it wouldn't have taken long, either. But you've spoiled that, haven't you, you dirty little cow? Just like *her*. Just. Like. *Her*."

The last three words were accompanied by an extra hard squeeze. Darkness engulfed her.

34

Ricky and Katie didn't bother with the formality of knocking when they burst into Nate's office.

"Got something, guv," Ricky said. "Simon Younger's car. There's a VW registered to a Simon Younger in Wilstone on DVLA, and the same car was in the vicinity last night, not long after Izzy gave Bethany the brush off."

"Plus," Katie said. "We found his pic on Downes's website and it matches the picture on this guy's driving licence. It's him, isn't it?"

Nate squinted at the photograph. "It's him all right."

"It works, doesn't it?" she said. "He'd have been heading that way to get home after failing to abduct Courtney in Watford and could easily have made a detour via Tring. Maybe to look for another victim, maybe for some other reason."

"So do we know anything about him yet?"

"Aliya's still checking police records even as we speak. Libby's trawling the Internet. But come on! It's got to be worth a follow-up. And quickly, if he's got Bethany."

"I agree. I can just hear the Super, if it turns out to be a massive coincidence and we go in all guns blazing. But I'll worry about that later. We might have wasted too much time already." He thought for a moment. "Ricky, can you help Aliya and Libby? It'd be nice to have a bit more justification if it all goes wrong, plus I want to know what we're dealing with. Let me know the moment you get anything else. Katie, can you get some uniforms on board, including armed response?"

"Will you tell DCI Sharp?"

"I can do that en route. And did you get hold of Izzy?"

"I tried her again. Straight to voicemail. I was about to try again when Ricky brought me this news, and it went off my radar." She made a face. "I hope she hasn't gone on to Simon's already, without phoning in."

"Shit," Ricky said abruptly.

"What?" Nate demanded.

"Guv, she was moaning about her phone the other day. Battery knackered, by the sound of it."

"Why didn't you say before?" Katie said sharply.

She had gone pale, and a familiar sickness was settling in Nate's gut, but he reached for calm. "We've all got a lot going on in our heads," he reminded her. "She'd have called in on an Aylesbury station phone, surely, if hers wasn't working?"

"You'd think. But then, she had no reason to be concerned about Simon, so who knows?"

"I don't like it," he decided. "Call Aylesbury now and see if she's still there. Meanwhile, I'll get everything else ready to roll *if* – and only if – we have serious cause to suspect Simon."

As he picked up his phone to make the necessary calls, he found himself praying that Izzy hadn't done anything stupid. She blamed herself for what had happened to Bethany. What might she do to make it right?

He'd barely made his calls when Katie came into his office, her face taut with concern.

"Izzy left Aylesbury twenty-thirty minutes ago."

"Fuck," he said with feeling.

"I think Izzy's gone over to Simon's with no phone, no backup, and no idea what she might be dealing with."

And nothing had been seen or heard of her since.

"I'm not waiting then," he said. "You're with me. Now."

He practically sprinted out of the building, Katie matching him step for step.

The thoughts going through his head made him feel so sick, he could vomit on the spot, but he couldn't allow himself that luxury.

Not now.

"I'm going to drive towards Wilstone," he said when she terminated the call. "But you need to get directions to the house for me. Then get onto Aliya or Ricky. Anything at all they get on Simon Younger, we need to know immediately, if not sooner."

"Should we get onto the guys at Tring station, tell them to get uniforms over there? They're nearer."

He thought fast. "Yeah, okay, do that first." Although the difference in journey time was maybe fifteen minutes, and he and Katie were already on their way. But then, even a few seconds could be crucial, if his fears were justified. He prayed he was overreacting.

Katie made the calls, then sat in silence for a few minutes while he threw the car around bends and finally barrelled onto the A41, flooring the accelerator and immediately moving into the right-hand lane. He could hear and feel the old car protesting at the abuse.

"She was only going to ask a couple of questions about Adam Downes's movements," Katie said. "She had no reason to suspect him. It could be fine."

"Unless she picks up on something," he said. "If she does… well, I'm not sure she's been thinking straight since Bethany disappeared. She thinks it's somehow her fault Bethany was in the wrong place at the wrong time." He shook his head furiously. "I should have seen this coming."

"How could you?"

But he wouldn't let her sugar the bitter pill.

"I should, that's all. Now, have you got those bloody directions?"

"Yep."

"Make sure you tell me when to come off this road. I've got such a bad feeling about this, Katie."

She was quiet for a moment. Then, "Me too," she said.

*

Bethany is weeping so hard she thinks she might choke behind the gag.

Izzy is dead.

Last night, she rejected Bethany. Then the car broke down just outside Tring on the way to her parents, and the nice guy offering to help turned out to be a psycho. But, like some crazy, impossible dream, Izzy found her. She found her and she came for her.

And now she's dead.

He steps away from the body, panting from the exertion. And looking angry. So angry.

"Fucking little cow!" he says. "Little *whore.*" He locks eyes with Bethany. "She's ruined everything. *Everything.*"

He wipes his hands on his jeans. "I knew the police might strike lucky one day, but I always thought I'd have more time. Now who knows how far they are behind this bitch?"

He looks down at Izzy's body. "I'd have loved at least the pleasure of locking her in the freezer with you. Two live women in there together... like an upgrade." He looks at Bethany again. "You wouldn't begin to understand. There's nothing like it. Fucking them, cutting and hacking them... that's not where the excitement is. It's all about putting them in that freezing coffin, closing the lid. Locking them in. Listening... until there's no more sound."

Bethany has no idea what he's talking about. What freezing coffin? All she knows is she's numbed by grief and, at the same time, beyond terrified.

Izzy is dead, and she will be following her soon.

"And then the transformation. The *translation.* From whore to ice maiden. Now all that's ruined. I daren't hang around to see you afterwards. When you're beautiful."

He kicks the body. "Why did she have to come here? Why did she have to go and make me kill her? Women always spoil things in the end. I never lose control like that, not since that one at uni. Even then, I was too clever to get caught, but I didn't enjoy it, and I haven't enjoyed this either."

He kicks out again, then shakes his head.

"I could put her body in anyway and then lock you in with it... but that will eat up time. Besides, I've done it twice before. The second time wasn't as good as the first. If only this bitch was still alive. That would be worth the risk."

He looks at Bethany again, still sobbing.

"What are you so upset about? It's almost as if you care about the little dead whore. Well, I'd be more concerned about myself, if I were you."

He steps over Izzy's body and moves to the bed, where he deftly unties Bethany's wrists. She knows she should struggle, but she's just too shocked to resist as, using one of the cords from the bed, he secures her hands in front of her.

"Pathetic," he says, shaking his head again. "Even now you won't put up a fight. By the time I threw the others in, they were weak and stiff from being tied to the bed so long. But you've not been here long, and you're younger than some of the others."

He checks the knots and grunts, apparently satisfied. "All the same, I won't untie your hands to put you in, not like the others. You'll just have to scrabble at the lid with tied hands. I've no time to wrestle with you if you decide to find some backbone."

The words sting her, and she realises how right he is. She *is* pathetic. She fell for Matt's charm and manipulation, cheated on her best friend with him, stood by, knowing he was screwing them both and assuming – wrongly, as it turned out – that Izzy still didn't know what was going on. She probably cottoned on to Matt cheating on her way too late in the day, and that dissolved her into a jelly that must have been easy meat for this monster. Christ, he probably smelt her weakness from the other side of the roundabout.

And now she's still being pathetic, when Izzy lies dead a few feet away, when she should be angry.

That anger finally starts to rise as he releases her feet and lift her off the bed. She pummels at him, all too ineffectually, yelling at him behind the gag.

"That's more like it," he chuckles, and she realises that her struggles probably excite him, heighten the anticipation.

He carries her past Izzy, onto the landing, and into a room with a table and some chairs, but dominated by a chest freezer. That reference to an icy coffin is all too clear now. As he dumps her down on a chair, she vows to herself that she won't make it easy for him.

As he moves swiftly to the table and opens his tool roll, she strains to loosen the cord, but he's tied it too tight. He turns around and shows her a hacksaw.

"Don't make a sound or move a muscle," he says, "or I'll be using this on you. I don't have much time, thanks to that little bitch in there, but it won't take long to cut your feet off, believe me."

Just putting the thought in her head threatens to dissolve her into fresh terror.

He shows her the secateurs. "I usually take a finger, as a souvenir, but it takes more time, and besides – what would I do with it?"

He busies himself getting the padlock ready, then he opens the lid of the freezer. Steam rises.

"I read up on it," he tells her. "Normally you'll run out of air before the cold gets you, so in theory, the less you move, the longer you'll last. But there, in the freezing cold and the dark… none of the others could stand it. They were all screaming, trying to get out. In the end, they were all translated. At peace."

He smiles, almost fondly. It sickens her. "I hope you will too, but I can't stay to the end, so you'll have to die alone. You might get really lucky and have the police arrive in time, but I wouldn't…" he giggles, as if the words he's about to say tickle him. "I wouldn't hold my breath if I were you." He giggles again. "See what I did there."

He removes the gag. She's crying, trying to be brave, but seeing no way out, unless the police really are on their way. But she doesn't want to be in there. The picture he's painted is beyond her darkest nightmares.

"Please," she whispers, but he presses a finger to her lips.

"Shh. No talking now. You can make as much noise as you like in the freezer. I'd be surprised if anyone heard you and besides, no one cares about anyone else these days. People say humanity is the poorer for it, but I say it makes us stronger."

He hefts her into his arms again.

"Please," she tries again, "please don't." She pummels him again.

He ignores her, seeming to revel in her fear. "The others were so weakened, so broken, they put up next to no fight. I thought you were already broken, after such a short time. But see? You're already transforming. You're growing stronger."

He sighs. "I wish I could stay to the end."

He holds her over the open freezer. She struggles again.

"No," she moans, "no. Please…"

He lets her fall.

35

Like a diver rising slowly from the floor of some ocean, Izzy slowly surfaced from the depths of unconsciousness. Her eyes opened and more pinpricks of light danced before her for a moment.

He neck felt bruised and tender and her throat raw. Through the disorientation, she felt those fingers around her throat again, squeezing, squeezing.

She thought she was lying exactly where she had been when Simon Younger had been throttling her.

When she'd thought she was going to die. Felt her life ebbing away.

She heaved herself into a sitting position. Where was he? She looked at the bed, one of the ties still dangling from the headboard. More importantly, where was Bethany?

She forced herself to think. Simon had talked about wanting to put her and Bethany, alive together, in the chest freezer in the next room. He said she, Izzy, had spoiled that for him.

So had he intended to choke her to death? When she passed out, did he think he'd killed her?

Surely he'd have checked, if he was half as meticulous as he seemed. But then her arrival at his house, her suspicions being raised, and her discovery of Bethany, all must have put him on the back foot, needing to tidy up here and get out. Maybe he'd just assumed she was dead and had been in too much hurry to make sure.

Bethany. Unfinished business. 'Tidying up'.

She rose groggily to her feet and swayed, taking deep, sawing breaths, getting her breathing under some sort of control. She checked her watch. She hadn't been out for as long as she feared. Now she strained her ears, she could hear a low voice not far away.

Moving as quietly as she could, she moved towards the door. Simon was talking, presumably to Bethany, inside the freezer room. Occasionally, he heard the tiniest of responses. Bethany was alive, but it was obvious what he intended.

Izzy wished she didn't feel quite as much like a woman recently risen from the dead, but a fresh determination to save her old friend gripped her, and she could see only one way she might manage it. She closed her eyes and tried to re-visualise that room. All she'd have on her side was surprise, and she had to make every nanosecond of that advantage count.

She slipped off her shoes and padded across the landing. The door was open and she could see Simon, with his back to her, holding a struggling Bethany over the open chest freezer. Mist was rising from the white metal box.

"No," Bethany moaned, "no. Please…"

Izzy was moving, fast and silent, as he dropped her in. She went straight to the tool roll on the table, which he'd evidently opened. There was no time to speculate on why. She selected a box cutter and closed the distance between the table and Simon.

He was about to shut the lid when she gripped his arm with one hand and held the blade to his throat with the other.

"Step away. Now. This is sharp enough to slice through your carotid, and I know what I'm doing."

He didn't lower the lid, but he didn't step away, either. "You're *dead*."

"Seemingly not, you narcissistic bastard. You fucked up. You should have made sure. How does that feel?"

Now she had him at her mercy, her fury was rising again. It would be so easy to slash that artery and paint the room red with his blood.

"Now step away," she repeated. "Carefully."

She guided him away.

"Now get on your knees. Slowly. Don't make my hand slip."

As he did so, she glanced at Bethany, now standing up in the freezer. "You need to get yourself out of there, Beth."

"It's so cold, it burns, Iz. I'm sticking to it, and it's slippery."

Izzy made eye contact with her. "Come on. You've got this."

It was only a momentary distraction, but it was enough for Simon. He twisted his neck away from the blade and jerked an elbow back into her kneecap before rolling away. He rose like a cat, hurtling towards the bench. Pain screamed in her knee, but she went after him, too late. He turned to face her, holding a large chisel.

"This is like that film," he grinned. "Call that a *knife*?" He brandished the chisel. "*This* is a knife."

"No it's not, you twat," she said, "it's a chisel," but her confidence was evaporating.

"I'll count to five," he said. "Here's the deal. You drop the box cutter and I'll be on my way." His gaze flickered between the two women. "You *do* know each other, don't you?"

"My colleagues will be here any second. Don't make this worse for yourself."

He laughed humourlessly. "I'm not sure how I could do that if I tried. Now drop it. Or I'm going to have to take it from you." He took a step toward her. Then another.

Every one of her senses was urging her to run away, but she made herself ignore it. But should she stand her ground or go on the attack?

She chose the latter, launching herself at him. He didn't even attempt to cut her with the chisel. He swung it like a club at the hand that held the knife, hitting her hard. Sick pain ripped through her fingers. She lost her grip on the box cutter, but she was close enough to grapple with him. Close enough to bring her knee up into his groin.

He bellowed in pain and she seized the moment to grab his right wrist with both hands, ignoring the hot throbbing in her own right, and twisting away, digging her nails into his wrist. Even as he lost hold of his own weapon, he used his free hand to grab her hair, jerking her head back. She felt her grip loosen, then he fell over backwards, taking her with him. They hit the floor in a tangle of limbs.

Just for a moment, she was on top, but at an awkward angle. With his superior weight and strength, what followed was inevitable.

Like a recurring nightmare, he was straddling her once more, his hands squeezing her already sore throat. Once again, spots were dancing before her eyes as her oxygen-starved brain fought for the air it craved.

He was staring intensely into her eyes.

"This time, I'm taking your advice," he told her. "I'm going to make damn sure you're dead."

*

Nate had always prided himself on his driving. If he'd witnessed his own catalogue of reckless actions on the way to Wilstone, he would have thrown the book at himself. But he'd shaved several minutes off the journey time.

Aliya called just as he was passing a farm shop on Lower Icknield Way. Katie told him to take the next right, then put her phone on speaker.

"Sir, I think we've got something," Aliya said. "We need to verify one hundred per cent that we're talking about the same Simon Younger, but the age is about right."

"Tell me."

"The name comes up in two news stories. Assuming it's our man, then when he was sixteen, his mother died in a freak accident. She was a prostitute and a drug addict, and she somehow managed to lock herself in an understairs cupboard while Simon was away at some sort of summer school. By the time he got back she was dead."

"In a confined space?" murmured Katie.

"Exactly. Not a cold one, but..."

Nate made the turn.

"He was the one who found her," Aliya said. "So now fast forward. He's twenty and at university, and a girl in his year dies in suspicious circumstances. There aren't enough details, but it seems she either strangled herself by accident, or someone else was involved. The story crops up relatively recently, because her parents are still looking for answers."

"Right, then right again," Katie directed.

"And Simon?" Nate demanded.

"One of the last to be seen with her. Oh, he wasn't the only one questioned and released, and no one has ever been charged. But if you put it with the rest…"

"Anything else?"

"Still digging."

"Great work, make sure you thank everyone."

"We're about there," Katie said as the call terminated. "Next left."

Nate spotted the patrol car immediately. Izzy's car was in front of it, and he shoved the Volvo into the inadequate space behind it at an angle, half the rear end hanging across the road. There were two uniformed officers on the doorstep, a woman and the ubiquitous PC Harrison, who was hammering on the door.

"Police! Open up! *Now!*"

Nate joined them, Katie at his elbow. "How long have you been here?"

"Couple of minutes, sir. No response yet."

"Try again."

Harrison pounded on the door again, while his colleague rang the bell incessantly.

"*Police!*" Nate yelled through the letter box. "Open the door." Then, "Okay, stop," he ordered the two uniforms. "Stop."

He held the letter box open and put his ear to it. He looked at Katie and shook his head.

"Can't hear a thing."

"Depends where they are in the house."

He stepped back and looked across the length of the building, supposing that it would be difficult to hear anything going on upstairs at the far end from here.

He reached for a calm he didn't feel. The front door was nothing special, but looked solid enough.

"Katie," he said, "you and PC…" He looked at the female officer.

"Khan," she supplied.

"You and PC Khan see if you can find another way in. We'll try and get this door open."

217

Katie was pale, as if she knew what he expected to find and felt sick inside at the thought. But she merely nodded, her mouth a grim line, and headed off, the other woman in tow.

"Right," he said to Harrison, "how are your lock-picking skills?"

Harrison frowned. "Non-existent, sir."

"Don't suppose you've got anything we could use as a battering ram?"

The other man shook his head.

"Then we'll try to kick it in. You up for that?"

"For Izzy? Yes, sir."

"We concentrate on where the lock is, yes?"

Harrison nodded, stepped forward, and slammed the sole of his shoe against the spot. And again, and again. They examined the door for damage and found only scuff marks.

"Let me try," Nate said.

He stepped forward and prepared to aim a kick at the door.

"Hold on, sir," Harrison said. "What was that?"

36

Izzy knew she really was dying, and that this time there would be no coming back. Her brain felt ready to explode yet, at the same time, a sense of peace and tranquillity was stealing over her, as if her body was already surrendering to the inevitable.

Simon's fingers on her throat felt like twin vices. Attempts to prise them off were as ineffectual as her efforts to harm him with her fists. If he even felt the blows, they seemed to make no impression on him.

She only hoped that DI Quarrel and the team would realise what she had seen too late: that they had overlooked Simon. And, whatever Simon might imagine, they would find him and bring him to justice. But it would be too late for Izzy. Too late for Bethany, who he would surely lock in that freezer once and for all, as soon as he'd finished with Izzy. She wished she'd had a proper chance to make it up with her friend. That she'd had a chance to say goodbye to her family.

Darkness was closing in on her when his fingers first relaxed their grip and were then ripped away. Then he was off her.

Clutching her burning throat, gulping in agonising mouthfuls of air, she sat up to see an astonishing sight.

Bethany, naked and wild-faced, like some vengeful ancient goddess, was kneeling behind Simon, the cords binding her wrists across his throat. Despite her ordeal, something seemed to have given her a strength that was impervious to his bucking and threshing. Her eyes, locked onto Izzy's, blazed with an avenging intensity. Her teeth were bared and she was snarling.

Izzy tried to speak, but could only manage a croak. Getting onto her knees, she shoved her hand in her jacket pocket and yanked out her handcuffs. She got a cuff on one of Simon's wrists, twisted the arm behind his back, did likewise with his other arm, and snapped the second cuff on.

Simon was helpless, but Bethany went right on throttling him. He was making hideous gagging noises.

"Bethany," she cawed. The noise sounded like nothing human to her own ears. She leaned across and, with her uninjured hand, gently removed Bethany's from the man's throat. "Beth. Enough," she whispered.

Bethany withdrew her hands and started to cry.

"You found me," she sobbed. "I can't believe you found me."

Izzy moved closer to her and caught her in a hug. Bethany was so cold.

"Of course I found you," she whispered, the most noise she could make. "But we need to warm you up." She looked at the handcuffed Simon. "I just need to make sure he's going nowhere."

She untied Bethany's hands and used the binding to secure the man's ankles. Then she led Bethany to the room where she had been held and swathed her friend in blankets and sheets from the bed.

"He's probably got your clothes somewhere," she croaked, "but our forensics guys will most probably want those, and won't want things disturbed. And I don't imagine you want to put on anything out of his wardrobe?"

Bethany shuddered as she huddled in her blankets. "Anything *he's* been wearing? My skin wouldn't stop crawling. I'm fine for now." Her face crumpled again. "As fine as I'll ever be again." She burst into tears.

Downstairs there was a banging and shouting.

"There's... someone at the door," Bethany said between sobs.

"They'll have to wait a moment. Will you be okay here? I'm going to formally caution him."

Bethany's eyes narrowed. She swiped tears away. "Just do what you have to."

Izzy returned to the other room and stood in front of Simon. "Simon Younger," she said, so hoarse she wasn't sure he'd hear her. "I'm arresting you on suspicion of abduction and attempted murder." That would do for now. The murders of Lynne

Redding, Donna Mason, Angela Andrews, Kimberley Wade and their unnamed victim could be added later. "You do not have to say anything. But, it may harm your defence if you do not mention when questioned something which you later rely on in court. Anything you do say may be given in evidence. Do you understand?"

His only response was a look of venomous contempt.

"Do you understand?" she repeated.

"Oh," he said, almost as hoarse as Izzy, "you're loving this, aren't you? A whore bitch with a bit of power?"

"Say you understand, or you'll be picking up a few injuries that," she made speech marks with her fingers, "'might have happened in the struggle'. What's it to be?"

He sighed. "I understand."

The cacophony downstairs had abated for a few moments. Now it sounded like someone was trying to kick the door in.

"I'd better go," she told him, "before one of my colleagues hurts their foot."

*

"What was that?" Harrison said.

Nate paused, listening. Footsteps approaching from inside the house. Seconds later, the door swung open and he sagged with relief at the sight of Izzy Cole, dishevelled but very much alive.

"Jesus, Izzy, you scared us."

She grimaced, looked on the verge of tears. "Sorry, sir." Her voice was croaky, and it didn't sound like she simply had a cold. "How did you find me?"

"Never mind that." He could see blotchy marks on her neck. He'd seen them before, on strangulation victims. It chilled him to the bone. "Are you all right?"

"I'll live. So will Bethany. She's upstairs, but we need to find her some clothes."

"And Simon Younger?"

"I just read him his rights. He's upstairs too, handcuffed. I ought to get back to them, in case Bethany decides to kill him."

"Are you serious?"

Her gaze strayed to the stairs. "A bit, actually. I was tempted myself."

"Go on then. I'll be right behind you." He hesitated. "You said she needed clothes?"

"Oh, she's decent. Rocking a sheet and blanket."

"And she's okay?"

"I wouldn't go that far."

Nate suspected that the point would come where Izzy's apparent swagger no longer carried her through. There was a story to tell, and those marks on her neck said it wasn't going to be a pretty one.

As Izzy headed for the stairs, Nate turned to Harrison. "Go and get our colleagues, before they break in at the back. Get DS Gray to join me upstairs, then call for paramedics. I want both those women checked out."

He nodded and departed, leaving Nate alone at the foot of the stairs. He was a tangle of warring emotions. His overwhelming feeling was relief that Izzy seemed okay, if the worse for wear, and that Bethany Kerr was safe. And he could hardly be displeased that Simon Younger had been apprehended. The full case against Younger had yet to be built, but Nate was as confident as he could be that they'd got their man.

At the same time, he was absolutely furious with Izzy for the scare she'd given them. She might not have known Younger was a suspect when she turned up on his doorstep, but her being out of contact could have had a much more nightmarish outcome.

As it was, he strongly suspected most of her casual bravado was a front. He'd make sure she got the counselling she needed, but part of him was sorely tempted to kick her off the development scheme and send her back to uniform with a recommendation that she be put on traffic duties.

But he wouldn't.

Maybe her normally clear head and sound judgement had been uncharacteristically fogged by a mix of guilt and concern for someone who'd once been her best friend – maybe still was

– causing her to put speed ahead of common sense. It was a set of circumstances that, it was to be hoped, would not arise again. If a similar set or circumstances did occur in the future, he would make sure Izzy knew better than to make the same mistake a second time.

And, after all, Nate knew he didn't always play it by the book. He'd conducted an illegal, ultimately pointless, search of Pete Savage's mother's house. He'd obtained and copied a case file he had no business with, and had roped a colleague into his wrongdoing. Because his feelings had overridden his normal professional instincts. Human beings often did the wrong thing for the right reason. He couldn't be too hasty in condemning Izzy.

He headed towards the stairs, realising he'd spent several minutes woolgathering.

"Nate?" came Katie's voice behind him. "It's true? They're both safe?"

She was standing just inside the front door.

"Seems that way, yes. I was just going up. Come with me. Is Harrison arranging medical attention?"

"Yep." They started to climb the stairs together. "Don't be too hard on Izzy, Nate," she said.

He stopped and smiled at her. "I wasn't going to. She's been through a lot, and I suspect she's a lot more fragile than she's letting on. Oh, I'll read her the riot act in due course, but we'll be chalking this off as a lesson learned."

"Sounds about right." She grinned at him. "I guess a commendation is out of the question?"

He briefly considered it. "If it was up to me, I might be persuaded, but I don't think our masters would be impressed. Best not push our luck."

37

One last mystery had been solved in the aftermath of Simon Younger's arrest. The final victim had been identified as Jennifer Poole, who'd been a familiar sight begging in Newham, East London until her disappearance last March. And yes, Newham was on the list for high concentrations of homeless people.

Younger himself was saying nothing. When he was asked, during an interview, if he'd like a break for a drink and something to eat, he'd started to say, "No comment," to that as well.

Not only was he not cooperating, but he seemed to see himself as being above the process, as if it simply didn't apply to people like him. Certainly, he looked down on everyone who attempted to engage with him, and he'd flatly refused any kind of legal representation.

The full story of what had forged him into the cruel killer he'd become might never be known, but he'd been less reticent when he'd been with Bethany, both when he'd held her captive and when he'd thought he'd killed Izzy.

He'd never known his father and his earliest memories had been of keeping quiet in his room while his mother entertained what she referred to as 'uncles', but were actually clients. Most of the money she earned went on drugs. One time, he'd burst in, convinced his mother was being hurt, and had been beaten by the furious man while she looked on.

She had first taken him to her bed when he was twelve, something he knew was wrong but felt powerless to resist until he was sixteen – ironically the age of consent. The experience had evidently twisted his thinking so that all women were whores in his mind.

And then he'd found her dead.

One of the things Dr Ross had apparently said when he was showing off to Katie was that it was often hard to tell where, in the case of violent criminals, the line could be drawn between nature and nurture. Later, at home alone, Nate came back to the old adage that every action had a reaction. A consequence. It was simple to surmise that the young Simon's early experiences had ultimately been the catalyst that had unhinged something inside the young Simon.

Too simple?

When did a story really start? His thoughts returned to Izzy, who he knew still felt she was in some way responsible for Bethany's ordeal. But the seeds of her rejection of her old friend last night had been sown more than a year before when Bethany had started sleeping with Izzy's boyfriend. Because both of them had been attracted to the same two-timing shit.

Nate wondered about himself. One of the reasons he'd become a cop, he knew, was that he wanted to protect the public, and that was because he'd always thought he should somehow have prevented his father's death and had failed. Laura insisted that was a ridiculous notion – that there was nothing a small boy could have done.

He'd known in his heart that she was right.

Now he wasn't so sure.

His grandparents had told him the horror of witnessing the murder and being covered in his father's blood were the reason why his mind had blotted so much out.

How he wished he could recover those memories now.

A stab wound that had followed an upward trajectory, as if from below. At least a suggestion that it could support his mother's self-defence plea. Yet there had been no mention of that whatsoever at the trial.

Why?

As to that, he had the ghost of an idea of how he might finally uncover the truth about a day that had cast such a long shadow over his life. Maybe it was time, finally time, to confront that truth head-on. Either it would confirm everything he ever thought he'd known. Or he would find out just how much of his whole life had been based on a lie.

He didn't know if he was ready for that. He didn't know if he would ever be ready. But he knew he'd be incomplete until he'd laid that ghost once and for all.

And he knew what he had to do.

*

Bethany was being kept overnight in hospital as a precaution. Izzy had been checked out. Her right hand was sprained but not broken, and she'd been given some drugs to help with the pain in her neck and throat, then allowed to spend some time with the woman she had rescued.

And, she'd realised in a moment of clarity, she really *had* rescued her. She couldn't deny that only sheer luck – a thud from upstairs that could have been anything – had raised her suspicions of Simon Younger. And it was also true that the team had, by more conventional means, been only a step or two behind her in those suspicions.

But who was to say the outcome would have been the same if she'd not somehow communicated her unease to Younger? If she'd simply taken her leave of him and phoned her suspicion back to the station. She liked to think the team would have swung into action, but what if they'd taken precious time digging into Simon's background and checking his movements before being ready to confront him? At best, Bethany could have endured more torture in the meantime. She might not have all her fingers. At worst, she might still have died inside that freezer – or Simon just might have decided to dispatch her at the first sign of the police at his door.

Now she sat at Bethany's bedside, holding her hand as though the past year, when all her thoughts of her best friend had been venom, had been washed away, and they were just Iz and Beth once more.

"They gave me the morning after pill," Bethany said. "He used condoms but just in case, you know…"

Izzy squeezed her hand. "I'm so sorry, Beth."

"Hardly your fault. I've been lucky. *Lucky,*" she repeated, laughing hollowly as her voice broke. "Every time that door opens, I think it's going to be him. I don't think I'll ever sleep again."

"I'm the same." Tears spilled from Izzy's eyes too. "I'm so tired. But every time I close my eyes, I'm back there in that room, and he's strangling me again. I really thought I was going to die."

"I thought you *were* dead." Izzy could feel Bethany's hand shaking in hers. "He would have cut my finger off, you know. He even had a pair of secateurs in his hand. All that stopped him was, he said he was short of time, and he couldn't take it with him."

Izzy knew that amputated fingers, presumably from other victims, had been found in the freezer compartment of Simon Younger's fridge freezer. But she chose not to mention that. Not now.

"It *is* all my fault," she said miserably.

"*Your* fault?" Bethany stared at her, tears rolling down her face. "But... you were amazing. You saved my life."

"Yeah, well. You saved *mine*, in the end."

Bethany managed to grin through the tears. "We saved each other. Like old times. But *your* fault? How do you make that out?"

"You came to me and I told you to piss off. You even tried to tell me you had car trouble."

"So?"

"So if I'd just forgiven you, like I should have, that bastard wouldn't have got within a million miles of you. Instead..."

"Don't be so bloody stupid. How could you possibly have known what would happen? Besides, I'm the horrible little cow who slept with your boyfriend. I never really expected you to forgive me, not just like that. I don't even know why I came round at all. I guess the guy who'd come between us was off the scene and I thought..." She shook her head. "I dunno."

They were both crying. Izzy rose from her chair and caught Bethany in a clumsy hug. "Well, I forgive you now." She might never *forget*, but she knew that much was true, at least. "Like you said, it was like old times. You and me against the world." She chuckled through her tears. "The world never did stand a

chance against us. We'll get through this together, somehow."
She pulled back and looked her friend in the eye, the months of
animosity melting away. "I've missed you, Bethany Kerr."

Bethany looked right back at her.

"And I've missed you too, Izzy Cole."

*

Courtney ends the call and hands the old pay as you go Nokia
back to Rosie.

"They're almost here."

If her brush with a killer had told her anything, it was that
Paul, or whatever his name was, had been right in one respect –
as had Rosie: she didn't belong here. Not on the streets in
Watford. Not in this life.

It was time to give her old life another chance.

Rosie had been happy to lend her her phone to call her
parents. There had been tears on both sides, and they'd said
they'd drop everything to come and get her. Although they were
coming by car, it was Rosie who'd suggested they meet at
Watford Junction train station – a fifteen-minute walk from the
town centre, but easier to find than some arbitrary spot in the
centre, and no parking hassle. She'd given them Rosie's
number, and they'd promised to phone when they were close.

She looks at her friend, at that mad, untamed hair, at an
upright posture that has refused to bow under hardship. "Are
you sure you won't stick around and meet them?"

Rosie smiles. "Nah. No offence, but I don't do goodbyes.
Tell you one thing, though. I've decided to move on again. I've
had enough of Watford."

"Really?" Courtney feels more upset about this parting than
she could have imagined. "But you know the place so well. You
know the outreach people. You could maybe try a hostel again."

But Rosie shakes her head. "Nah," she says again. "That's
not for me, not just now. Maybe I'll tell you my story some
time, if we keep in touch – you've got my number." She looks
serious. "Look I know the idea that many of us are homeless by

choice is a myth, but right now, this minute, that *is* what I choose. And I'm okay. Really. I can look after myself, okay?"

"You certainly looked after me." Courtney feels tears welling in her eyes.

"I'll miss you," Rosie says. A single tear creeps down her cheek. "Now look what you've done." She laughs and swipes it away. "Look, I'm off, okay?"

"Can I at least give you a hug?"

For a moment, Rosie looks hesitant. The she smiles. "So long as you don't say goodbye."

They embrace, holding on tight. Then Rosie pats her on the back, disengages and, without another word, turns and walks away.

Courtney watches her until she turns a corner and is out of sight. She wonders what secrets her friend is keeping – secrets she hinted at, but is clearly not ready to share. She doesn't know how things will work out with her parents this time, but it feels like a second chance. Maybe a last chance. One thing she does know for sure. She will keep in touch with Rosie.

She doesn't think she'd be here without her.

Earlier on, they overheard people saying an arrest had been made in connection with the Wigginton murders. She wonders if they helped. If so, maybe they prevented a few more deaths. She likes to think so.

She spots the car coming along the road. As it turns into the drop off area, her mother sees her and starts waving madly. A lump forms in her throat as she realises, in spite of everything, just how much she's missed them.

38

Three weeks later

It was a very long time since Nate had been here, yet the winding road, separated from fields on both sides by drystone walls, was as familiar as if it had been yesterday. He could see the former farmhouse up ahead on the right. That too looked the same as the image in his memory, but somehow quite a bit smaller than he remembered it.

His passengers were as silent as he was. Laura, in the front passenger seat, seemed to be taking in every inch of this slice of her partner's past. From behind him, he fancied he could feel waves of apprehension radiating from Sandra Bowman.

His mother had seemed reluctant to make this trip. It had surprised him, not so much for her scepticism about the whole venture – he wasn't sure himself that it wouldn't prove a massive waste of time. But, after all her attempts to get a foothold on his life, he'd thought she might jump at the chance to spend the best part of four hours each way with him in his car. Instead, she'd been withdrawn and mostly monosyllabic, even when Laura had attempted to engage her in safe small talk.

But then, he supposed, few people are wild about visiting a haunted house.

He pulled up on a grass verge outside the property and got out. It was unseasonably mild for the time of year, but he shivered. What was one of his grandfather's favourite sayings?

It felt like a grey goose walked over my grave.

The women had also left the car and came round to flank him.

Laura's hand found his. "You're absolutely sure about this, Nate?"

He shrugged. "No. And yes. I feel like I've been running from this place for the best part of forty years." He glanced at Sandra. "I've no idea where this is going to get us. Nowhere, most like. But I don't know what else to do."

She tried to take his other hand, but he pulled away. At least he managed to do it gently.

He pushed open the gate then, and began walking up the flint path to the front door. He couldn't pretend to remember the old front garden, but he was pretty sure the current owners had put their own stamp on it.

They stopped at the door. That had definitely changed. UPVC, duck-egg blue. But more than the door, the path took his attention, continuing on round the side of the house. Fatally stabbed, his father, Philip Bowman had staggered out of the converted Yorkshire farmhouse and round that corner, where he had collapsed. Six-year-old Nathan had cuddled the dying man as he bled out, getting covered in blood in the process.

At least, that was what he'd been told. What he'd read in the reports, even though his name – a name he no longer wore – had been withheld 'for legal reasons'. Because of his age.

How do you forget a thing like that? How do you remember it again?

He recognised the big old-fashioned doorbell, with its pull cord, immediately. It should have been erased with so many other memories. Yet the feel of the cord in his hand and the clang of the bell seemed to resonate inside him. He realised that his untameable hair felt as if it was standing on end, even more than it usually did. A dog started barking within.

He stole a glance at Sandra. She was ashen. He sensed she might bolt at any second, but then the door opened inward and a middle-aged couple stood there.

"Hello," said the ruddy-faced man. "You must be Nathan." He held out a hand.

He wore an elderly brown sweater and dark blue cords. His wife, blonde curls out of a bottle, had teamed a sage green cardigan with denims.

Nate shook the proffered hand. "It's good of you to let us come." *Coom.* How easily traces of his old Yorkshire accent

231

resurfaced. "As I said on the phone, I lived here a long time back, and I thought, since I was going to be in this neck of the woods, I'd like to have a look at the old place." The rehearsed lie slid off his tongue like honey.

"I'm guessing you must have lived here before the murder?" the man suggested.

"Yeah," he said glibly. "I heard about it, of course. Terrible business."

"Well, it's never bothered us. It's a bit of fun, having a notorious house."

Fun.

"I suppose it must be." Nate disguised how much the comment irked him.

"Well, come in. Will you have a tea or coffee? And there's homemade fat rascals. My wife makes them better than Bettys, I promise you."

Nate doubted anyone could better Yorkshire's iconic tea rooms, but, "Sounds great," he said. "Although I wonder... could we ask a really big, cheeky favour? Any chance we can have a moment to ourselves. Just a couple of minutes? You know, soak up the atmosphere?"

Just for a second, the couple exchanged glances. The man looked dubious, but the woman was immediately all smiles.

"Of course you can. We'll just be in the garden. Take as long as you need."

Stepping over the threshold was like an electric shock. For all he could remember, he might as well never have been here, yet something tugged at him, seeming to sing him a song whose melody was indistinct, and whose lyrics were unintelligible. He shivered again as the owners trooped out the back door.

Nate stood in the space that made up the single living area that took up most of the downstairs. The front door led straight into it, the back door led out from it, and the stairs went up at the back. The room itself served as both living room and kitchen. One further door led off, and Nate knew, even though he shouldn't, that behind it lay a utility space with a toilet.

Was it imagination? Or could he really feel the years rolling back?

He looked through a front window and half-expected to see snow falling.

Red blood on white snow.

That image, the tiniest fragment of a flashback, was the nearest thing he had to a memory of his father's death. His paternal grandparents, who'd raised him after his father's murder and his mother's imprisonment, had told him what had happened when they deemed him old enough to know. He'd loved and trusted them, and had no reason to disbelieve them.

Much later, feeling as if a building block was missing from his identity, he'd been compelled to research the case, finding no inconsistency between newspaper accounts and what he already thought he knew.

After his mother's release, his reaction to her desperate attempts to re-establish contact had been extreme. He'd changed his name and moved south. But last year she'd found him again, and Laura had finally persuaded him to listen to her.

She'd told him nothing she hadn't told the jury. Certainly, nothing contradicted the basic established facts, which seemed to have been common ground between his mother and her prosecutors. Except her version was that, yes, she'd been drinking when his father came home, but that had been merely a little Dutch courage, anticipating his likely mood when he walked through the door. He, not she, had been the aggressor. She'd picked up the knife to keep him at bay, but he'd attacked her anyway, running onto the blade in his fury

The jury hadn't believed her, and Nate hadn't either, not even when she'd asked him to look at the case again, through dispassionate eyes. Yet he'd not been able to resist picking it over again, this time getting hold of the case file. And it had led him to that one nagging loose thread.

For all he knew, the kitchen had probably been upgraded more than once since the Bowmans' time. This incarnation looked fairly recent, light, glossy, handleless doors and drawers, space age appliances, a black granite worktop.

Yet somehow he also knew that the basic layout had changed little, if at all. His gaze travelled to the kitchen work surface, and he instinctively knew where his mother's knife block had once stood, close to the sink. He moved closer to the spot.

"Anything?" Laura said.

He held up a hand for silence, while he took it all in, tried to sense something of the atmosphere. Sandra had said not a word. He wondered if she had breathed since they arrived.

There was a fear in her eyes, and it was a look so unfamiliar and familiar at the same time that the ground seemed to shift beneath his feet. The temperature seemed to have plummeted to winter levels, and Sandra's tension seemed to infect him. He felt a little like that scared little boy again.

He squeezed his eyes tight shut, and waited for things unremembered to come to him.

*

After what felt like an age, his eyes flew open again. The two women were watching him. Concern, maybe even fear, was naked in Laura's eyes. Sandra's – *his mother*'s – face was unreadable.

He looked at her. Locked eyes. And he knew.

He *knew*.

He felt like his knees were about to give out. He would collapse here in this kitchen that was both alien and in some way home. Either that, or he would throw up. Or both.

He was so cold, he might have been in one of Simon Younger's chest freezers.

He tried to reason with himself, to tell himself there was no reason to believe that what was in his mind cancelled out the version of events he'd been told. The version he had carried with him all his adult life, handed down to him by the people he'd trusted more than anyone.

This was what she'd feared would happen, he realised. Had tried to protect him from. Not just this trip, but forever.

Emotions warred and tangled inside him. Anger at her. Anger at his grandparents. Guilt.

And, above all, despair.

"What?" Laura was grasping both of his upper arms, staring anxiously into his face. How long she'd been doing so, the white noise in his brain perhaps rendering him oblivious, he wasn't sure now. *"Nate?"*

His mother was no longer looking at him. For some reason, that infuriated him. He pushed Laura away and stepped across to Sandra.

Oh, God...

"Why?" he whispered. Still she wouldn't listen to him. *"Why?"* he yelled in her face.

"Nate..." Laura protested.

"No!" he shouted. Then, "No," he said again, more quietly. "You wanted me to hear her out, and I did." He reached for calm. Found it. "But let's go outside."

Laura inclined her head towards the door out to the garden. "What about them?"

"I'll tell them we have to go. Something's come up."

Outside they stood by the car. Sandra seemed to have shrunk. Her hands were thrust deep in her coat pockets and she was staring down at the pavement.

Nate addressed Laura. "She asked me to take another look at the case for her, and I did. And all the time, she knew the truth. You *knew!*" he said to Sandra. "Better than anyone. Why didn't you just come out and tell me?"

"How could I?" she whispered. "How could I tell anyone, and ruin your life? You'd have always been that boy. *That boy.* You'd have carried it with you forever."

He laughed harshly. "And now I'm stuck with it anyway, after all these years." The knowledge was almost overwhelming. "I don't even know what I'm supposed to do with that. You went to prison..."

"Nate?" Laura said. "Please. What's going on? What are you saying?"

He glanced at her, shaking his head. *Not now.*

"I never thought it would go that far," Sandra said. "I never thought I'd even be charged. I said it was self-defence, hoping you were too young to be questioned. Then, when it turned out you'd blanked the whole thing, I thought that was for the best.

A child shouldn't have a thing like that in his head, and now there was no way you were going to contradict me, even if they *did* question you." She was crying. "I thought you'd never need to know. My story would be accepted and we could both move on. So I stuck with my story."

"But then you *were* charged."

"It turned out no one was interested in my self-defence plea. Not when there was just enough there for a murder trial, with your father's parents filling in the blanks. Not when your granddad had influence."

"But I don't understand," he persisted. "Once you saw the story wasn't working. That you were *going* to be charged. Why did you persist with it?"

Her mouth twisted into a mirthless smile. "I still thought it would work in the end. That at least the jury would believe me. But no one did. Besides, what was I supposed to do? I *told* you. I couldn't tell them what really happened. I couldn't do that to you."

He felt like he was living some mad dream.

"Christ!" Laura finally exploded. "Isn't anyone going to tell me what this is about? What is this 'truth' you keep talking about?"

"Tell her," Nate said, but Sandra shook her head, tears beginning to flow.

He turned to face the woman he loved, sick at what he was about to say to her.

"Sandra didn't kill my father," he said. "I did."

Laura stared at him, her mouth open.

He'd said it.

He looked at Sandra again, swallowed a great lump in his throat, and said, "Tell her what happened."

"You *remember*," she said. "*You* tell her."

"I want to hear it from you," he whispered. "The truth. Finally."

She let out a shuddering sigh, tears continuing to flow.

"It was an accident," she told him. "Your father's fault. I knew he would be in a mood when he came in that day. It had got so I could almost sense it. And there he was, swaying on the threshold, scowling. Taking a heavy step towards me, with that leering look he had. It usually meant we were going upstairs and closing the bedroom door, whether I liked it or not.

"And then his foot landed on your red fire engine. He crushed it, and he almost fell over. He flew into one of his rages. Stamped it to pieces, swearing and shouting. Then he turned on you. The temper he was in, I thought he'd really hurt you, once he started.

"I remember getting in between you, and that was when he switched his attention to me. I'd often thought he'd kill me one day, and I honestly thought this was the day. I tried to grab the knife I'd been using off the worktop. To scare him, make him back off, I suppose. But I fumbled it and it fell on the floor.

"And there was the great irony. I'd always taught you to pick things up for people when they dropped them. Good Manners. And there you were, holding up the knife, crying, begging Daddy not to hurt Mummy.

"It's like he didn't even see you. He stumbled again and he managed to fall on the blade. It stuck in him, and then he was going out the front door, staggering and stumbling. I stood there shocked, but you followed, saying, "I'm sorry, Daddy, I'm sorry, I'm sorry, I'm sorry…"

"I followed you out, and I'll never forget the red blood, soaking into that white snow." *Nor had he.* "And there you were, cuddling him, still saying sorry."

He absorbed it all. Silence hung around them like a fog.

"Nate?" Laura ventured finally.

He barked out a harsh laugh as tears welled in his eyes. "*My father.* My grandparents – *his* parents – made a saint of him. But he really was a drunk and a brute, wasn't he? And I…" He took a gasping breath. "I killed him, and she went to jail. To protect me." He laughed again, a bitter sound, even in his own ears. "But you know what?"

"What?"

"She said she didn't want me to remember. Well, I *don't*. I didn't remember a bloody thing just now. But I'd guessed. Worked it out. It was the only thing that made sense." He looked at Sandra. "I just needed you to confirm it."

"But…" her eyes were wide. "You insisted we come here. You hoped it would jog your memory."

"I did and I didn't. You know, just like you, I've read up on suppressed, or repressed, memories. Dissociative amnesia, the scientists call it. Thing is, the notion that those sorts of memories can be recovered by psychotherapy, or by trying to trigger them like we did today, has been widely rubbished. A lot of experts believe that attempts to do so will more likely create false memories than trigger real ones. But you knew that." He shrugged. "Did I hope something would come to me anyway? Maybe. But I guessed if you really thought it had, you might finally tell me the truth."

"I just… couldn't."

He sighed. "Then what I don't get is – why didn't you leave it at that? You were out of prison, you'd served your time. Okay, I get why you came looking for me, trying to patch things up between us, but what was the point of asking me to have a look at the case?"

"I just wanted you back in my life so much. You didn't trust me, didn't want anything to do with me. But I knew the case was flimsy, just my word against the prosecution. I couldn't afford much in the way of representation, and I think even my lawyer thought I was guilty. I just hoped, if you took a look at the case, maybe you'd come to doubt the verdict. Maybe you'd finally give me a chance."

"Except I did a bit better than that. I found something that could have helped your case, maybe tipped the balance with the jury, hadn't even been mentioned at the trial. First of all, I just couldn't see why not. Then I could only see one explanation. You refused to have your defence introduce it, in case it raised other questions. In case the whole truth came out. And the prosecution weren't about to make anything of it and weaken their case."

His world really had shifted on its axis.

"Dear God," he said bitterly. "I grew up without either of my parents. You didn't want me to be known as 'that boy', but there were other ways round that. When you kept trying to contact me, I changed my name, moved to a new area. Nathan

Bowman effectively disappeared. We could have done that back then, you and me, if you'd said what really happened."

He was sobbing now. "All my life, I've thought I could have stopped it happening. Saved my dad, somehow. And all the time, it was me who killed him."

Laura put her arms around him, and then he was sobbing. She shushed him gently.

"But you didn't kill him," she soothed, "not really. It sounds like it happened exactly as Sandra always said it did. He ran onto the knife. Except you were the one holding it. You were only six."

He released himself from her, swiping at his eyes.

"Don't you see? My whole life is based on a lie, told to me by people I loved and trusted. What am I supposed to do? I don't even know who I am any more."

Laura's own eyes were glistening. "Don't know who you are? Nate, look at all the things you've become. The man I love. A brilliant police officer and a great friend, when you let people in. Who knows? If you hadn't erased that memory – if you'd grown up blaming yourself for your dad's death – how might you have turned out then?"

"I don't know," he admitted.

"Sandra kept it from you out of love. It's what a mother does."

"Yes," he said, "I think I believe that."

"But put yourself in her shoes. The sacrifice she made – one you never asked her to make, that's true, but you were a child and she was trying to do what was best for you. All that time in prison, no contact from her child. Rejected even when she came out. Think how that must have hurt."

"I should have just accepted it," Sandra said. "Accepted I'd lost you forever. Not come trying to push my way in. I'm so sorry, Nathan."

He held up his hands. "Look, I need time to process all this, but one thing's for sure. I need to tell the truth. Clear your name. What do they say about the truth? It sets you free."

Laura hugged him, dropped a kiss on his cheek, then held him at arm's length. "I've never been prouder of you. I just told you all the things you've become, maybe because you didn't know what really happened here that day. Maybe you should try adding 'son' to that list, after all."

"Maybe. I've never thought of her as my mother. Maybe it's too late. Maybe not. I don't know."

"Just remember," she cautioned. "It'll be like all she went through was in vain. And everyone will finally see behind that wall you've built around yourself. Are you ready for that?"

He felt as if his head was about to explode. "I've had enough of this place, and I noticed a nice looking pub about five miles back. Shall we get some food? Talk some more?"

"I'd like that," said Sandra.

Nathan Quarrel took a last look around the place where so many destinies had changed so long ago. Where his future might just have changed again. A place where his father wasn't the only ghost. He fancied a little ghost named Nathan Bowman still haunted this house too.

Or maybe they'd all just been exorcised.

He slipped an arm around Laura's shoulders.

"Let's go, then," he said.

THE END

ACKNOWLEDGEMENTS

Whether you're a long-standing reader or *In Ice* is the first book of mine you've read, I hope you enjoyed it. A book is just words on paper – it only comes to life when someone starts to turn the pages.

As always, huge thanks are due to the many people who have played their part in helping me make this the best book I can. Sue Black, Lisa Cutts, Clare Houston, and others have been extraordinarily generous with their professional expertise. Any inaccuracies are either intentional in the interests of the story, or my mistakes.

I am ever grateful to my wonderful, insightful beta readers, Chris Sivers and Debbie Porteous; their insights and criticisms are an essential part of my writing process, as is the gimlet eye of Helen Baggott, who again helped me to give the book a final polish.

Thanks to individuals who lent their names to some of the characters in *In Ice*: Archer and Baines 'veteran' Lara Moseley for a cameo crossover, and Pete Savage and Margaret Lunn, who both made generous donations to charities to have characters named after them. I hope they like their namesakes.

The support and friendship of all my mates in the crime writing business – too many to name, but they know who they are – as well as the Oxford Crime Writers, Chiltern Writers, and my friends and followers on social media – all help to keep me going.

Since my last book was published, my father, and head cheerleader, Fred Sivers, and my father-in-law, Maurice Kennard, have both left us, and this book is dedicated to them.

Last, but anything but least, my thanks and love to my wife, Chris, who supports, encourages and loves me every day. I couldn't do this otherwise.

Buckinghamshire, 2022
www.davesivers.co.uk
Twitter: @davesivers
Facebook: @davesiversauthor1

Printed in Great Britain
by Amazon

16427142R00144